CLAIMING THE BEAST

HOLLY ROBERDS

Editors: Theresa Paolo, Athena Franks, & The Havoc Archives
Sensitivity Readers: The Havoc Archives

BOOKS BY HOLLY ROBERDS

VEGAS IMMORTALS

Death and the Last Vampire

Book 1 - Bitten by Death

Book 2 - Kissed by Death

Book 3 - Seduced by Death

The Beast & the Badass

Book 1 - Breaking the Beast

Book 2 - Claiming the Beast

DEMON KNIGHTS

Book 1 - One Savage Knight

Book 2 - One Bad Knight

LOST GIRLS SERIES

Book 1 - Tasting Red

Book 2 - Chasing Goldie

Book 3 - Igniting Cinder

THE FIVE ORDERS

Book 0.5 – The Knight Watcher

Book 1 - Prophecy Girl

Book 2 - Soulless Son

Book 3 - Tear in the World

Book 4 – Into Darkness

Book 4.5 - Touch of Hell

Book 5 - End Game

* For recommended reading order, visit www.hollyroberds.com

Dedicated to anyone who struggles with mental health issues. Rebrand yourself as a spicy disaster and conquer this world anyway.

But maybe take a nap first...

CHAPTER I

THE BADASS

"Here kitty, kitty." I psst psspt'd into the dark.

It was three in the morning, and I prowled through the back alleys behind the Vegas hotels that served the best breakfast buffets. The pungent odor of rotting shellfish, meats, and sweets grew so intense, my eyes watered and I had to hold my breath.

Why was I here?

Because I was hunting a god spawn.

A dangerous divine being that chose to stay in his primordial animal form. And the last thing Vegas needed was for humans to run into an otherworldly creature with fangs and realize gods and monsters walked among them.

Grim, my former boss and god of the dead, shared that my target's name was Sheshem, a lion-like spawn of the goddess Sekhmet. Unlike Sheshem's distant, vampiric ancestor, this fanged creature had a sweet tooth for syrup and an appetite for shrimp—raw, fried, you name it.

Back in the ancient days, the big scary cat god spawn had inadvertently released a plague of darkness on the earth so he could extend his hunting grounds, and the only way to stop him had been to kill him and his connection to the dark plague.

But in the present day and age, he seemed quite happy with his hunting forays in the city of Las Vegas. He mainly left a trail of ravaged dumpsters, metal peeled back in strips.

While Sheshem's return to this world hadn't caused anything so dramatic like a plague, he was a dangerous entity that couldn't be allowed to roam free.

And Sheshem only set his paws on this earth again because of me. Guilt sliced through me as I paced up and down the stinking alleyway. I deliberately opened a dumpster to attract Sheshem's delicate and discerning senses. The longer I waited in the dark, the more antsy I got.

"Oh Bob, I wish you'd give me a few words of encouragement," I whispered to the blade I held erect, ready to slay or defend myself. The sword remained stubbornly silent, causing a pang of guilt to spear through my gut.

It's my fault the Blade of Bane didn't speak anymore.

At first, I was freaked out to have a psychic connection to a weapon with a French accent and a strong aversion to blood, but I'd grown accustomed to having him in my head.

His silence was only another damning side effect of my massive mistake. One that stole Bob's voice and released Sheshem into the world.

A low rumble vibrated through the air, resonating from the deep, shadow-clad recesses of the alley. My pulse quickened, a tumult of adrenaline and foreboding surging through my veins. I tightened my hold on the blade as I retreated several steps, my gaze piercing the darkness in anticipation.

The moment stretched, taut with expectation, until the shadows themselves seemed to shift and coalesce. From their depths, Sheshem emerged into the scant light of the moon.

My breath hitched, caught between awe and fear. Its fur, if one could call it that, shimmered with a spectral quality, translucent and flowing like liquid obsidian, edged with a luminescence that hinted at otherworldly origins. Its eyes, twin orbs of chaotic energy, burned with a fierce intensity, a swirling maelstrom of colors that defied the natural order.

I felt small, vulnerable—every inch the mortal I was.

But I wielded the most powerful weapon in the world, the Blade of Bane, aka Bob, the only sword that could kill a god. My duty was to make penance for my mistake as well as protect this world, and I'd fulfill those responsibilities no matter what.

As I reoriented myself, blade in hand, all I could think was: *Bring it on, Sheshem.*

Fangs bared, the god spawn roared—a sound that was a grotesque cross between a lion's roar and impossibly, a rattlesnake. It lunged, and my blade swung up, narrowly blocking its claw from my face. I staggered, almost tripping over some errant trash.

Dodging another claw swipe, I managed to thrust my blade toward its face. But Sheshem dodged with such speed, it was like trying to spear a shadow. It leapt at me, and I jumped back. My head smacked against brick with a sickening crack. My vision turned black for a second as dizzying pain exploded in my brain.

I was cornered against a graffiti-covered wall. Sheshem readied to pounce, its claws fully extended, eyes locked on me like the final piece of shrimp on a brunch platter. This was it. I was going to die at the paws of a pancake-loving, kitty-cat god.

A blur of motion swept through my peripheral vision, landing between me and my would-be killer.

It wasn't an illusion. A figure landed in front of me, a barely contained tempest of power and agility. For a moment, the world fell away, and there was only the silhouette bathed in moonlight, standing like a sentinel ready to protect me from certain death—Xander.

The man—the god—I lost everything for.

CHAPTER 2

THE BADASS

Xander didn't bother wearing shoes or a shirt, making him look almost as feral and out of place as the god spawn. The neon lights from the Strip filtered through the alley, casting a contrast on the contours of his muscled body.

Scars once riddled the entirety of Xander's body—a body that I'd touched every inch of—but they'd all disappeared. He was flawless now, courtesy of his rebirth from the Blade of Bane. Whereas I was now damned by the same action.

Xander spared me a glance, and for a split second, our

eyes met. A myriad of emotions passed through those turquoise depths—worry, relief, anger? Whatever they were, I severed them from my mind, like hacking off a gangrenous limb. He was the last thing I should be thinking about.

Xander clenched his fists and let out a challenging roar, meeting Sheshem's intensity. What happened next was nothing short of incredible. He lunged forward, fist meeting claw in a blur of motion and raw power. They clashed, Xander ducking and dodging the deadly swipes with the grace of a dancer, landing punches that actually made the hulking god spawn stagger.

Finally, with a growl that shook the alley, Xander landed a punch square on Sheshem's snout. The creature reeled backward, let out a ferocious snarl, and then bolted, vanishing into the labyrinthine maze of darkened alleyways.

"What were you thinking, Miranda?" Xander turned back to me, panting, his eyes ablaze. "If Sheshem hadn't been in a playful mood, you could've been killed. Your military training didn't cover sword fighting and gods. You are way out of your depth."

Playful mood?

Emotions welled up in me, all mixed and tangled so I couldn't pull any one of them apart.

How long had it been since I heard his raspy voice?

A month.

So why did it feel like an eternity? I'd been starved of hearing words spill from those frowning lips. It'd been forever since I'd been captivated by the way his hair hung loosely over those striking azure eyes. They held a permanent disdain, as if he didn't care about one single goddamn thing in this world.

An ache yawned inside of my chest so fiercely, my breath caught.

Xander once cared about me. A gaping hole formed in his ruthless indifference, and that's where he held me. A literal god looked at me like I was the only woman in the world. The only one worth his attention.

I swallowed past the large lump that lodged itself in my throat.

Calm the fuck down, Miranda. Of course, he looked like heaven and hell, saran wrapped in sex. He's a literal god. The Egyptian god of primordial waters, once called Nun. Any and every person would be gripped by the desire to fall at his feet and beg to worship him.

The image of him between my legs, worshipping me with his tongue zapped me with a white-hot electricity I tried to shake off even as my skin turned feverish.

But I fucked up.

And when I last saw him, his gaze burned into me with such rage and resentment, it burned away every last bit of what we had together.

I tried to ignore how frustratingly captivating his face is even when he's irritated. *Especially* when he's irritated. Like he can't decide if he wants to fight or fuck me.

We usually settled on a combination of both.

I gritted my teeth. "No, the army didn't teach me how to fight gods with a sword. But I'll adapt. I always do." With that, I turned on my heel and made my way down the alleyway.

Energy crackled along my spine, letting me know he was following me. "Adaptation won't keep you alive against gods," he shot back, his voice tinged with concern that did nothing but fan the flames of my already complicated feelings for him.

He was right. But admitting that would hurt more than Sheshem's claws ever could.

Xander had tried to train me to wield the blade. Yet too often, our sessions morphed into something else—something sexual and forbidden.

My heart hammered in my chest, heat building in my veins, forcing feelings to the surface.

Lop.

There, I cut them off again. Another gangrenous limb gone.

I felt nothing for him.

"Thanks for the save," I said flatly, even as adrenaline pumped through me. "Now, if you don't mind, I have a kitty-cat god to hunt."

"Kitty-cat god? Are you crazy? It's not a house pet. You could have been killed." Xander's expression changed; no longer a dangerous, feral scowl but something else. He looked regal, as if he'd changed from the beast I first met in the Grim Reaper's basement, and into his godly persona.

Ignoring his protest, I picked up Bob and turned on my heel. "You can't do this, Miranda," Xander insisted.

"That's where you're wrong," I replied, not slowing my stride.

Two strong hands gripped my shoulders, forcing me to face him. Instantly, he was too close. My skin tingled, my head went fuzzy, and I involuntarily wet my lips. Xander's pupils dilated, as if he too sensed the undercurrent of desire throbbing between us, between all the places we'd been and lost.

"Why are you here?" I asked, shrugging off his grip and stepping away. "I thought you hated me."

His brows furrowed. "Hated you?" he echoed in confusion. His eyes cleared as he looked away. "I was upset."

"Upset," I scoffed, throwing my braids over one shoulder. "For four weeks, you've been *upset*." I hated the way the pitch of my voice rose at the end of that sentence.

"I didn't ask you to bring me back, Miranda," he murmured, a soft growl imbuing his voice.

With Xander's dying act, he saved me from stabbing my own child in a supernaturally-induced hallucination.

When the dream cleared from my eyes and I found Xander pierced through the heart by my own hand, I thought he would regenerate like he did every night I killed him. But whether fate is a cruel bitch or his sudden desire to live triggered it, Xander's power had ebbed enough that I was able to kill him for good.

Right there, right then, he died a true death at the end of my blade.

I couldn't leave it at that.

"I know you didn't ask me to save you," I said stiffly. "Believe me, I realize my mistake now." I threw away my life the day I revived him.

I regretted ever asking for outside help, allowing myself to be manipulated by Sunny—the fae who performed the spell—who clearly had ulterior motives.

Not only was Xander released from the prison of the blade's steel, so was everything the blade ever killed. It was a massive jailbreak of all the destructive gods and monsters that had been destroyed and trapped into the steel of my blade. All thanks to my feeling-clouded idiocy.

Now the most primeval deities this world had seen since the beginning of time walked this earth again. And it was my fault because I had a crush on a beast in a cage with a death wish.

The purge had also robbed Bob, my talking blade, of his voice. We'd known each other a short time, but I felt bonded to him, and now that my sword was silent, I felt more alone than ever.

My hands clenched against the stupidity of my own actions.

"What do you think you are doing then?" he asked even softer now.

That's when I spun on my heel and backed Xander up against a wall, the sharp end of my sword pricking at his throat. His eyes remained impassive even as he lifted his chin. As if he didn't believe I'd do it.

He should. I killed him every night for weeks.

But if I did it now, he would die instantly, his soul trapped in the blade I held.

"I am dealing with the consequences of my actions," I said, only growing angrier when I heard the tremor in my own voice. "I have to kill every one of those monsters I let out. Perhaps I should start with you, since you are here."

But this wasn't about Xander. He wasn't slain because he was a threat to this world. He was only a threat to my good sense.

"They can't expect you to do this." His eyes bore into me, until I felt his penetrating gaze travel all the way to my toes. "It's suicide, Miranda. You can't fight immortals as a human."

My arm dropped, the blade going with it. "It is my duty, my penance." I paused. "Put on a shirt and some shoes. You look like some damn homeless maniac." My irritation was way too apparent. Hopefully he'd think I said it because I think he's indecent, not because it's distracting as all hell.

I hated the way his stupid carved abs flexed at my comment.

"You didn't know what you were doing. It wasn't your

fault," Xander argued on, ignoring my commentary on his dress—or rather the lack of it.

I narrowed my eyes. "Didn't seem to stop you from blaming me either."

The moment the searing light of the purging spell lifted, Xander appeared there in my living room with a look in his eye so full of hatred it was a live wire electrocuting me.

Then he took off, and I hadn't seen him since.

Until now.

Xander's jaw went slack with surprise before he recovered a moment later. "Miranda. I was upset. Angry. Not at you, but at the situation. To exist in a world with *him* again..." Xander's blue eyes spiraled off into a place I couldn't reach him. The feral edges of him returned as I watched him enter the personal hell of his past.

The stately god receded, once more becoming the beast I met in the basement—a god driven insane by an over-abundance of power that kept him alive and in pain for thousands of years. But he'd apparently preferred that hellish existence over living in the same world as his nemesis again.

Aten, the sun god, was roaming around somewhere, and it would only be a matter of time before he made his move. To him, there could only be one God, and he'd do anything to wipe out the other immortals. And judging by the magnitude of their fear, he might have the power to do it.

The other gods whispered and fretted. They wanted my head before Grim stepped in. They blamed me for releasing Aten. They should.

A vise clamped around my heart and squeezed so hard I expected my ventricles to pop like balloons.

When Xander's eyes refocused on me, I looked away.

He whispered, "You can't go after him."

I repeated the little poem-like order given to me by Grim. "I am to kill every god who'd been slain by the blade before."

Before I could turn and walk away, Xander stepped in front of me again. "He'll kill you, Miranda."

"Maybe," I said, staring at a spot on his chest, breathing in the intoxicating scent of the salty sea and sandalwood. "But this is my duty, my penance. No one but me can pay it."

I risked touching him so I could push by him, but Xander grabbed my shoulders again, dragging me close. "Miranda, I can't let you do this. I can't let anything happen to you. I..." The oceans in his eyes roiled as he fought to get the words out. "I *love* you."

All the cells in my body stilled, petrified by his impossible words. My throat thickened until I couldn't swallow. I pursed my lips to keep from drowning in the tormented depths of his cerulean eyes.

Gone was his indifference. All his intensity, his desire, was trained on me, and it drilled through me like a power tool, gutting me.

How fucking dare he?

How dare he try to play on my emotions after being absent for a month? I thought my heart broke the night I killed him, but I'd barely tasted heartache until he stared at me with such accusation, such open hatred before disappearing into the night.

Sure, I'd made my bed and I had to lie in it, drowning in my own mistakes. But if someone loved you, they either tried to pull you out or lie down with you.

He did neither. I sacrificed so much for the god in front of me, and he'd rejected me.

It had been a miracle he'd pried himself into my heart in the first place. There was absolutely no way he would get in again. I'd sealed all the cracks, and no one would breach that barrier. Ever.

Envisioning ice swirling out of my eyes to freeze him in place, I said, "I thought I loved you, but I was an idiot. It was only because you'd awoken feelings I thought I'd never feel again. But I don't need those feelings, and I don't need you." I enunciated those last words with extreme prejudice.

He didn't back down. Instead, he stepped in closer.

"You want me," Xander insisted, his face lowering until his mouth was mere millimeters from mine, causing my lips to tingle in anticipation and my belly to flip-flop wildly.

Chemistry, nothing more, I insisted firmly to myself. There was nothing sexy about vinegar and baking soda, and that's the sum of what we were to each other. Chemicals.

"I want to kill gods and be left alone." I struggled against his grip, but Xander held me fast.

His lips pressed against mine in a fierce possessive kiss that bent my body backward, even as he held me to him.

Sharp pricks scratched at the back of my eyes as his mouth molded to mine. My chest felt like it was going to blow apart until my heart was scattered in gruesome red ribbons at his feet.

The same time Xander broke the kiss, I wanted—*needed*—him to keep kissing me even as I hated him more than I ever hated anything or anyone in my life. Even more than reckless drivers, more than the last remake of *Pride and Prej-udice*, more than people who chewed with their mouths open.

I shoved him away.

"Don't come near me again," I warned, even as I stalked away, never looking over my shoulder.

No matter how every fiber of my being begged me to.

CHAPTER 3
THE BEAST

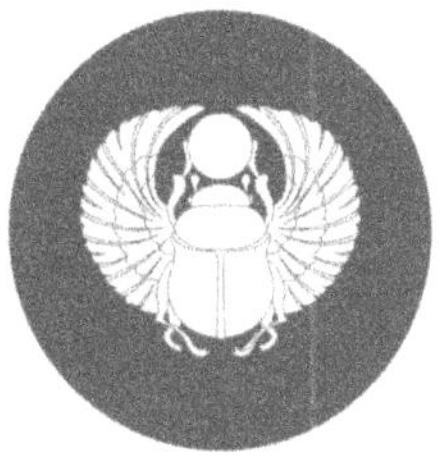

When Miranda entered Grim's penthouse, she stopped in her tracks as soon as she saw me. Eyes narrowing, she looked back and forth between me and the god of the dead with accusation and wariness.

Fuck, the taste and feel of her mouth against mine still burned me like a ghost. I craved her so badly my fingertips itched.

Instead of the Blade of Banee being sheathed on her back this morning, it resided inside her duster. In skintight pants that rose up past her belly button and a crop top, both in army print—a nod to her past—she looked every bit the delicious little badass I remembered and more.

Gone were the suit jackets and façade of professional courtesy of a woman who worked for others. Her shit-kicker boots and leather duster only added to the visage of her fully embracing what she was. A warrior.

The god of the dead stood next to me in his pressed black suit, hands laced behind his back. "Hello Miranda," he greeted formally.

The old boy was nervous.

Who knew even the Grim Reaper could be intimidated by a five-foot-four mortal with glowing brown skin and cat-like eyes that flashed with live fire? Maybe it's because her tensed jaw promised death?

His, specifically. But I had no doubt I'd be next.

After spending thousands of years in my underground prison and grotto, Grim's modern and luxurious penthouse atop the Sinopolis hotel was a sight to behold. The decor featured sleek eggplant-colored couches, black marble, and state-of-the-art appliances—all of which showcased his wealth and moodiness.

Had I been amongst my brethren all these years, I supposed this might be how I would be living now too.

After years of living in a dark, damp place both physically and mentally, I had reached my limit. If I lived here, I'd ditch the gloomy hues and decorate with more bright pops of color.

But the only luxury, the only home I recognized or desired, stood twenty feet away from me, and was looking progressively stabbier.

Gods, the sight of Miranda made my body riot with desire, pride, and raw need. I wanted to wrap my hand in those long, thin velvet braids and toy with her until she punched me or fell apart in my hands. But mostly, my body vibrated with agitation, knowing I couldn't have her.

Not yet anyway.

"What is this?" Miranda asked, her suspiciously slit eyes bouncing between Grim and me.

"Miranda," Grim started, but paused when her scrutiny drilled into him. "I've decided you could use some assistance with your endeavors."

Miranda arched an eyebrow. She wasn't buying this. I didn't expect her to, my clever girl.

Her shoulders rolled back as she regarded him coolly. "No."

"No? No, what?" he asked, hands falling to his side.

"No, I will not be working with Xander."

I couldn't help the grin that spread across my face. Nothing got by her.

"Sure you will, sweetheart," I mocked. Those molten brown eyes turned to me, openly incensed.

That's it my little badass, put all the energy here. The more you give me the anger, the more you'll fall into my gravity until I've captured you entirely. The same way you've ensnared me.

"Xander," Grim warned in a low voice before addressing Miranda again. "I know things have changed considerably—"

"Are you talking about the part where I lost my job working here at Sinopolis?" she asked drolly. "Or the part where the entire immortal community holds me personally responsible for the biggest disaster since the bloodthirsty goddess Sekhmet went on a rampage turning mortals into vampires?"

"Miranda," Grim sighed, taking a seat on one of the black leather chairs while pinching the bridge of his nose. "You answer to a higher calling," Grim explained. "You were chosen by the fae to wield the Blade of Bane. This was always to be your fate. I simply helped elongate the normalcy of your life for as long as I could."

Neither Miranda nor I moved to sit, standing across from each other at either end of an invisible tether.

"I'm not a child. You don't need to coddle me." Her hand curved tightly around the blade's hilt.

Bob. She called the Blade of Bane Bob.

Grim opened his hands. "Of course you aren't, but Miranda, you were the one who insisted on clinging to mortal responsibilities, and we allowed it. But in lieu of what's happened—" He stood up again, as if remembering he is the boss. "—you must kill all of the gods who escaped the blade. They were slain for a reason, because they were a threat to our world and left unchecked—"

Miranda cocked a hip and tilted her head toward me. "So you're saying I should kill him again? For the safety of the world?"

The only one in danger is you, sweetheart. I'm coming for you.

"He's not exactly the threat I'm referring to," Grim said dryly. "And as Xander is not only adept in swordsmanship, but also has a familiarity with a number of the most dangerous gods you are now in pursuit of and lacks an occupation at the moment, he can help you hunt."

"Listen, I know what I've done." Miranda's composure broke as real panic entered her eyes. "And I'm paying for it. But I don't think I deserve this punishment."

Grim crossed to Miranda, standing between us even though she and I never broke eye contact.

"This isn't punishment, Miranda. The other gods raise their voice in outrage, but it is because they are scared.

Scared of what's out in the world now." He took her hands in his.

Instantly my hackles rose, but I worked to keep my possessiveness in check.

I'd convinced Grim to arrange our partnership and I wasn't about to screw over my chance at being near my dark angel again.

Grim's word was final, so I followed Miranda to the elevator where we stood side by side, her eyes trained on the changing floor numbers. I opted to bite the inside of my cheek to keep from saying anything smug that might compel her to stab me.

"Don't you know the rules of civilized society?" she mocked. "No shirt," her eyes scanned my chest, leaving a trail of heat in their wake, before lowering, "No shoes, no service."

"I'm more interested in providing service," I leered at her.

Miranda's eyes flashed with anger as she turned to fully face me. "Keep your service to yourself, Xander." Her hand tightened around the hilt of her blade even as her cheeks turned a beautiful rosy shade. "I don't need you tagging along, and I certainly don't need to be distracted."

I simply chuckled, taking a step closer to her. "Oh, but you do need my help," I replied, my voice low and dangerous. "And as for distractions," I leaned in, my breath hot against her ear, "you know you can't resist me."

Miranda's face twisted with anger as she shoved me away from her. "You're disgusting," she hissed, and the elevator doors opened. We stepped out into the lobby of the hotel, and I could feel her eyes burning holes into me as we walked towards the exit.

Outside, the sun beat down on the city, and the unfamiliar rumbling, bleating sounds of traffic filled the air.

My ears began ringing and my throat tightened as the caustic stench of exhaust filled my senses. The urge to escape to a dark and quiet place intensified as the chaotic surroundings threatened to overwhelm me.

But there was something I wanted more than peace.

Now that I was in Miranda's orbit, I didn't want to break away.

The tension between us was thick and palpable as we made our way down the street. I didn't know where she was going, but I'd follow her to the ends of the earth if she let me.

"You know," I said after a moment, breaking the silence between us, "you're even more beautiful when you're angry."

She growled. Actually growled.

"You may be the chosen one, but you'll need my expertise if you want to survive in the world of the gods," I replied, my voice low and menacing.

Miranda stopped at a parked, sensible silver car, and turned to face me, her jaw clenched. "I can handle this on my own."

"You can't possibly believe that," I retorted. "You may be strong, but you're not invincible. The gods are dangerous, and you'll need all the help you can get."

Miranda's eyes narrowed, and the tension rose between us once again. I knew she didn't trust me, but I also knew that she had no choice but to work with me.

I'd made sure of that.

Setting both hands on the scalding metal of the vehicle, I boxed her in. "Trust me, Miranda." My head tilted down toward her as my voice softened. "I won't let anything happen to you."

Miranda stiffened at my nearness. Oh fuck, I was close enough to inhale the heady mixture of bergamot and her skin.

Miranda hesitated for a moment, her eyes searching mine as if looking for something. A reason to believe me?

"Never," she said, her voice cold. "I suppose I *have* to tolerate your presence for the sake of completing my mission, but nothing more."

I couldn't help but grin at her stubbornness. It only made me want her more.

"Don't worry, sweetheart." I reached up to smooth my thumb over her tense jawline. Her skin was like warm silk. "I can handle a little hostility."

I knew that I was getting under her skin, but I wanted to get deeper. I wanted to dig into her heart and nest there for all eternity.

The way she now lived inside of me.

Miranda pushed my hand away so violently, I knew I was in danger of losing the appendage. "Touch me again, and I'll show you hostility." The way her teeth were bared promised violence.

That's fine my little badass, as long as I get to be close to you. For now...

I nodded and shoved my hands in my pockets to keep from reaching out and doing it again. Rocking back on my heels, I asked with all the innocence in the world, "So when do we go hunting?"

THE BEAST

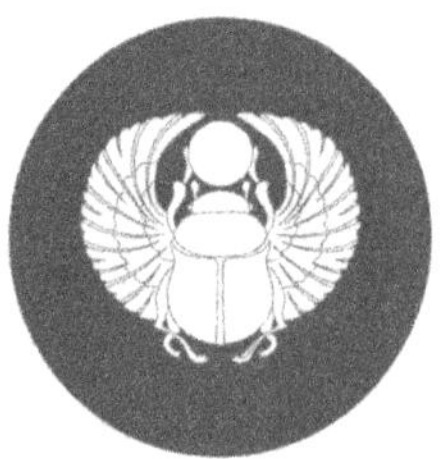

"What in the hell are you wearing?" The whites of Miranda's eyes nearly swallowed her dark irises as she stared at me, slack-jawed.

We agreed to meet in the Sinopolis lobby at dusk to go god hunting.

Looking down, I pulled out the edge of my shirt, checking to see if I got anything on my new purchase.

"What?" I asked, not seeing whatever horrified her. "You said to get a shirt and shoes."

Miranda's head slowly shook, the horror on her face fixed in place. "And *that* is what you chose?"

I frowned. "The shopkeeper said red was my color."

Plus, I liked the big white tropical flowers on the Hawaiian shirt.

It still felt strange to cover up. My clothes never lasted long when I was locked in my cell. My madness would drive me to claw at my own chest until I pulled out my own heart, deranged with the need for a death I could never reach. After a while, I stopped fighting my near constant state of undress. But Miranda had a point about regular people looking at me like I was crazy or dangerous.

I was, but they didn't need to know that at first glance.

"He lied," she said drolly, her face going flat, still scanning me from head to toe with open judgement in her eyes and twisted lips. "And anyone wearing socks with sandals should be shot on sight."

My frown deepened. On that point I couldn't entirely disagree. I'd modeled my look after the street vendor, and while I loved the bright cheerful colors and floral shirt design, the socks and sandals immediately proved to be impractical.

Miranda chewed on the inside of her cheek, irritation flashing in her dark eyes. "And could you at least button that thing the rest of the way up?"

Again, I glanced down. I'd only done half the buttons to offset the claustrophobia I felt at being covered so entirely. I settled on telling her a half-truth. "It's hot."

That wasn't a lie. While summer was coming to a close, the days were only heating up carrying over into sweltering nights.

And I didn't have to guess at why. The sun god's presence was all around me, even if I didn't know exactly where yet.

Miranda rolled her eyes at my reluctance to button up, shrugging her shoulders as if she suddenly felt uncomfortable. If I didn't know any better, I'd swear I saw a spark of lust in her eye before irritation drowned it out.

I followed her as we made our way through the bustling lobby and out onto the city streets. The sun had dipped below the buildings, casting a golden glow over the strange garish buildings on the Strip. I'd seen them in pictures and on video through the years, but I'd only been on the streets for a short time and the adjustment was... intense.

My teeth automatically gritted as my senses endured the onslaught of color, sound, and smells. A bachelorette group screamed in excitement as they passed by in an overwhelming cloud of different perfumes. An overweight, sweat-soaked family of tourists who stank of irritation and hunger trudged by, one of them clipping my shoulder with theirs without any follow up acknowledgement. Several poorly dressed men lining the street forced little slips of paper depicting barely censored naked women into my hands without so much as a smile. The irrational urge to retreat back to my cell yanked at my guts.

"You good?" Miranda asked. It took a second to pull my fractured senses together so I could focus on her. Eyebrow raised, Miranda looked genuinely concerned.

Keep it together Xander. Stay calm, stay cool, let her see how you've changed.

"The best you ever had, baby," I quipped back. My lips slid into a lascivious smile though the sheen of sweat now covering my body had nothing to do with the pressing Vegas heat.

I'd expected Miranda to roll her eyes so hard they'd threaten to fall out of her head. Instead, she kept that unerring gaze trained on me, as if she could see right through me. It both thrilled and terrified me to capture her complete attention.

To further the picture of ease I was trying to sell, I slipped my hands into the pockets of my shorts. It was also so she couldn't see them shake.

Keep it together, you crazy fuck.

I couldn't let her see the loose threads that I feared would continue to unravel.

Finally, she nodded and turned her attention back to our walking path.

I removed my hands from my pockets, clenching and releasing my fingers to try and shake off the tremors.

Miranda's eyes continually scanned the crowd, always on high alert.

"So, exactly how have you been choosing which god to target?" I asked, needing to focus on what we were doing rather than the busy Vegas Strip.

"They usually leave behind a general trail of chaos, and the longer they've been left to run wild, the more reckless they become."

"How so?" I asked, if nothing else, to keep her talking to me. I was addicted to every word that fell from her lips.

Godsdamn, those perfect lips.

She sighed. "The Obelisk hotel disappeared for several hours before reappearing, all the casinos in the Martini went off with jackpots at the same time, it rained *inside* of the Menaggio, and of course, strange animal sightings are showing up on the internet from people recording with their phones. Usually, the activity picks up once the sun goes down."

I nodded. "Sounds like my asshole brethren. So are we going after any one of them in particular?"

And how can I keep you as far away from them as possible?

I knew I didn't stand a chance in hell of keeping Miranda out of danger when she was determined to run headlong into it, but that didn't mean I couldn't do anything about it.

Miranda's jaw tensed. "I still plan to go after Sheshem, since he has an easily discernible pattern. Even though you stepped in and ruined my chances last night." She grumbled her last words.

I stopped at that. "I *saved* you."

There was Miranda's classic eye roll I knew so well. She didn't bother replying to that. We both knew it was true, but it must gall the shit out of her that I saved her perfect, shapely ass. I had to jog a few steps to catch up to her again. I followed until we were cruising the back alleys of restaurants. Miranda deliberately unlocked or opened certain dumpsters as if to draw a path directly to us.

With my heightened senses, the stink of garbage was enough to make me toss my last meal, but I muscled my gorge back down.

"This is disgusting," I finally said after our long stretch of silence.

Miranda shrugged. "Consider it all one big cat trap. There isn't a night when a hotel brunch restaurant doesn't complain of the garbage being splattered across the alleyway and the dumpster ripped into shreds. So, this is our best bet."

Even though we turned off the Strip a while ago, there were still too many odors. Too many lights. Too many sounds.

Everything pounded into the side of my brain like so many nails. My fists clenched tight in my pockets.

Don't let her see. Don't let her know. She can't know how fucking broken your brain is.

A bowl of broken spaghetti.

A rotting meat pile.

You're shit. You're nothing. You don't belong. This world isn't yours. You have no world. Worlds won't swallow you—

A blessed breeze swept by, and Miranda's scent engulfed me, clearing away the incoherent jumble of stabbing thoughts.

I almost shuddered in relief as I breathed in the singular scent of her skin and bergamot. That sweet, refreshing citrus scent wafted from her skin that was also somehow deeply complex and round.

Sweet fucking hell, I wanted to bury my face in her throat, lick her from ankle to chin, until she had completely saved me.

I wanted to save her too. Save her from the hardness that was turning her brittle.

"Do you really think this is the best idea?" I asked. "A stakeout at the dumpsters, waiting for Sheshem to show up like a rabid raccoon? Maybe we could go patrol the Strip, check out a show, search the wax museum for evil," I teased, trying to inject some levity into our tense mission.

Miranda shot me an irritated glance. "We stick to the plan. It's not about what's fun, Xander. It's about what works."

I raised an eyebrow, a challenging smirk playing on my lips. "But what if I have better ideas? Something less... dumpster-divey?"

Her response was firm, unwavering. "We're not improvising. I've mapped this out. We follow the plan, Xander. No deviations."

I probed further, testing the boundaries of her resolve. "Ever think your plans are a bit... rigid? There's a whole spectrum between dumpster diving and going off-script, you know."

Miranda's tone turned defensive, her words laced with

an icy chill. "Rigid keeps us alive. And I don't recall your improvisations ending well last time."

Softening my approach, I said, "Hey, I get it. Control feels safe. But sometimes, a little chaos can be our ally. Trust me."

"It's not about trust." Realizing she'd raised her voice, Miranda closed her eyes and took a calming breath before continuing. "It's about minimizing risks, now shut up and be patient."

So that was a no on getting her to relax around me. But we were stuck together for the foreseeable future, so I had time. For once, time was an element in my favor.

Miranda may be a no-nonsense badass, but I knew her vulnerabilities, her fragile humanity even if she wanted to deny she possessed any weakness.

Whenever she spoke of killing a god, a frenetic kind of desperation entered her eyes. She'd hadn't achieved her goal yet and it was killing her.

The more she reinforced her walls of protection, the more she tried to expunge her vulnerabilities, the more delicate she became.

I'd be fucking damned if I let her crack. Or if she does crumble, I'll either be the one to put her pieces back together, or better yet, I'll be the one to make her fall to pieces, my tongue between her thighs, pushing her over an edge so pleasurable she forgets anything and anyone other than me.

Fuck. If I didn't get myself together, I'd end up sporting an obvious hard on. And she might get the idea I get randy over trash.

As if sensing my shift in focus, Miranda turned toward me.

She licked her lips slowly, maybe even nervously. "Don't look at me like that."

"Like what?" My voice was husky even to my own ears.

"Like you want to devour me." Her brows were pinched in a frown, but her breath hitched. My little badass *liked* the idea of me eating her up.

"Would that be so bad?" I asked, taking a step closer. Miranda started to step back but stood her ground at the last second, letting me invade her personal space.

A ray of streetlamp light sliced across her eyes, turning the deep, fathomless dark of them into the color of honey. The pressing dry heat also had her covered in perspiration, making her warm brown skin glow and sing like a siren. The song beckoned me to slide my hands over her muscled, toned arms, into the dip of her tank top to find the generous swell of her breasts.

Instead of answering, her lips tightened. I groaned. It only made me want to cover her mouth with my own and coax that beautifully full mouth apart.

Something about my thoughts must have broadcasted on my face because Miranda's eyes widened, and her hands pushed against my chest as if to keep me at bay. But the beast in me was taking over, and I wasn't sure if anything could stop me now.

Right then, I knew nothing could stop me. I was going to kiss her so deep, so thoroughly, I wouldn't stop until she was dripping between those thighs.

CHAPTER 5
THE BEAST

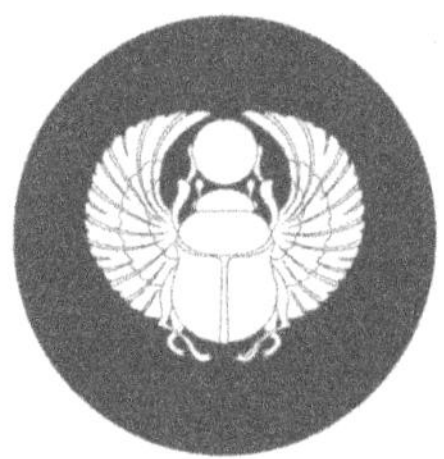

Dipping in, I tasted her sweet breath. She didn't move away. Tingles swept across my lips and pressure built in my cock. I was millimeters from heaven again.

A crash boomed from nearby, and both of us jumped back. Before I registered what happened, Miranda charged off in the direction of the sound.

My instincts kicked in and I followed her, pushing through the narrow alleyway. The smell of garbage intensified with the sickening stench as we neared the source of the commotion.

Ahead, a massive shadow loomed, its outline unmistakable even in the dim light. Sheshem rummaged through a dumpster with a voracious appetite. The sight of the deity, feasting on leftover pancakes and shrimp from the trash, was both surreal and pitiful.

We were once gods that ruled the lands and all humans. Now, Sheshem was a dumpster cat, and I couldn't seduce the only woman in the world that mattered. Pathetic.

Miranda moved with stealth, drawing her blade with silent precision. She was a warrior in her element, every muscle tensed for the strike. I readied myself, preparing to flank the creature. I had no intention of letting Sheshem's claws get anywhere close to her.

We crept closer to the hulking cat god, carefully coordinating our steps to avoid any noise. Miranda's blade gleamed in the dim light, a silent promise of a swift end.

Suddenly I was heartened by the idea this could all be over rather quickly.

Maybe we'd have time for a midnight swim in a pool after this?

Just as we were about to pounce, a large, clumsily set cage, draped with a net and various shiny objects, crashed down from above. It landed with a loud clang a few feet away from Sheshem, missing its mark entirely.

The cat god, startled by the sudden intrusion, let out a roar that reverberated off the walls. In an instant, it bounded away with supernatural speed, disappearing into the darkness.

Two figures stumbled into view, both dressed in cheap glittery magician costumes, complete with capes and top hats. One wielded a net, while the other brandished what looked like a toy wand.

"Hey! You ruined our trap and scared off our star attraction!" the taller of the two magicians exclaimed, frustration evident in his voice. He was a young, lanky fellow with a greasy ponytail and acne scars, and his outfit looked like it had seen better days.

The other, shorter and rounder with a fast-receding hairline for his age, chimed in, "Yeah, we've been planning this for weeks! That cat was going to be the centerpiece of our new act at The Mystical Mirage."

Miranda's eyes narrowed as she sheathed her blade, her posture radiating annoyance. "You two were trying to catch *that creature* for a magic show? Are you out of your minds?"

"I know I've been out of circulation for a while," I said to Miranda, eyeing the two morons, "but exactly how dumb have humans gotten over the years?"

"Excuse me, we are professional magicians," the taller magician retorted. "We are Marvelous Max," he gestured to himself then his friend, "and the Amazing Alfonso, and we're going to revolutionize Vegas entertainment with a real-life mystical beast." He wiggled his fingers at us in a way that made me want to rip them off his hands.

His companion, "Amazing Alfonso", piped up, "Yeah, and we would've caught it too, if it weren't for you guys charging in like a bull in a china shop!"

The situation was absurd; the two wannabe magicians in their shabby costumes and their botched trap were like something out of a low-budget fantasy film.

They must have dumped cologne on this morning and it made my stomach turn until it was difficult to think.

Miranda stepped forward, her body language all business. "Look, this isn't some game. That *beast* is a dangerous animal. You're lucky it ran off instead of turning you into its next meal."

I'd like to think Sheshem would have better taste, but he was already rummaging in dumpsters. These two looked like they crawled out of a glittery trash can themselves.

Max's frown was downright petulant, reminding me of a five-year-old child about to throw a tantrum. "We... we have a system. We're setting traps all over the city. High-tech stuff."

Alfonso nodded eagerly. "Yeah, high-tech. With nets... and, uh, shiny things cats like."

Miranda turned to me, a mix of frustration and resignation in her eyes as if to say, "Can you believe these two idiots?"

In a dry, matter-of-fact tone I said to them, "You are both going to get eaten."

Over my limit with irritation, not only because we lost Sheshem but because I almost had a perfectly delicious moment with the goddess to my left. "Here's some free advice: Leave hunting to the professionals. Go play with your card tricks and leave the real dangers to us."

Max bristled at my words, his pride wounded. "We are *not* giving up. This is our big break!"

Alfonso, however, seemed less convinced, his eyes darting nervously around the alley. "Maybe we should rethink our strategy, Max..."

Closing the distance until I stood right in front of the two morons, I bared my teeth and said, "This is our hunt, and if you two don't back off you will both end up either in that cage or in the big cat's stomach. Get it?"

"Yeah, right." Alfonso curled his lip as he looked me up and down. "Like we are going to let a low-rent Magnum PI intimidate us."

I stuck a finger in both of their faces, packing all the menace I could muster into my words, "I'll take the compliment of even resembling a handsome beast like Tom Selleck, but that's not going to save you from an ass kicking if you don't back down."

While my bouts of pain locked in a cage usually had me senseless for most of my days, my body had given up just as often, too tired to shift or think, and the invention of television had been one of the few blessings I'd appreciated. That and the age of books on tape helped keep me from tearing the pages out of paperbacks or splitting hardback spines in half during a sudden fit, or accidentally ruining the books in either of the pools of water I recovered in.

I knew better than anyone that Tom Selleck was a gift. And while I was pissed as hell at these two idiots, I was seriously considering how I'd look with a mustache.

"We don't have time for this," Miranda said behind me, clearly done with these two idiots. I couldn't agree more.

"Last warning," I growled. "Stay out of our way."

"This is YOUR last warning. Stay out of *our* way," Max threatened.

I turned on my heel, shaking my head, walking with Miranda before I cracked their stupid skulls against each other.

Miranda kept pace with me as we strode out the long alley and toward the Strip. "Have all humans become so idiotic over the years?"

"Were we really all that smart in your day and age?" Miranda asked with genuine curiosity in her voice.

"Good point. You, my little badass, have made the exception seem like the rule."

Her lips twitched as if she were trying to hide a satisfied smile. She didn't even balk at my nickname for her.

There. Miranda had relaxed just a little, and I reveled in the victory.

"Magicians trying to catch a god spawn for a Vegas act,"

Miranda muttered, her voice tinged with disbelief. "What's next? A circus ringmaster trying to tame a sphinx?"

I chuckled, despite the irritation still simmering inside me. "In this city? I wouldn't be surprised."

Miranda glanced at me, a wry smile briefly flashing on her face. "You know, for a second there, I thought you were going to lose it with those two."

I shrugged. "The thought crossed my mind. But then I remembered I'm trying to be a civilized god now."

"Civilized? You?"

"Hey, I'm wearing a shirt, aren't I?" I gestured to my Hawaiian shirt. "And it's... mostly buttoned up."

Miranda laughed, a genuine, unguarded sound that filled the night air. It was a rare moment of levity in our usually tense interactions. For a fleeting moment, I saw the woman behind the warrior, the vulnerability behind the strength.

But as quickly as it came, the moment passed, and Miranda's expression hardened once more. "We can't let those two interfere again. Sheshem is dangerous, and they're clueless."

I nodded in agreement, my gaze fixed on the bustling crowd ahead. "We'll keep an eye on them. But right now, we need to focus on our own hunt. They are a distraction."

Miranda sighed, running a hand through her braids. "Yeah. Let's keep going and maybe, just maybe, find you a shirt that doesn't scream 'tourist', or Magnum PI." She paused. "Though you might look dashing with a thick mustache."

I knew it!

CHAPTER 6

THE BADASS

My hands closed around my red-eye, a blissfully large cup of coffee topped with two shots of espresso. After the oppressive heat of the night, I was grateful to be back in the air-conditioned bliss of Sinopolis, sitting at Perkatory, the cafe in the lobby.

I told Xander I was going home after our night of fruitless hunting to make sure he wouldn't try to tag along for my morning routine.

Where he headed off to, I didn't know, and I tried not to care. I really tried, but questions like where was he living, and what had he been doing the last several weeks hammered into me with relentless force.

I certainly wouldn't admit to him or myself that when he walked in silence next to me I felt less alone, and intrinsically understood. That he'd reached inside of me and nestled in right next to my heart, making me feel at home in his presence.

I'd never admit those things.

I toyed with the cup sleeve. On it was a printed skull in a coffee cup logo with the slogan—*good to the last drop*. This little coffee stand had become a regular part of my routine. Perkatory was an oasis smack dab in the middle of the gleaming black marble and gold filigreed lobby of Sinopolis.

Lush greenery created a canopy of tranquility and isolated the coffee stand. The gentle rustle of leaves in the air-conditioning forced the subtle floral scents to mingle with the aroma of freshly ground coffee beans. This little spot always felt like my own personal sanctuary.

Vivien slid into the chair across from me, also finished with her nocturnal duties. Though my vampire best friend had a better night than me, judging by the fact her fishnet stockings were still intact and her auburn hair maintained volume and style as if she'd just done it. While I felt like a limp, exhausted noodle. Stains from the trash bins and nasty alleyways marked up my dark tank top. I felt disgusting, but I needed a moment to decompress before I went home and woke up Jamal to get him ready for school.

"How'd it go?" Vivien asked.

"Y-yeah, how'd it go?" a second voice chimed in as Aaron sat down. He adjusted his black apron with the Perkatory logo as he sat in the last chair. The coffee line was low enough that he could let the other barista handle it and join us, completing our little trio of friends.

"Fine," I said, sipping the dark brew.

Aaron and Vivien exchanged a glance.

"Did you f-fuck him?"

"...in a dumpster?" Vivien added, her nose wrinkling.

My jaw dropped as I turned to face Aaron. "Okay, I'd expect that from her," I pointed at Vivien, "but from you? Et tu Aaron?"

He shrugged his muscular shoulders up into the tips of his wavy, sun-bleached hair. "I-it's a v-valid question." Aaron's stutter had been getting slightly better from speech therapy, but ever since his surfing accident years ago, the stammer was his constant companion.

"No," I said icily, my shoulders stiffening. "He has absolutely no effect on me anymore. And I have zero intention of ever letting him touch me again."

Except for that moment when he almost kissed me... again.

A growl of frustration escaped me.

Aaron and Vivien leaned back from me a couple of inches.

"Yeah, no effect whatsoever," Vivien said airily, giving Aaron a look.

I gave them a rundown of the hack magicians who ruined my chances of slaying Sheshem. "After that, I couldn't get a bead on any gods or monsters the rest of the night."

"So... it was just you and Xander hanging out until dawn?" Vivien poked and prodded like a nosy little kid. It was hilarious when she did it to others. Not so much when she did it to me.

"Yes. It was... fine."

"Y-you said that," Aaron pointed out.

Usually, my friends gave me a sense of peace and pleasure. Staring into my coffee, I considered chucking the rest of it at both of them.

"What happened to getting back in the dating game?" Vivien asked. "When Xander disappeared a month ago, after the… incident, you said you were going to."

I did say that, didn't I?

I'd said I was never really in love with Xander after all, that it was only infatuation. We'd been in an intense, stressful situation that was sexually charged, but after some reflection (unfortunately only after I brought him back and released havoc on the world) I had come to the conclusion I was only in lust with the god.

Determined to fall in lust with someone else—anyone else—to prove my point, I'd gone on a couple dates. Every time my stomach would lurch with nausea almost as soon as the meeting began, and it wouldn't let up until I parted ways with whatever perfectly nice man I'd met. It was like I was repulsed by any man who wasn't Xander.

God damn it.

And now that he was back, invading my space, teasing me, protecting me, my body hummed with that same intense satisfaction and need rolled into one big ball that lodged itself under my ribcage.

I'm not in love with him. I never was, I insisted to myself. That would be crazy.

"Have you heard anything about rogue gods or monsters wreaking havoc?" I asked Vivien, changing the subject. "I lost the trail of the one I was tracking last night and nothing else came up." Which meant a full night of stalking the streets with a god who looked at me like he wanted to throw me against the nearest wall and ravish me until I died.

The kind of stress that inspired must have originated from the fourth or fifth level of hell. I'm usually adept at keeping my emotions under wrap, but Xander made it so damn hard, digging his hooks into me until I wanted to explode… one way or another.

The intensity in Vivien's green eyes let me know she was aware of my evasive tactics, but she let it slide. "Nothing concrete, but the gods are restless. Nervous."

"Because of Aten," I finished for her.

Vivien drummed her fingers on the table. "Apparently, he's one scary motherfucker."

Aaron shook his head. "I can't imagine what k-kind of god would scare the shit out of the other immortals." Then with a look at Vivien, "Other than Grim of course."

Vivien grinned at the mention of her hot husband and god of the dead. "He's just a pussycat underneath all that dark, gloomy death stuff."

"Yeah, sure." Aaron drew out the words with evident disbelief.

Vivien's impish smile faded, her fingers playing with the edge of the table. "They are all freaking out though. Grim is afraid that gods will start to turn on each other in fear."

"Why?" Aaron asked. "Are they worried some of their own are working for Aten like that little fae girl did?"

My hand tightened around my cup. The memory of trusting the wrong person still sliced through my chest with a triple helping of shame and regret.

Vivien shook her head. "None of the gods support Aten's monotheistic agenda— aka murdering the shit out of all the gods until he's the only one left. But when gods get upset, they get unpredictable and temperamental."

"Turn bitchy and childlike?" I offered.

Vivien pointed a finger at me like a gun. "Bingo. So Grim and Timothy are cooking up a way to pull them all back together. Like a big *rah rah* morale boost."

The downturn at the corner of her lips showed she was less than thrilled.

"How does that work?" I asked.

Vivien shook her head and gave me a wry smile. "They are still working on a plan, so I'll let you know when I do."

By the way she avoided my gaze and fidgeted, I had a suspicion she knew exactly what they were planning.

I had to leave her explanation at that as I had to get home before Jamal woke up. Parking my car in the driveway, I was surprised to find a man I didn't recognize pulling my garbage can to the edge of the street. As I stepped out, the man turned and unleashed a powerfully beautiful smile. It hit me like a tractor beam.

Well over six feet tall with light brown skin and shocking green eyes, the black man's head was shaved clean and he was as handsome as all get out. This may well be the finest man I had ever seen in my life. He belonged on the silver screen next to some leading lady he effortlessly wooed. Yet all his attention was directed at me, warming me from the inside out.

"Hi there," he said, striding forward to close the distance and shake my hand. "I'm your new neighbor. I hope you don't mind. I was worried you'd miss the trash pick up, so I thought I'd pull yours down."

The gears in my brain that came to a grinding halt began again with slow ker-chunks. "Oh, uh, thank you. I appreciate that." The knowledge I was still wearing dumpster-stained clothes suddenly made me self-conscious.

"My name is Michael." My neighbor still didn't let go of my hand, and I suddenly found myself not minding so much as I got caught up in his gaze. The light olive hue of his eyes made a striking contrast to his skin which was damned near mesmerizing.

"My name is Miranda," I said, suddenly remembering myself.

The curve of his lips somehow made me feel like he was bestowing a special smile patented just for me. "Miranda." The sound of my name from his mouth sent heat spiraling through my stomach.

My reaction surprised me, but then again, I supposed it was rare I was the object of such a handsome man's attention.

Turquoise eyes made of crashing oceans flashed in my mind.

Okay, maybe not so rare these days.

The front door opened, and a face etched with lines of age and frizzy white hair stared out at us with curiosity. "Miranda?"

I dropped Michael's hand. "Hey Mama Jean." Then I nodded to Michael. "Sorry, I've got to—" I gestured to my house, words failing me, but still indicating I needed to get inside.

"Of course," he said, holding up his hands with another dazzling smile. "It was enchanting to meet you, Miranda."

Again, the way my name rolled off his lips did a number on my spine, so I had to suppress the need to shiver under his gaze. I hurried inside, shutting the door behind me.

"So you met the new neighbor," Mama Jean said, pointing out the obvious.

My mother-in-law's brown, near black irises melted into the whites surrounding. While her back was starting to bend, her brain was sharp as steel. She'd had Rashon much later in life, which put her closer to the age of my own grandmother.

I feared Mama Jean noticed my reaction. Rashon passed away many years ago, when Jamal was practically a baby, but it felt disrespectful to ogle someone in front of her. Though she'd said many times life was for the living, and I couldn't let the memory of Jamal's father hold me back.

"Yeah, he seems nice," I said, hating how breathy I sounded. The attraction I felt also unsettled me.

Maybe because I wasn't used to all this male attention, and after a night with Xander, I was starting to crack. But I had to put all that away in a box and switch on mom mode.

"Is Jamal awake?" I asked, heading toward my room to change my shirt real quick. I'd shower later.

A genuine smile broke out on her face, making her look so much like her son. The pang of pain I used to get no longer reared its ugly head when I saw the likeness. I only felt an appreciative fondness and comforting nostalgia in my brief time with Rashon.

"Yes," she said. "He's showering now."

My shoulders fell, releasing tension I didn't realize I'd been holding there. "I don't know how to thank you, Mama Jean. You've been a godsend since I started this night shift." I rubbed my forehead. *And before that.*

Rashon gave me a child and a parent.

Mama Jean waved a dismissive hand at me. "Honey child, you don't need to thank me. We are family. It's what we do." She stood in the doorway to my bedroom as I stripped the disgusting tank top off.

Mama Jean had always been adamant about staying in my and Jamal's life. While my parents retired to Florida years ago, Mama Jean moved out here from Georgia to be close to us. She took care of Jamal when I was still on active duty.

After I got out of the army I did my best to stay independent, but her constant presence somewhat accustomed me to counting on her, and after my massive cosmic mistake I had to lean on her more heavily than ever. Thankfully, she didn't mind.

I pulled on a soft T-shirt. Instantly, my battery filled fifteen percent. Soft, clean clothes was one way to my heart.

Not that I'd ever tell Xander that little tip. I needed to keep that god far away from my fleshy blood-filled organ.

I finished changing and stepped back into the living room, where Mama Jean was setting the table for breakfast.

Jamal came bounding out of the bathroom, his toothbrush still in his mouth. His bright eyes landed on me, and he gave a muffled, "Mmng!"

I chuckled, ruffling his short crop of hair. "Good morning, kiddo. Ready for that math test?"

Jamal nodded vigorously, foam from the toothpaste dribbling down his chin. "Mm-hmm!" he mumbled, before dashing off to spit and rinse.

Mama Jean shook her head affectionately. "That boy. He's growing up too fast." Mama Jean's gentle hands moved with practiced ease as she buttered pieces of toast. The rich aroma of the coffee enveloped the room, mixing with the gardenia scent of her favorite hand cream.

"Yeah, he is," I agreed, watching Jamal with a combination of pride and wistfulness. I loved being his mother almost more than anything.

Jamal returned, his face clean, and sat at the table after dropping a kiss on his G-Ma's cheek. He glanced at me, his young face suddenly serious. "Did you catch the bad guys last night, Mom?"

"Bad guys?" Mama Jean said, halting her pour of coffee abruptly.

I gave Jamal a meaningful look to lock down his comments around his G-Ma.

He turned away and gritted his teeth. While Jamal

knew far too much about the immortal underbelly of Vegas, Mama Jean was blissfully unaware, and I planned to keep it that way.

"You know, people who want to scam the casinos. Bad guys," I supplied to Mama Jean. She thought I still ran security at Sinopolis. I didn't love lying to her, but I'd learned long ago that there were necessary lies to keep loved ones and civilians safe as well as at ease.

"Well Lord have mercy, because you came in smelling like a garbage truck honey. Are you sure they are paying you enough?" She held out a steaming mug of coffee to me. I really should pass on more caffeine if I wanted to sleep, but truthfully, I didn't want to.

I'd only dream of *him*.

"Uh." My thoughts raced as I looked down into the dark elixir of life as I took it. "A high-profile patron lost their jewelry in the trash, and we helped dig it out for her."

"Oh well, that was awful good of you." Mama Jean nodded.

As Jamal chattered about his upcoming test, I smiled and listened, treasuring these mundane yet precious moments. They were my anchor in a life filled with chaos and danger.

Tonight, I'd face the supernatural again. But for now, I was just a mom, sharing breakfast with her family.

CHAPTER 7
THE BEAST

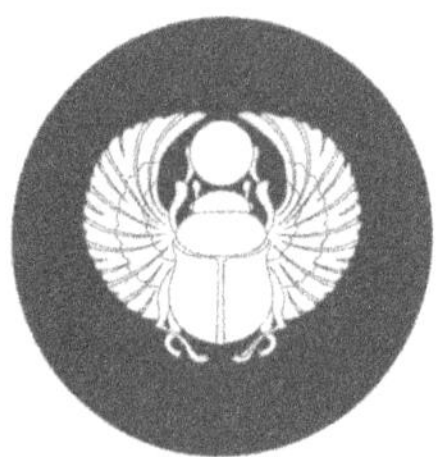

The daytime passed in a torturous crawl, every second a burning needle piercing my sanity. I was practically vibrating with anxious energy as I paced the opulent lobby of Sinopolis for two hours before Miranda even showed up.

The clack of polished shoes against the smooth marble floor grated against my eardrums, a constant reminder of the passing time. More than once, someone bumped into me, not bothering to look up from the little glowing phone in their hands. People were more like zombies now.

The bright lights overhead seemed to buzz loudly in my ears, creating a sense of disorientation and unease.

Desperate for some relief, I had resorted to wearing sunglasses even indoors, hoping they would offer some reprieve from the harsh lighting.

Growing more agitated with each minute that ticked by, I started to fear I'd neared a snapping point.

Which is why it was absolutely the fucking worst when a primly dressed Timothy clipped his way directly toward me in expensive shoes and a lush verdant green suit. Per usual there wasn't a hair out of place framing his Asian features that were arranged into a cool mask of control. Grim's second-in-command had a strong distaste for me, always barely tolerating my existence. I didn't care for his neat freak routine either.

"To what do I owe the pleasure Thothy-pie." I bared my teeth at my fellow immortal, belying the levity of my words. I bastardized his ancient name, Thoth, just to see his jaw tick.

His back stiffened. "I heard Grim has aligned you with Miranda in her pursuits. No doubt a situation you manipulated to get close to her again."

I rolled my eyes and sneered. "Come to warn me away from her again?"

Because now that I'd gotten a taste of her, I couldn't let go. I *wouldn't* let go. I'd spend the rest of eternity trying to claw my way back into her heart.

Timothy regarded me with a gaze that cooled the temperature around us by several degrees. "I suppose my wisdom would be lost on you then?"

"It's called an opinion, and they are like assholes. Everyone has one and they all stink."

Timothy visibly recoiled at my crudeness. I deliberately laid it on thick to offend his sensibilities. I knew I wasn't good enough for Miranda, but I didn't need Timothy rubbing that in my face.

"Fine." He held up a hand. "You don't need my opinion, but how about a few facts?" Before I could stop him, he barreled forward. "Miranda is mortal and you are not. How do you think this ends, Xander?"

Despite all the hot tension pulsating in my body, I coolly observed my nails and replied, "With us living happily ever after."

"You'll stay with her until she grows old and gray and crosses over to the afterlife?"

My stomach churned.

"If need be," I said, though truthfully I hadn't considered the future..

Timothy sighed, his shoulders dropping several inches. "I know you think I am your adversary, but we aren't so different." We mutually sized each other up, him in his perfect suit and controlled lifestyle and me in my loud Hawaiian shirt, messy hair overdue for a cut, and raging mental instability.

Still, he went on, his voice lowering. "You don't know the pain of loving someone so hard you'd turn yourself inside out, only to blink and find they are gone with an eternity stretched out before you, absent of their lifeforce."

The scowl remained on my face even as I swallowed hard. I didn't want to give Timothy any space in my brain, but I could already feel his words burrowing into my neurons like tiny mites that would eat away at me.

Even the thought of an existence without Miranda's lifeforce in it made my skin crawl and acid rise up my throat. It would be unbearable.

"Why do you hate me so fucking much?" I rasped, my fists tightening into balls.

Timothy's expression softened, surprise flickering in his eyes. "Don't you see, Nun?" he asked, using my old name, causing a spark to ignite in me. A hand fell to my shoulder, imprinting a level of sincerity I'd never experienced from him before. "I don't hate you at all. I am still trying to protect my friend and you from yourselves before it's too late." Timothy's eyes flickered over my shoulder.

I knew without looking that he'd spared a glance at the man who worked at the coffee stand. The mortal with the beach boy looks and the damaged voice box.

The one Timothy yearned to be with.

The sincerity in his voice made me all the angrier. Though whether I was angry because he kept trying to interfere or because he had a point was unclear.

I shrugged his hand off and stalked away from him, wanting to put as much distance between me and Timothy's words as possible.

Yet they clung to me, like a sticky patina. Even long after the god had left, the words sunk into my pores infecting me with ideas that combated the feelings I had for Miranda.

She was mine, and I had to make her see that.

But the future looked bleak even if she was the briefest shining light of my existence. Not to mention, I wasn't sure what she would think of our coupling. Mortals were sensitive about aging in contrast to the immovable nature of gods.

Maybe there was a solution. An eternity with Miranda, one where we were bound together for all time. Like Grim and Vivien. A god and his sekhor.

My palm slammed into my temple several times with rapid blows.

No. I could not think of asking her to become a vampire when she didn't even believe we belonged together. Still, my thoughts jumbled into muddled spirals, causing anxiety to rise in every strand of muscle until I was sure I'd explode. I had to get out of here. I had to collect myself or things would get messy.

Just when I'd been about to turn and head back to where I'd been retreating during most of my days, she strode through the door.

Miranda stole the breath from my lungs before ripping my beating heart out. Maybe it was my madness, but I swear I could feel my brain drip out of my ears as my eyes devoured her lithe figure dressed in dark, form fitting combat clothes.

The sleek material clung to every curve and muscle of her body, accentuating her toned arms and legs. Her tank top revealed the defined lines of her shoulders and the dips between her biceps and triceps. Even as her dark eyes bore into me with hard scrutiny, they were the most mesmerizing feature I had ever seen.

Not to mention they were a perfect juxtaposition to the soft near over-fullness of her mouth.

Fuck. That mouth.

Every aspect of her being exuded a raw violence and sexuality that left me reeling. Her expression always broadcasted that she'd suffer no fools and not even the strongest god or man could tame her.

In that moment, I wanted to beg her to kick my ass because it would give me a sick kind of satisfaction to have her unleash all of that strength on me.

Apparently, the long torturous years of seclusion had turned me into a masochist.

Walking right up to me, Miranda had no clue I was crumbling before her.

"Ready?" she asked.

I shoved my hands in my pockets and gave her a mute nod.

With a cool glance down at my feet, she gave another sharp nod. "Better."

I followed her gaze to the heavy boots I now wore that were far more practical than the sandals. Miranda scanned back up to my chest where my bright turquoise Hawaiian shirt was only fastened by one button, since I still felt claustrophobic wearing shirts.

Miranda whirled around and I had to take several long strides to catch up to her quick pace as we walked out into the evening, the sun quickly setting with fiery oranges shooting into the sky as the day died before us. Instantly, we were both shining with sweat from the baking heat.

"That color looks good on you. Brings out your eyes," Miranda said, keeping her focus forward.

The lump in my throat doubled in size.

A normal person would say something like, "Thank you," but all my brain could pound out beat after beat was, *I'll make you mine, I'll make you mine, I'll make you mine.*

So I kept my mouth shut and matched her pace. Perhaps a little hunting would clear my mind. And if I was very lucky, a little violence would work off this extra energy before I took it out on Miranda.

THE HEAT WAS A TANGIBLE WEIGHT, pressing down on us as we moved through the streets. It felt like the city was holding its breath, waiting for something to happen. We were on the hunt for Sheshem, but the massive cat god remained elusive, slipping through our fingers like smoke.

We'd hear rummaging in dumpsters around the corner,

but once we got there, the devastation had been done, leaving rotting food exposed and used napkins rolling around free.

Miranda coiled like a spring, pulling in tighter with each missed encounter. She moved with a predator's grace, her eyes constantly scanning the alleys and shadows. Despite the odds stacked against her, her determination only grew.

While I only became crankier, unhappy I couldn't work out the extra energy thrumming through me.

I should be grateful. Not that long ago, this level of agitation would have power ripping me apart, turning me into my monstrous god-likeness, out of my mind with violence and pain.

I wouldn't do it again though. I'd managed to keep myself from turning into the beast for weeks now. I had to make sure it was safe before I approached Miranda.

While my power had normalized, I was anything but balanced. It had taken brutal hours, days, weeks of pushing the jumbled parts of my mind into a working lump of control.

But right now, I was beginning to think control was overrated.

"We're chasing shadows," I grumbled, scanning the rooftops. Sheshem could be anywhere, watching us with those big, feline eyes and mocking our efforts. "Maybe you should go home."

Miranda shot me a look. "This is my responsibility, Xander. I can't turn away from this."

I scoffed. "That's only because the other gods are putting pressure on you, letting a mortal do their dirty work."

She stopped, turning to face me. "*I'm* the one who made

this mess. I take full responsibility and will deal with the consequences."

I turned on her, fury filling me up like a kettle beginning to boil. "You shouldn't have to deal with the consequences. You're a human."

Even as I said it, Timothy's words reared up and slapped me in the face. I did my best to squash his reservations back down into the dark recesses of my mind. The details of our future could be figured out later. Right now I was trying to win her back.

Though right now she was looking at me like she wouldn't deign to spit on me even if I was the last being on earth and fully on fire.

"Stop underestimating me."

I could practically hear her grinding her teeth.

"Fine." I stepped closer, my nostrils flaring as I breathed in her heady scent. "You think you can take on the gods. Let's see what you got."

I lunged at her. Miranda reacted instantly, her blade flashing. But I was faster, a blur of motion, godly speed at my disposal. I dodged her strike, my hand closing around her wrist, pulling her close.

Our eyes locked, inches apart, and the heat radiating off her body drilled into mine. Her heart raced, her breath quick and shallow. The air was charged with something more than just the tension of the hunt—something deeper, primal.

I released her hand, stepping back. "You're too slow. You need to anticipate, react faster."

Miranda's eyes flashed with frustration, and she attacked again, her movements fluid and calculated. But again, I was faster, evading her strikes with ease.

We danced around each other, a deadly ballet in the

empty alleyway. Every touch, every near miss, sent a jolt of electricity through me. I could see it in Miranda's eyes too, that fire, that undeniable spark.

"You're holding back," she accused, panting.

I grinned, adrenaline pumping through my veins. The irritation had given way to excitement as we sparred. "Wouldn't want to hurt you, sweetheart."

Something flashed in her eyes at the pet name I gave her when she'd visited my cell nightly to kill me. It rolled off my tongue like sugar, and I could almost taste her even now.

She growled, lunging again, and this time I let her get close, close enough that our bodies almost touched. Our gazes met, and for a heartbeat, the world stood still.

"You can't win this, Miranda," I said in a low husky tone, even as my focus drifted down to her lips. For a minute, even I wasn't sure if I was talking about her suicidal hunt for the gods, or this thing between us.

She shook her head. "This isn't one of your games, Xander. It's not about winning, it's about doing what's right."

"Is it right if you get killed trying to track down immortals? What happens if you come face to face with... him?" My guts wrenched up into a tight ball, heat gathering in my forehead as flashes of her burning up under his powers slammed into my temple.

I watched Miranda's throat swallow hard as if something thick was stuck in there. "Then I'll deal with that too."

"Over my dead body," I snarled, before lunging at her again. She quickened her pace.

Aten was as vicious as he was cruel. He would take her apart piece by piece with zero remorse. It's what he did to me. Aten flayed me alive, sending me back to the cradle of life. I emerged from the cradle thousands of years too soon, corrupted with too much uncontrolled power where I remained in a living hell until my mistress of death came along.

Aten had wreaked havoc on me for the past five millennia, and I was a god. Miranda was mortal. I wouldn't let him anywhere near her.

"That's how we got here, isn't it?" she threw at me.

A wry smile pulled at my lips. At least she could joke about what happened. After all, she'd been around my dead body quite a bit.

With that, I gained a couple inches closer to her inner defenses without being shot down.

It took everything in me not to try to claw off her armor, but I knew it would get me nowhere. Miranda's defenses had become a second skin, and she hated being naked. But fucking hell and godsdammit, I wanted her naked in every way. Bare and vulnerable, just so I could show her I'd be the only armor she ever needed from the world.

We circled each other, the tension palpable in the dimly lit alley. Each of Miranda's attacks was faster, more precise, pushing me to dodge with a grace I reserved for battles of a higher stake.

"You are mortal. You can't depend on speed to save you," I coached.

When she lunged with a particularly aggressive thrust, I sidestepped, using her forward momentum to spin her towards me. The move was calculated, intended to disorient, but she was quick to recover, launching a high kick aimed directly at my chest. I caught her leg, the contact a spark in the charged air between us.

Our eyes locked in a heated gaze, her chest heaving in quick bursts.

"You're going to need to be smarter. Monsters only answer to their base instincts. Gods are arrogant. They will underestimate you, which you can use to your advantage to exploit their weaknesses."

Her response was not verbal but physical—a twist and a pull that should have sent her stumbling away from me. Instead, the momentum crashed her into me, pushing us both off balance.

My arms shot out and instinctively wrapped around her to prevent us both from falling. Our faces were inches apart, her breath warm against my skin, stirring something within me that had nothing to do with our combat.

For a long moment, we just stared at each other, the air thick with unspoken words and suppressed desires that shimmered before us like heat waves. I could feel her heart beating against my chest, fast and hard.

Then, slowly, almost hesitantly, Miranda tilted her head up, her mouth parting slightly. My gaze dropped to her lips as she licked them slowly before whispering, "You said to exploit their weakness against them." Her voice was soft, her breath tickling my face, pulling me deeper into the moment, into her.

Her words didn't penetrate my brain as it went fuzzy from her closing the distance between us, my lips parting in anticipation of tasting her.

In a swift movement, Miranda slipped from my hold, her leg sweeping out under mine, sending me crashing to the ground. I blinked, finding myself on my back, the hard ground pressing against my shoulders and my breath jettisoned from my lungs with a tight, painful squeeze.

Miranda, quick to capitalize on her advantage, straddled me with a grace that belied the deadly intent of the blade she now held to my throat. The metal was a chilling touch against my skin.

"You mean like that?" she asked, tilting her head with haughty triumph.

Despite the blade at my neck, despite the precarious position I found myself in, I couldn't help the surge of admiration that went through me. I grinned at her.

That's my girl.

Pinned beneath her, I was acutely aware of every point of contact between us. The pressure of her thighs around my torso threatened my sanity.

The desire to close that distance was overwhelming. I saw the same longing mirrored in her eyes. I leaned up onto my elbows and surprisingly, she allowed me to brush the blade aside before reaching up to push her braids back behind the perfect shell of an ear I wanted to nibble on until she gasped and shivered.

Her breath was warm against my face, a tantalizing hint of closeness that drew me in, the world narrowing down to the space between us.

As I leaned up for a kiss that promised to shatter the walls between us, our moment teetered on the edge of becoming something more.

Just as our lips were about to meet, an exasperated, nasal voice shattered the moment.

"Oh no, not you two jerks again!"

The voice snapped us back to reality like an icy splash of water.

We were on our feet in seconds as Max and Alfonso emerged from the shadows of the alley, annoyance etched on their faces.

They didn't know the *meaning* of annoyance. The urge

to rip off their faces and throw them away like bits of trash overwhelmed me. My brain thundered with violent images as my emotions roiled with disappointment.

"What are you doing here?" Miranda snapped, her hand instinctively readjusting around her weapon.

Max, in his glittery magician costume that seemed even more out of place in the stark reality of the alley, rolled his eyes dramatically. "We were on the trail of our star act again, but it looks like we've stumbled upon a different kind of show," he said, eyeing us with a mix of disdain and lewd suggestion.

Alfonso, fumbling with his toy wand, chimed in with evident frustration. "Yeah, and we probably would've caught him if it weren't for you two always popping up and ruining everything! You are chasing off the star of our show."

Miranda's expression turned thunderous with irritation. "What did I tell you two idiots? You should not be tracking the massive murder cat." She enunciated the words as if explaining to a couple of slow minded children.

"You should stop getting in our way," Max shot back, before giving Alfonso a slight nod.

The moment Alfonso waved that cheap plastic wand, muttering some half-cooked incantation, I was hit by the urge to laugh.

"You are bound by the chains of the Houdini's heir, unable to break free until the moon kisses the sea."

It sounded like something out of a bad fantasy novel.

I scoffed. "Really? That's your big—"

A wave of dizziness hit me like a punch from a drunken boxer. My legs buckled, and the world spun. Miranda's concerned face blurred into a kaleidoscope of colors before darkness swallowed me whole.

When I came to, it felt like only seconds had passed, but I was laying down next to something warm. My right arm was cut short of movement with the rattle of something metal.

A pair of sparkling brown sugar eyes blinked back at me. Miranda.

We were chained to a bed that seemed to have been stolen from a medieval torture chamber placed on an otherwise empty stage.

CHAPTER 8

THE BEAST

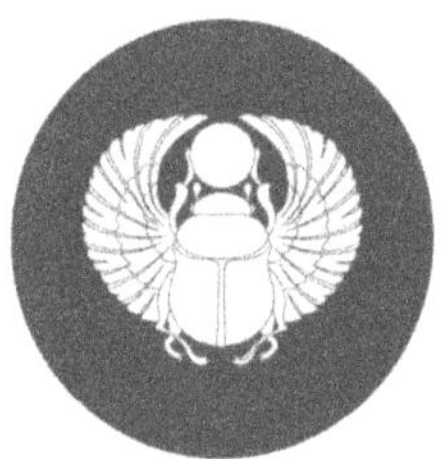

"Xander," Miranda's voice brought me back to the present, her tone clipped with irritation. "Tell me you can break these."

We were trapped together, handcuffed to a bed in an empty theater. I wish I could say I'd woken up in a stranger situation, but this kind of took the cake.

I shot her a smug grin and a flirty wink. "Of course I can, sweetheart."

My hubris got the best of me. I instantly realized I should have lied because I had my mistress of death exactly where I wanted her. Miranda lying next to me, her warm curves pressed into mine where she couldn't run away.

Also, I got a strange reassurance from being restrained. It likely had something to do with being locked up for most of my days. The sensation was akin to how someone else would feel with their grandmother's handknit blanket wrapped around them. Downright cozy.

But there was no taking advantage of this situation now, not that I let my mouth run before my brain caught up.

I tugged at the cuffs, expecting them to snap like twigs. Nothing.

My brows knitted in a frown. That can't be right. I pulled again, but something was holding some of my strength at bay.

"Hold on," I grunted, rolling over, pressing more firmly into Miranda's prone body. She turned her head, the only part she could move away from me.

Another jerk of my wrists. Nothing.

"Problem?" Miranda asked, her voice tight with impatience.

"No," I huffed. "No problem... Just..."

I twisted and rolled until I straddled Miranda's hips, covering her completely with my own body. The heat of her body scalded me even as she inhaled sharply.

Caught between my need to capture that sigh in my mouth and my pride, my pride won out as I refocused on getting us the fuck out of here.

I pulled at the handcuffs again and again. The chains rattled a mocking tune to my attempts to break the weak mortal metal. My agitation ratcheted upward as my efforts to break the chains grew near violent.

"Okay, okay, okay," Miranda practically yelled over the cacophony of my frustrated grunts and rattling metal. Her hands steadied my elbows even as I panted.

She took a deep breath. "What's going on? Is it some kind of god-proofed set of handcuffs?"

I searched my muddled thoughts.

Alfonso's ludicrous incantation echoed in my head, and I realized, with annoyance and disbelief, that it had worked. My godly strength, seemingly nullified by the power of bad acting and worse magic tricks.

"He's a hypnotist," I growled.

Miranda's brow rose in a skeptical arch. "And that works on gods?"

My lips twisted and a low growl vibrated from my throat.

"Oookay then," she drawled out. "Guess that's a yes."

It works when the god in question is weak of mind. I didn't want to admit that to her though. She didn't know. She couldn't know. It's why I stayed away for so many long weeks until I was strong enough to get back to her. I wanted to be normal, reliable, for her.

"Seems like we're stuck," I admitted, trying to ignore how close Miranda was. Her warmth, the scent of her, it was all a bit too much for a god who was supposed to be focusing on escape, not the way her velvet braids brushed against my skin.

Our faces were inches apart, our bodies aligned in a way that was both uncomfortable and electrifying. I could feel every breath she took, each little movement sending a new wave of awareness through me.

"Do you have your phone? Mine isn't in my pocket," she asked.

"I believe they are over there," I said, pointing off to an edge of the stage where keys, phones, and even Miranda's blade sat on a chair, well out of reach.

"This is ridiculous," Miranda said. "We're supposed to

be hunting a god, not playing out some magician's twisted fantasy."

"I know, I know," I replied. "But you have to admit, there's something poetic about us being chained together. Like fate is telling us we belong together." I waggled my eyebrows at her.

She scowled. "Don't get any ideas, Xander. As soon as we're out of this, it's back to the mission."

"Of course, the mission." Then I repeated the magician's dopey words, "You can't break free until the moon kisses the sea. So that means until dawn?"

"Great, just great," Miranda muttered, shifting slightly. The movement sent a ripple of awareness through me, every sense heightened by our proximity. "It's a ridiculous thing to say about a landlocked state."

"I estimate we have a couple more hours trapped here together."

At that, pure panic flittered across Miranda's face, widening her eyes and quickening her breath, causing her chest to heave. "That's unacceptable."

With that, she rolled us until she was on top. Miranda plucked a hairpin from her braids as if performing a magic trick herself. She directed the makeshift lock pick to the keyhole on the cuffs, but her hand stopped abruptly an inch away. Miranda's hand shook as she gritted her teeth, trying to push the hairpin into the hole. It was as if some invisible force was keeping her from getting any closer, the same force that held my strength back when I tried to snap the chains.

We were both under that doofus's spell.

Miranda growled and threw the hairpin aside, resorting to pulling and rattling the chains like I had. Her motions grew jerkier and more desperate as her panic mounted.

The urge to calm her down was overridden by a more powerful problem of my own.

Though it wasn't her intention, Miranda was riding and rubbing the part of me that had already grown to attention. The ache to thrust inside her gripped me like a massive fist.

My hands fell to her hips as I stopped breathing all together.

"You're gonna have to stop that, sweetheart, or we are both going to be in for more than you bargained for," I choked out.

Miranda's head tilted down at me, her braids falling to brush over my chest with alluring caresses. Annoyance gleamed brightly in her features, but realization dawned on them as she took in how I gripped her hips and the hardness that pressed into her inner thigh.

"Or," I licked my lips, daring to press my luck. "We could make the next few hours at least interesting and see how many times I can get you to scream my name." My voice was hoarse to my own ears.

I waited for the slap to ring out across my face and for the consequent sting of her rejection.

"Oh really?" Miranda said. Her voice and face were tense, as if she rode on the edge of something sharp. Something she would likely stab me with. "How many times do you think you could make me scream?"

My head snapped up so fast, it nearly flew off. Am I still caught in that ridiculous magician's thrall and in a full blown hallucination?

She asked the question as seriously as if she were asking about a cancer diagnosis. Miranda took everything too seriously.

I lifted my hips, hitting the soft warmth of her sex with my hardness. The contact dragged a groan from both of us.

Miranda threw her head back as her hands curled around the bed's iron frame, the heat intensifying between us. "I'm betting at least five," I said roughly.

My hands found their way to her hips again, pulling her closer. The heat of our bodies pressed together was incredible, and my desire for her grew to near maddening hardness. We were both breathing hard, our hearts pounding in sync.

"You want to bet me?" Miranda dared me, her eyes challenging me to make good on my words.

We'd tried playing games in the past, but both of us were too competitive to relax into the frivolity normal people get from play. But I did discover she couldn't resist a wager, and I found that far more delicious a concept to play with than a board of Candy Land. Though that game really ended in my favor too...

My hips rocked gently up into her scalding soft heat. "What do I get if I win?"

Her dark orbs narrowed, even as her free hand fell onto the exposed chest of my unbuttoned shirt. It scalded me, my nipples wrenching up with tight anticipation.

"Wouldn't winning be satisfaction enough?" she asked.

A feral grin kicked up at the corner of my mouth. I was far more hungry than she could have guessed. If she knew how I wanted to possess her utterly and completely, she'd drop the bet all together. She'd likely break her own wrist to slip it from the chains and get far away from me.

As my straining cock rocked right into the dip of her cleft again, lust fogged my senses.

"If I make you scream my name five times, I get to take you on a date. You'll dress up, we'll have dinner, the whole real deal."

Miranda's glistening full lips parted in surprise before

her face contorted as I rocked into her again. That hand clutched and clawed at my chest, leaving scratch marks.

Fuck. Hell. That felt so good, I almost forgot to stay focused on closing the bargain.

"And if I win?" she rasped, her fathomless pupils nearly swallowing her irises up.

"What do you want?" I asked. My fingers dug into her hips so I could roll up into her harder, faster. Miranda's head fell back with a gasp and her sweet, honeyed arousal filled the air until my mouth watered.

Sweet afterlife, it was going to take all my strength to focus on driving her to madness instead of burying myself in her and fucking her like a savage. It felt like it had been an eternity. But I had too much on the line.

"You throw away the hideous Hawaiian shirts," she finally got out.

"Deal," I barked, as soon as she stated her terms. Our lips crashed into each other, and the world around us faded away. All that existed was the heat of our bodies and the ravenous desire that drove us.

And if she truly thought she was winning this bet, she was the crazy one.

CHAPTER 9

THE BADASS

It's just a bet. It doesn't mean anything, I tried to tell myself. But I couldn't hold onto my own reasoning as hot tingles rushed throughout my body, bringing me to life in a way only Xander could evoke.

The god met my mouth with hot open mouth kisses of fierce intensity. His tongue explored my mouth, tasting and savoring as his hand gripped the back of my neck, drawing me even closer. I kissed him harder, trying to reassert the dominance I somehow lost even though I was on top of him.

Through our clothes, I could feel his desire for me. His need was just as powerful as mine in the hardness rocking against my aching wetness. The pure, raw sexuality between us sent shivers down my spine.

The hand holding the back of my neck released and scooped under my ass, pulling me up until I sat on his upper chest. "Get these fucking things off right now," Xander growled as he leaned forward and used his teeth to tug at the hem of my leggings, before he dipped lower and ran his tongue along the seam of my sex.

Blood shot to my head like a gun blast, leaving me dizzy.

Holy shit.

Urgency smashed into me. With our wrists still hand-cuffed to the bedframe, I un-straddled him, and we both pushed my pants off awkwardly and painstakingly. The skin-tight fabric stole my delicate yet soaked panties with them and I was no sooner free of them when Xander hauled me back up to his face, my legs splayed on either side of his ears.

He swiped his tongue up my wet slit, and the sound that escaped me was unrecognizable to my own ears.

Both my hands gripped the metal bed frame as Xander devoured me from below until I found a rhythm, riding his face.

The intensity built within me, like a wildfire raging out of control. My hips began to move in perfect sync with his mouth, riding him with a ferocity that matched his own.

"Oh god," I cried out as he brought me closer and closer to the edge.

"Fuck, Miranda," he rasped, his voice gruff and full of need. "You're so wet, so ready for me. Do you know how much I want you? I always fucking want you. You're in my blood now and I'll never get you out."

A fire ignited within me, fueled by his words and the

heated intensity of his touch. The rasp of his stubble on my soft wet parts only drove me crazier.

A strong, unstoppable need built within me, like a wildfire raging out of control.

"Oh fuck," I cried out as he brought me closer and closer to the edge.

He was a mess. Xander, a god who didn't bother shaving regularly, desperately needed a haircut, and wore ridiculous Hawaiian shirts with combat boots. Any woman could see the neon sign above him flashing 'man child.'

Although, I was also above him now, my hips bucking wildly against his face. I chased that upward slope of intensity with wild abandon.

My abs wrenched up tightly as I grew more tense, more wound up. The irrational thought that I might die if I didn't find release soon took hold of my mind.

Xander's fingers and tongue worked in perfect harmony to elicit the most delicious sensations from me.

Every movement, every flick of his tongue was calculated and precise, driving me closer and closer to the edge. As I neared my peak, my mind became consumed with the fear that only he knew how to make me feel this way, that without him I would never reach this level of euphoria again.

Then his tongue turned rigid and his touch quickened, pushing me over the edge so fast I didn't know where the ground was.

"Xander, oh god, yes!" I screamed, throwing my head back as the waves of pleasure crashed over and through me. My body shuddered violently, writhing in the throes of an agonizingly sweet release, each contraction pulling me deeper into the abyss of pleasure.

My body still buzzed with need even as my knees

relaxed from around his head. Xander looked up at me, licking his wet lips like the cat who got the cream. The devilish spark in his eyes radiated satisfaction that bordered on smugness. "That's one, sweetheart."

My competitive side reared up for attention. "That was your freebie. I didn't want you to think you didn't have a chance... even if you don't."

His thumb brushed against the sensitive skin where my inner hip and thigh met, as he stared at me like he could see straight through my bluff. Like he knew he was going to win.

And we both knew he wanted to win more than my body. I couldn't allow that though. Not when he hurt me so badly already.

No one hurt me twice. I was smarter than that.

Is that why you let him lick you to a bone shaking orgasm? my senses asked.

Before I could get into the debate with myself, I was on my back.

Xander's free hand pushed up my tank top.

The way we were chained, neither of us could divest ourselves of our tops, but I unbuttoned his shirt the rest of the way. My fingers trailed down the washboard of his cut muscles, making my chained-up hand jealous.

The fabric bound tight above my freed breasts, perking them up for him to drop and wrap his lips around my nipple. Electricity jolted from behind my bud of flesh, striking down between my legs, causing another rush of desire to coat my thighs. Fuck, why did I feel like I was even more desperate to come a second time?

Xander shoved his shorts down. Sure enough he wasn't wearing underwear, who could be surprised? The man clearly had a grudge against clothing.

I hated how I found that detail of him going commando so fucking sexy. I knew it would burn me up whenever I saw him in the future.

My mouth went dry as his thick cock sprung free, the tip glistening with his desire.

A smirk pulled his mouth in that sinful manner that made me want to either kiss or punch it off. Maybe both.

"You know what's going to make this easy, sweetheart?"

I scowled at him, openly communicating I wasn't interested in chit chat right now.

He dropped his hips, nudging at my lower lips with his cock, causing me to gasp and dig my hand into the sheets.

Xander kept nudging at my wet entrance even as he kissed his way over to my other nipple then up the sensitive column of my neck until his hot breath washed over my ear.

"Because I know you think of me when you touch yourself. I know when you grow wet, my name is already bouncing around your mind. And because it's already balanced on the tip of your tongue, I can push it out whenever I want."

As he said that last part, he thrust his rigid cock into me, filling and stretching me in ways I'd forgotten were possible.

"Oh god," I hissed between my teeth, my chained-up hand gripping the bed frame so tight my knuckles shook as he filled me.

"That's right sweetheart, I'm your god now and I'm going to fuck you into oblivion." His hand covered mine, even as he pumped in shallow, teasing motions. "Say it, Miranda. Say my fucking name." His words came out in a pained hiss.

My brain turned into a white fuzzy haze as all my

senses were engulfed by pleasure. His words echoed around me even as I lost track of where I was. I was floating, flying higher and higher but not fast enough. I wanted more, I needed more.

"Do you want more, sweetheart? Say. My. Name." The words were thick hot honey, pouring into my brain and turning my blood molten. My hips bucked, trying to get more.

"Say it," his command came rougher this time as he pinched one of my nipples, giving me a white hot zap of pain and pleasure.

"Xander," I keened and moaned. "Please, I need more."

He immediately obeyed, his hips slamming into mine, shooting my breath up into my throat.

As we kissed, our bodies moved in a frenzy of passion, our lips and tongues exploring, our hands roaming, our bodies colliding again and again. He was my drug, and I couldn't get enough.

Something inside me cracked, and it was like meeting a part of myself I'd tried to forget. I tensed around him, on the verge of breaking.

He stopped fucking me so abruptly, my head spun.

Hovering over me, still, and dripping with sweat, he smelled liked soap, fresh sea air, and sex. He was unreal. "Fucking say my name, Miranda. Say it and I'll let you come, sweetheart."

I closed my eyes and whimpered. "Xander."

His next words came out through gritted teeth. "Beg me."

I shook my head, keeping my eyes wrenched shut tight. No. I'd already moaned his name a third time, but I wouldn't beg anyone.

"So we are back to that, are we?" he asked in a cold voice. "Fighting me while we fuck?"

He wasn't wrong. I suddenly didn't want to give him any more of me. It was all too much. I halted my orgasm, freezing it in place, trying to control myself.

"Fine," he snarled. "I'll fucking take it from you then." With that, he resumed a punishing pace into me. "You're my girl, and you know I'm completely and utterly yours. You feel that, sweetheart? That's my name pushing its way back into your mouth."

There was no sense or reality, just Xander's words and cock filling me up until I felt it... his name. It tasted salty and delicious as it landed on my tongue. The harder he fucked me, the closer it moved toward my lips.

"Say it, Miranda. Say it, like you know you're mine."

My body seized as I fractured on Xander's cock, his name wailing out of my mouth like a prayer.

I forced my heavy lids to lift and met his eyes which were stormy waves of cerulean blue. Sweat coated his skin, highlighting his ferocious intensity. Xander didn't just fuck me, he claimed me from every cell inside and out.

His pace didn't relent, overstimulating my over-sensitized body, rocking me into an acute spike of pain before I swung like a pendulum back into pleasure.

"It's been too fucking long," he rasped, face contorted in ecstasy so intense he seemed to be in agony. "Too fucking long. I can't—not without—I need you, Miranda. You are fucking air. Fucking water. I want to drown in you."

My responsibilities slipped away, my guarded nature dropped, and I met his thrusts as moans with senseless primal instincts. I was free, soaring, and surging with more power than I knew possible. Xander not only set me free, but he could handle all of me unleashed, just as I could handle him.

Then his powerful hands flipped me, pulling me up and onto my knees. The handcuffs tightened on both of us, drawing him even closer as he slid into me from behind. I cried out as he penetrated deeper than should have been possible. He covered both of my hands on the bed frame as it creaked wildly, threatening to collapse under us. He covered my back with his flexing torso. There was no one in the world but us.

"Xander." His name came out in a half-choked sob this time. I felt complete, alive, in a way no one else could make me feel—not even myself. Even though he was here, as close as he could get, I missed him so fiercely my insides threatened to blow apart. Whether the feeling of missing him was from before or in anticipation of him leaving my body, I couldn't tell.

His lips kissed gently along my spine even as his cock speared me deeper. My pleasure dripped down my thighs, and over his balls that smacked into me, causing a secondary jolt of pleasure.

"That's four, sweetheart," came his husky whisper in my ear. "Give me one more."

I shook my head, not even sure what I was trying to deny any more when he made my body sing and break so completely, but it was my nature to fight. It's who I was.

His hand slipped down, and two fingers pushed onto my clit with a firm grinding motion as if it were my own hand that knew exactly where to touch.

"Please," he begged, voice hoarse. "Say it, sweetheart. Say it so I can fill you up. I can't unless you let me." Xander's breath hitched, his pants becoming ragged and shallow.

A literal god was begging me to let him come by simply

saying his name. A girl's brain could explode from that thought alone.

"You want it, don't you, baby? You want my cock to fill you up?" He pleaded, almost desperate. He was the hypnotist now and suddenly I wanted that more than anything.

"Yes," I gasped, my voice hoarse and strained. "Fuck me, Xander. Please, just—"

And then he was coming, his hips jerking wildly as he filled me with his seed with a long, wretched roar that echoed throughout the empty theater.

I couldn't help the rush of pleasure as he spilled inside me. Xander was nothing short of a wild animal, driven and untamed, and I wanted to take in every ounce of that energy. His warmth coursed into me, warm and thick, satisfying some part of my brain I rarely used.

The peaks of my breasts screwed up and electrified into tight buds, my stomach clenching and releasing. My body buckled beneath him, quaking in yet another release as he claimed me in the most intense way possible.

"Fuck, Miranda," he groaned, his body shuddering as he collapsed onto his side, pulling me with him. His arms wrapped around me tightly.

The sheets were soaked from either our sweat or desire, and we lay there, panting until the air cooled our overheated bodies.

"Sushi or Mexican for our date?" Xander asked, breaking the moment.

CHAPTER 10

THE BADASS

The reality of what I'd done hit me like a bucket of ice cubes over the head. I'd been determined to keep him at arm's length. I had control of myself and the situation... until I didn't.

My self-respect, or was it my self-preservation, scattered like a flock of birds.

How much time had passed? I jumped off the bed, wrenching Xander along with me as I seized the hair pin again. Unlike last time, it landed in the pinhole, and I quickly unlocked the cuffs.

I snatched up my clothes and had them on before Xander even got up from the bed.

"Miranda," he said, his voice concerned but weak.

"We shouldn't have done that." All the self-hate poured in with more intensity than that last orgasm.

Okay, maybe not *that* intense, but close.

"Miranda, slow down," Xander ordered, but I was back in control of myself.

He stepped in front of me, completely nude and sexily disheveled, that stupid Hawaiian shirt still open, barely hanging on his shoulders, brows set low over his piercing, concerned eyes.

"I can't. I have to go. Jamal will be up soon." I swept by him, grabbing my effects off the chair and quickly finding my way out a door and into the morning heat that already promised to be another scalding day.

My brain raced at a mile a minute as my legs carried me in a half walk, half run, obeying my every instinct that told me to get as far away from the god in that theater as possible. We'd ended up in a place a mile off from the Strip, but I recognized this part of town. Only when I'd put a good distance between me and the sex god, did I order a ride to pick me up.

Thankfully the driver wasn't chatty, and I was dropped off at home just as Mama Jean and Jamal's morning alarms went off. I jumped into the shower, trying to erase what happened before they got up.

"You okay, honey child?" Mama Jean later asked with a furrowed brow over her coffee.

"What?" My head snapped up.

She reached out a buttery soft, yet weathered hand and set it on mine at the breakfast table. "You've been jumpy all morning. Like the devil himself might be chasing you."

I blinked.

My cool demeanor had been shattered after a couple

hours in bed with Xander. I could actually feel the guilt and heat eat at my cheeks.

With a quick glance at Jamal, I saw he was absorbed with the game on his tablet while he ate his cereal. Normally, I'd force him to put it away and focus on his food, but I left him alone. I pulled my hand away from Mama Jean's.

"Too much caffeine I guess," I offered with a smile that felt shaky on my lips.

My phone buzzed in my pocket and I jumped several inches. Jamal even looked up.

"Whoa Mom, you okay?"

Now two people were giving me way too much attention. I shot up to my feet. "Gotta take this." I pointed to the phone before hastily beating a retreat to my bedroom.

"Hello?" I answered, not even bothering to screen who called.

"Miranda," Grim's low, steady voice filled my ear as dread landed with a thud in my stomach. There was something about the way he said my name, as if he was about to tell me something I wouldn't like.

"Could you come to Sinopolis? I need to have a word with both you and Xander."

I couldn't speak past the lump in my throat.

"I understand you've been up all night hunting, but there is something we must discuss and I'm afraid it can't wait until tonight."

"Uh yeah, sure."

Even as I gave my distracted consent, Jamal cracked the door to give me a smile and wave to let me know he was off to school. I blew a kiss at him before he disappeared.

"I can come now," I said, not hearing Grim's farewell before the phone hung up.

I threw the phone on my bed and covered my face.

Oh my god, did Grim know what happened? Was he going to talk to us about what happened?

About your failure to kill Sheshem or because Xander banged your brains out?

So far, I was painfully aware of what a failure I was. Unable to kill a single god and trap it back inside of the Blade of Bane, and unable to hold my ground on not fucking the feral god who got under my skin and hurt me.

"Oh Bob," I said to the silent blade that also lay on my bed. "I wish you were here."

Despite Bob's squeamishness about blood and death, he'd been dealing with all of this supernatural immortal nonsense longer than I had.

A REFRESHING AIR-CONDITIONED breeze blew over me as I entered Sinopolis, stepping on to the ocean of gleaming black marble. I'd spent so much time here, it truly felt like my second home.

That feeling did little to ease the knots of nervousness in my gut. Maybe one day I'd get over the feeling that meeting Grim wasn't the same as being sent to the principal's office, but apparently that wouldn't be today.

Grim strode out from the elevator, making his way directly toward me. The god of death was always a big, imposing dark mass in black suits, and though I worked for him before I knew what he was, I always felt that distinct undercurrent of danger around him.

My skin prickled and heated as someone stepped up next to me. Xander. The jackass still wore the same rumpled blue Hawaiian shirt and pants from last night. A memory of him curled over me, the shirt undone and flowing around his hard body as he fucked me senseless, slammed into my head like a baseball.

Knowing he was likely keyed into my every small motion, I focused all my attention on steadying my breathing so he wouldn't know he affected me.

I screamed his name five times as I splintered under his tongue, hands, and cock, and that was mere hours ago.

He probably knows he's affecting me right now.

Goddammit.

Grim got halfway to us before a child ran out into the lobby. She couldn't have been older than ten years old and she stopped directly behind Grim, giggling.

Grim turned around slowly before leaning down to her level. "And what are you doing here, little one?" he asked.

It was, in fact, a school day, so she should by all rights be in a classroom somewhere.

"My mom works at Wolf Town Club, and we are going to the dentist this morning." Even as she gave her explanation, her giggles only intensified.

"What do you have behind your back?" he asked, his brows furrowing.

Oh no.

Not again.

The little girl's arm whipped around, holding a child-sized pillow and smashed it into his foreboding face.

Then with a delighted scream, she tore off, leaving the pillow behind. "Vivien made me do it!"

I thought we might be beyond this, but the great pillow war raged on between Vivien and Grim. I believe the fight started as a way for her to unwind and focus on something other than the crushing duties of being Master Vampire and dealing with the tragedies and trauma of all the humans who were turned against their will and now learning to navigate a life with fangs.

But neither Vivien nor Grim did anything halfway, and their creative, sometimes almost lethal pillow attacks would come at the most unexpected times.

"That was... weird," Xander said, his brow deeply furrowed as he stuck his hands in his pockets.

I was going to explain the great pillow war, but standing next to him, after the things we did, robbed me of my voice.

Grim scooped the pillow off the ground and handed it off to one of his employees who walked by. His face now seemed to be made of stone, but his eyes gleamed with a fire that made me very, very concerned.

CHAPTER II

THE BEAST

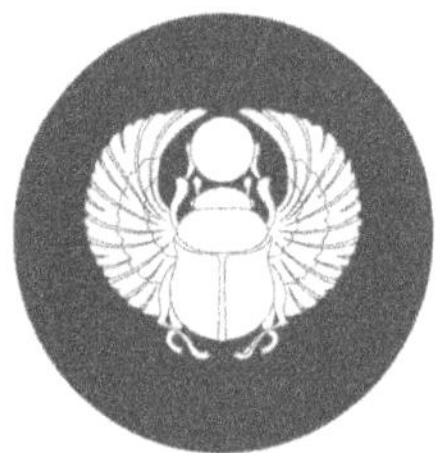

Because Miranda didn't reply, I couldn't be sure if what just happened was actually weird, or if I'd been kept below so long I didn't observe the normal social practice of swatting each other with pillows.

Would Miranda like that?

Getting used to living above ground among humans was more disconcerting than I ever wanted to admit. I chanced a sideways glance at Miranda. She'd showered off the sweat and sex I was still coated in. It intensified her clean bergamot scent which made my dick twitch even as a warmth spread from the center of my chest.

Instead of her combat clothes, she now wore high-

82

waisted jean shorts, and a black, long-sleeved crop top that displayed a thin band of her taut, glistening stomach. I wanted to drag my tongue along that strip of flesh, but there was no chance of that between Grim's cock blocking presence, and Miranda being locked down tighter than a bank vault.

She didn't let a single expression or tell escape her stony expression, and I knew she was doing it on purpose. Miranda's poker face was top notch, but I was learning to read the small twitches underneath that gave her away.

"Apologies for the interruption," Grim said through gritted teeth as he stopped before us. "Let us go somewhere where we won't be interrupted by my wife's insanity."

"Good luck with that," Miranda breathed.

Okay, someone would have to explain the pillow thing to me at some point, but everyone was acting as serious as a heart attack so it would have to wait for now.

Grim led us toward Wolf Town Club, the most exclusive club on the Strip. This early, it was deserted.

I could see why this place was so popular. The center-piece was a massive 360 degree bar, surrounded by a dance floor that I could feel the ghosts of writhing bodies on. Levels of balconies arose on all sides for those who wished to drink and look down at the fray.

Grim rounded the bar and pulled out a bottle of brown liquor and set it on the bar top.

"Can I offer either of you a nightcap? Seeing as all three of us just got off our duties?" The deep timbre of his voice echoed through the massive empty room.

Grim spent his nights judging souls for the Afterlife. But despite performing his duties, he looked as put together and slick as if he'd just arisen for the day.

I held up a hand. "None for me." There was no fucking

way I could keep my sanity together if I dripped even a drop of booze on my broken brain. Miranda needed to see I'd changed, that I could be whole. No matter what. She needed that stability.

Though we'd fucked like mindless, out of control animals, so we backtracked just a little.

It was hard to be sorry.

Miranda shook her head, declining a drink as well.

Grim shrugged and poured himself a small glass of the stuff, though he didn't take a sip.

He stared at the amber liquid as he spoke. "I have decided it is in all of the immortals' best interests to conduct a convocation."

The barest arch of Miranda's eyebrow told me she didn't know what that meant either.

"You sound like Timothy," I joked. "Why don't you just tell us what is going on?"

I didn't care for flourish or bullshit. It's one of the reasons why I worshiped the no-nonsense woman next to me so much.

Grim gave a sharp nod before tossing back the small bit of liquid. "In plain terms, we are going to hold a ball."

"And this involves us... how?" Not to say I didn't appreciate Grim getting me in proximity of Miranda again, but this felt like he was wasting our time.

Since I'd been released from the basement, I'd stayed as far away from immortal affairs as I could, that is until I joined Miranda on her mission. Even then, I had no desire to socialize with my brethren.

Grim leveled a gaze at me. "Word has finally spread of Nun's revival, and the immortals have grown anxious to welcome you back into the fold."

My hands slipped out of my cargo shorts at that. *Oh, fuck me off a waterfall.*

My tone turned stiff and cold. "Thanks, but no thanks. I'm not interested."

"Xander," Grim said, using his best 'be reasonable' voice. "Things have been tense with the release of Aten and any number of chaotic gods."

I didn't bother pointing out I was one of the original chaotic gods.

He went on. "A soiree to unite our kind in celebration of the return of one of our strongest will both assure and invigorate morale. You know as well as I do, we are best when we are united."

I took a step back, cognizant that Miranda was studying me closely. "Forget it. I am not some showpiece you are going to use to rally those spineless narcissists." The last words came out in a snarl.

"As much as you dislike it, you are one of us." Grim sighed. "I know the last time you gathered with the immortals it didn't end well—"

"Forget it," I spat out, cutting him off. My vision swam and blackness crept in on all sides, but I fought it back.

The very thought of being near those assholes, much less the center of scrutiny, threatened my senses I'd been working so hard to keep under control.

Grim's proposal echoed in my mind in a hundred taunting voices. My jaw twitched uncontrollably and a deafening roar filled my ears.

Pain.

Time.

Isolation.

They beat at me with so many bludgeoning rocks.

They were afraid, all of them. Afraid of Aten and what he was capable of. And they wanted to see me, the one who dared challenge him, the one who saw through his manipulations.

The anger swelled and raged inside me, consuming my thoughts and clouding my judgment. My body was coiled like a spring, ready to snap at any moment.

Grim's voice lowered, snaking under my rioting senses. "The days have grown hotter, a blaze that will only continue to grow as Aten runs loose. They are afraid, Xander. With Aten no doubt plotting somewhere, they want to see you. The one who dared challenge him, the one who saw his machinations for what they were."

A wave of hot fury rushed through me, threatening to boil over and consume everything in its path. Tendons and muscles swelled, attempting to lengthen and change. My primal instincts wanted to turn me into something else. Something unhinged and uncontrollable.

"They can all fuck each other right off a cliff!" Only after the words escaped me, did I realize I screamed them. In my periphery, Miranda recoiled. Self-hatred added its white-hot lancing pain to the mix.

Grim continued to meet my gaze with unflinching resolve. I dropped my voice to a low, gravelly tone, that still dripped with venom. "Or better yet, they can burn by Aten's hand. It's what he did to me."

The threads on my string of sanity were fast-fraying, so I turned and stalked out of the club before I lost control.

Each step felt like I was walking through fire, my mind ablaze with memories of Aten and his cruel actions.

The abandonment of my brethren pierced me deeply underneath that.

If they had helped me, if they had listened...

I died to save us all and now I was some kind of idol in their eyes.

Grim and Timothy had been trying to talk me into rejoining our kind, encouraging me to take my rightful place the last few months. Where my body had healed, the wounds in my mind and essence were still raw, still festering with betrayal and pain.

Grim believed unity among immortals was our greatest strength against the encroaching darkness, but the scars of the past ran too deep for me to easily set aside.

The only being I cared to be around nearly just saw me lose it over gods who weren't worth even a minute of consideration.

I'd thought being near Miranda so soon after what we did chained to that bed would be good for her. She could see it was safe to be around me, no matter what happened.

Instead, Grim tried to hurl me over the edge of my sanity in front of her. Fuck him. Fuck them all.

Once alone, my hands gripped at my head as voices and thoughts bombarded me so hard, I had to grit my teeth.

I needed a mission. Something to distance myself from the aggravation Grim caused.

In the long empty corridor leading to Wolf Town Club, a tiny black puppy appeared, jauntily stepping its way in the direction I'd come. It was rare to see a reaper puppy. It was even stranger to see one wearing a blinged out pink collar, as it would have required Grim to create one from the ether.

My mind suddenly flew in another direction, the only safe direction—toward Miranda.

In a moment of vulnerability, she'd once told me a tragic story from her childhood. One where she felt responsible for the death of the little dog she'd begged her parents for. When she'd been playing on her own, it had wandered out into the road and been hit by a car. The way she relayed the story, I knew it laid down an important pillar in her soul, one that taught her to never lose vigilance, to never play, and to be careful with who and what she loved.

A plan formed in my broken brain even as I made my way toward Grim's private elevator. Stepping in, I hit the black button that led to his judgment chambers.

What could help take my mind off his revolting proposition more than an ill-advised mission into the afterlife to retrieve the soul of Miranda's long lost pet?

I already knew I wouldn't be sleeping, even after spending my every ounce of attention and energy on Miranda in that theater. Thankfully I knew a ferryman who owed me a favor.

CHAPTER 12

THE BADASS

After Xander left, I turned to Grim. "I take it there was a reason you called me here too."

Grim's unerring focus remained on where Xander disappeared, deep in thought for a moment before he pulled his attention back to me. "Yes, I'm afraid you will not be exempt from this gathering."

I gritted my teeth. "Goodie." Suddenly I wished I had sprung for the drink. "I doubt they want me there to share a cup of tea and tell me what a good job I'm doing."

Grim shook his head even as his fingers flexed on the countertop. "I'm afraid they don't think they can trust a human, and I've come to the conclusion it would be best for them to meet you and understand what a considerable force you are."

I swallowed hard. That felt like a joke right now. I hadn't killed a single chaotic god in the preceding weeks. The pressure just doubled over on me.

"Vivien told me about the last ball," I said hesitantly, not wanting to set Grim off.

Vivien made a point to share what snooty meanie heads the gods, especially the demi-gods, were. My friend had a way with words.

One of the gods, Seth, had publicly presented Vivien with a collar inscribed with the words "Grim's Bitch," causing chaos and bloodshed that brought the party to a screeching halt. Vivien described Seth like an old George Clooney with an addiction to tanning, white suits, and gold chains who belonged on a yacht, throwing hundred-dollar bills at a bunch of young hoochies in bikinis.

Seth eventually lost his head to the Blade of Bane, but he was no doubt out on the streets again, thanks to me. Which also put him on my hit list.

I rose my chin to keep from letting my fear show. "Do you believe that this may be a setup to make an example of me?"

"I won't let anything happen to you, Miranda," Grim assured me. "Neither will Timothy or Vivien who will both be present."

Somehow that didn't feel nearly as reassuring as it should have.

Grim forced a smile that didn't reach his eyes. "Preparations are being made, and I've already entrusted Timothy and Vivien to see that you are properly dressed for the occasion."

I forced a smile. If the god of the dead thought playing

dress up would mitigate my fears about mingling with the literal gods I had crossed, he'd gotten the wrong memo.

I started to head out but paused and looked back. "You really don't think he'll show?"

Xander's reaction was explosive and violent, a storm of emotion that tore through the air around him. At Grim's suggestion, his newly calm demeanor shattered into fragments, leaving behind a raw, unbridled rage that seared my skin. I didn't fully understand the reason for his outburst.

Grim leaned his arms on the bar in a surprisingly human posture.

"The last time Xander was among our kind, he was attempting to rally us against Aten who was making moves to become the one true god. We didn't believe him. And it's what led to his death."

My heart suddenly seemed too big for my chest. Xander died some several thousand years ago when he went against Aten alone. I'd learned that the spirit or soul or whatever you want to call it—of the gods returned to a place called the cradle of life where they arise again centuries later. However, Xander almost immediately returned to physical form. Having not laid in the cradle long enough, his powers were volatile and overcharged, causing power surges that would continually fry his own brain and body.

He'd suffered more than anyone, all because he tried to do something about the danger when no one else would.

His sacrifice saved everyone else, but no one saved him. Not until I came along with the Blade of Bane, where he demanded I keep killing him until he's put to rest for good.

And then I brought back the god responsible for his death.

"How did..." I trailed off, thinking better of my question.

"Burned him to death I'm afraid," Grim said, his own expression contorted with pained lines.

Oofta. Not that I imagined being murdered in any way was pleasant, but imagining Xander burning to death made me positively sick.

Leaving Grim, I walked straight to Perkatory to order myself a quad shot red-eye from Aaron. There would be no sleep today. Because I'd be damned if I went to face the immortals without putting back at least one monster in the box.

Which meant I had to take a different tack.

Thirty minutes later, I parked outside Echo's warehouse. I traipsed by unused machinery to the back elevator, down past the cameras and automated guns that dropped from the ceiling as a security measure and into the secret lair.

Echo's massive space was half tech heaven with several dozen screens showing different anime shows, news programs, and surveillance cameras. The other half of the space resembled an old grandmother's living room. Antique floral couches spread out over a generous, patterned rug, protecting the living quarters from the cold concrete floor.

It looked like Batman's grandma had decided to move into the Batcave.

"What took you so long?" Echo asked in her usual clipped tone, and thick Filipino accent. Echo's face reminded me of a scowling bullfrog with her wide features and narrowed bulbous eyes. The short, stout woman's walking cane was set off to the side of her computer command chair. Short, pudgy fingers flew across the keyboard.

"You should have come sooner," she scolded again, without looking up. "We'll find them. We'll find them all," she promised.

The idea that I could use my fae contacts to help track down potential god targets only just hit me.

Apparently, Echo had been waiting for me to come to the realization on my own. My molars rubbed against each other in a punishing grind, as I accepted the extent of my own ignorance. It wasn't like me to overlook resources.

"Why didn't you call *me*?" I asked. That call could have gone two ways.

Echo's fingers paused for the briefest of moments. Then she went on typing, forgoing a real answer.

But then again, there was another reason I'd stayed away. Someone I'd been avoiding.

With a quick glance around, I found only Echo's two rabbit familiars, one the size of a medium dog, and a small white one with a dark circle around its eye. Lulu and Darth Vader. They were snuggled together on the couch resembling two different sized loaves of bread.

The door swung open to what I presumed to be the rest of their underground home. My heart jumped in my throat.

Echo's husband, Ryuki, tottered in with a tray of tea. The sparse Japanese man gave me an impish grin I couldn't help but return.

"She's not here," Echo said, still not facing me though her gruff tone softened.

"Oh," was all I said. I wasn't going to pretend I didn't know who Echo was talking about.

Echo's daughter had been the one to convince me to bring back Xander, with the help of her girlfriend, Sunny.

They claimed to want to help in the name of love. But Aoiki didn't realize her girlfriend had ulterior motives in performing that spell on the blade.

Aoiki had been betrayed, like me, but I didn't know how I felt about her.

Even thinking of the girl, and that night brought waves of shame crashing over me.

"Come, come," Ryuki said, ushering me over. His English needed a lot of work, but his hospitality was off the charts, balancing out his brusque wife. Most surprising was how he doted on her like she was the queen of Sheba.

While Echo did her thing, Ryuki and I sipped tea in companionable silence while occasionally petting the soft rabbits I'd settled down next to.

Echo's hands smacked with a tremendous crack as she let out a victorious cry. I jumped in my seat.

"Aha! Gotcha sucker."

Echo waved me over then swiveled her chair to face a different screen. "Here, on the Strip." I stood next to her, and she pointed to a live feed showing the bustling heart of Las Vegas. The neon lights flickered in the background, casting colorful glows on the faces of oblivious tourists and locals alike. In the midst of the crowd, a small figure darted between people, causing mischief.

"That's Bes," Echo clarified, her eyes narrowing. "According to Egyptian mythology, he's a protector, but now the little shit is just stirring up trouble. To mortals, he'll look like a particularly unruly child."

On the screen, the figure identified as Bes was no taller than a six-year-old, but with an unusual appearance—a wide, grinning face and hair that seemed to stand on end.

Every person he reached out and touched suddenly seemed overcome by some kind of emotion. Two people fell into a fist fight. A trio of strangers all disrobed and began to grope and fondle each other. Several people curled into balls on the ground, sobbing their faces off.

"He's in the pedestrian area near the Menaggio fountains," Ryuki added, his voice tinged with concern.

I grabbed my gear, feeling a mix of adrenaline and resolve. Bes needed to be stopped, immediately. "I'm on it," I said, heading for the door.

"Be careful, Miranda," Echo called after me. "Bes is tricky and unpredictable."

The city's pulse beat like a drum in my ears as I navigated through the traffic, the neon lights painting the night in surreal colors.

As I approached the bustling area near the Menaggio fountains, the chaotic energy grew palpable. A couple of people recorded on their phones from a still-safe distance, confused expressions marring their faces.

Amidst the chaotic crowd, I caught sight of my target—Bes, the small, mischievous Egyptian god. His devilish grin sent shivers down my spine as I pressed forward, determined to stop his malicious games. Fists collided with faces and bodies crashed to the ground all around me, but I remained focused on my goal.

I weaved to avoid a man smashing his fist into someone's eye. I stopped up short when a woman fell to her knees before me, sobbing to the heavens. Hands clawed at my clothes, along with pleas to come fuck them. I shook them off.

Bes clapped his hands together, delighted by the outbursts, as if it were a special show being put on just for him.

As I closed in, the tension in the air thickened like a volatile bomb ready to detonate. Once I got within twenty feet, Bes finally took notice of my presence and his smile widened into a sinister smirk.

He raised his chubby hand and summoned a searing orange energy that crackled and sizzled with ancient power.

Laughter turned to hysterical shrieks as people started lashing out, their faces twisted with wild expressions.

The mass of bodies and emotions surged around me. If I didn't do something, I was going to be taken down by the riot.

"Hey Bes, you want to mess with someone?" I called out, drawing the Blade of Bane and elbowing people out of the way. "Come play with me."

The crowd's mood shifted to confusion and fear at the sight of the weapon, their emotions still being toyed with by the god. Many of them ran screaming from me, crying out that I'd killed them.

Bes laughed, a high-pitched sound that grated my nerves. He leaped towards me, surprisingly agile. I dodged, but not quickly enough—his sharp, diminutive claws raked across my arm, leaving a burning sensation that told me his touch was more than just physical.

Gritting my teeth against the pain, I swung the Blade of Bane in a wide arc, but Bes dodged effortlessly, his laughter echoing mockingly around us.

His touch burrowed into me like a venomous snake, injecting its poison into my veins and unleashing all of my repressed emotions. My skin seared with a primal yearning, every fiber of my being consumed with the need to find Xander. Memories flooded my mind, of being chained to that bed with him, our inhibitions stripped away in fits of laughter and desperate clinging.

But then, anger boiled within me, threatening to erupt like a volcanic eruption.

My fingers twitched around the handle of the Blade of Bane, its cool metal offering a small sense of grounding in this chaotic moment. My skin prickled with the heat of my own anger and the icy chill of fear, a physical manifestation of the emotions raging within me.

This wasn't right—Xander had brought out these wild and dangerous parts of me, but he had earned that privilege.

As Bes appeared before me, I struggled to keep control of myself, fighting against the explosive emotions threatening to consume me entirely. I took a deep breath and tried to push back the memories and emotions that Xander's touch had unleashed. I needed to focus on the present.

The taste of copper filled my mouth as I bit down on my bottom lip, trying to physically restrain the emotions bubbling inside of me. My tongue tingled with the metallic tang, a reminder of the sharp edges of the Blade of Bane.

Bes appeared before me as I struggled to control myself. His tiny grubby hands wrapped around mine, trying to wrench Bob away from me.

No.

Bes shot back, his ass smashing into the ground with a yowl.

I didn't have the bandwidth to make sense of what just happened, I was still fighting against the swirling tornados of emotions. But unlike everyone else around me, I'd gone as still as a statue, slowly but surely reigning it all in.

Bes wouldn't get the satisfaction of getting any of those parts of me.

Hell, even I didn't give *myself* permission to feel like

that, not without a pair of stormy cerulean eyes to be swept away on.

The surge of energy that had me nearly clawing my way out of my skin traveled through my veins to where I held Bob until it ebbed.

Just when Bes was in front of me a second time, taking another more careful chance at stealing my weapon, I came to myself.

"Don't toy with my feelings," I snarled at him.

Bes' impish grin fell.

With a swift movement, I feigned a strike to the left and then quickly reversed, catching Bes off-guard. The blade connected, and a look of surprise crossed his tiny face.

He disintegrated into a cloud of golden dust, the Blade of Bane absorbing his essence. The crowd around me had thinned, leaving a few stunned onlookers who were trying to make sense of what they'd just witnessed.

A couple of them clapped, unsure if they just witnessed a streetside attraction.

Vegas was so bizarre, people didn't question much. They usually just stood back and admired the spectacle.

The people released from Bes' power either blushed hotly, pulled their clothes on, or helped each other up before joining in the clapping. It was as if they believed they were part of some mass Vegas hypnosis trick meant for entertainment.

Pulling out my phone, I called Fallon. In ancient times, he was known as Horus. He was my contact to help clean up any matters that spilled on the street as he had a hypnotic way with people to make them forget any super-natural occurrences. He'd finish up here.

Clutching my wounded arm, I blended into the less crowded streets of Vegas as I waited for Fallon to arrive.

The cut was deep and needed to be disinfected and bandaged, but victory thrummed through my blood. I did it. I really did it. I killed a god, trapped him back in the Blade of Bane.

"Miranda?" A familiar French voice reached into my mind.

I stopped short.

"Bob?" Emotion hit me like a tidal wave, as relief and surprise nearly swept me off my feet.

The adrenaline of victory still coursed through my veins, but the sudden return of Bob's voice brought a different kind of rush, one of poignant relief mixed with the unexpected sting of tears threatening to breach my defenses.

"How long have I been asleep? Uck, and what is that taste? Whose blood did I just eat? Blech."

"It's good to hear your voice." My own words, betraying the depth of my concern for the pacifist blade who had been my constant, albeit reluctant, companion.

"Oh, please, don't get all sentimental on me now. You know I abhor melodrama almost as much as I do bloodshed. And speaking of, could we perhaps avoid any more... gory encounters in the future? My constitution is simply not built for such... barbarity." Bob's attempt at maintaining his usual demeanor of complaint couldn't fully mask the warmth underlying his words.

The corners of my mouth lifted in a wistful smile. "I missed you too, Bob. More than I thought possible."

"Missed me? I was merely dormant, not on a holiday in the French Riviera. And now, look at the state I'm in. I feel like I've been used as a... a... kebab skewer at a rather bloody banquet." Despite his grumbling, there was a lightness to Bob's tone that I hadn't realized I'd been missing until now.

"And do clean this nastiness off me, if you please. Maybe you could rub Tic-Tacs on me."

"Tic-Tacs?" That threw me.

Bob scoffed. "Of course I am kidding. I am a sword. I deserve proper care. It was a joke."

I laughed softly, the sound mingling with the lingering chaos of the Vegas night around me.

I wanted to ask him where he'd been, why Bes hadn't been able to take hold of Bob, and probably a dozen more questions, but they could wait.

"Alright, you over-dramatic cutlery, we'll get you cleaned up."

CHAPTER 13

THE BEAST

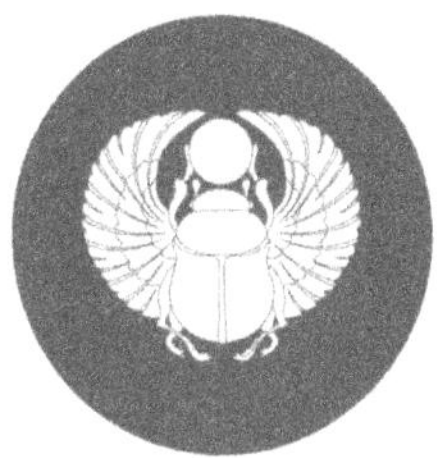

We planned to meet Sinopolis later tonight to go god hunting. That is, if Miranda even deigned to show up. But after what happened with us in that theater, I couldn't take the chance that she'd try to wiggle out to shy away from the discomfort. It was still only afternoon when I knocked on her front door.

The modest house sat on a patch of what used to be a perfectly curated lawn, though it was now scorched to dry brown blades from the heat. The autumn drought prohibited people from using water for the grass.

This street felt a million miles away from the busy, blinking neon streets of the Strip and something inside my chest unclenched, as if I could breathe easier. I wasn't sure if it was this part of town, a little slice of suburban bliss, or it was because I knew Miranda was on the other side of these walls.

As the door swung open, I was met with an elderly Black woman with white hair and smile lines at the corners of her eyes. She wore a floral shirt and stretch pants that were being put to the test by her expansive waist.

"Hello ma'am," I snapped out on reflex.

Had I gotten the wrong house?

No. I knew this was Miranda's house. I'd traveled here even when I'd been out of my mind. Looking beyond the older woman, I reassured myself that I recognized the furniture.

The older woman cleared her throat expectantly.

"Is Miranda here?" I finally followed with.

Shit, did I have the wrong house? The fear of not knowing my surroundings or my own mind began to cave in on me.

"Xander," a familiar young voice piped up.

Jamal pushed his way past the older woman to stand on the front stoop.

Relief swept through me. I was in the right place.

Jamal gave me a half toothy, half toothless smile, since he'd recently lost a couple baby teeth.

"Mom's not here," Jamal supplied.

"Oh." The need to slink away overwhelmed me as I suddenly felt I should not be here. Not without Miranda.

"Young man," the older woman snapped. "Where are your manners?"

Jamal's spine stiffened, and he bared his teeth in a silent 'uh oh.'

"Sorry G-Ma. Xander, this is my grandmother, Mama Jean. Mama Jean this is Mom's... uh, friend—"

"—from work," I smoothly supplied, readjusting the box I held to one arm, extending a hand to her.

She slipped a soft weathered hand into mine and I brought it to my lips, giving it a chaste kiss and smelling gardenias.

"Oh," she said in surprise, covering her chest with the hand I just kissed.

Fuck, was that wrong too?

"Sorry, I can be a little old fashioned." I gave her a wry smile.

"I suppose the world could use more of that," Mama Jean said in a more evident Southern drawl. The woman's posture and tense face told me she was sizing me up, and I wasn't sure what she was going to see. I sure as hell didn't have a good idea on how to cultivate a certain appearance for her. All I could hope was she didn't come to the conclusion I was an immortal with no social graces and severe mental health issues.

"What's in the box?" Jamal asked, pushing up onto his tiptoes to see inside. The flaps were mostly closed, but not all the way.

"Uh, a gift for your mom." Again, I got that extreme discomfort of knowing I wasn't supposed to be here. Somehow, interacting with Miranda's family felt entirely too intimate and private, and I knew she wouldn't like it.

"Well, come in and set it down." Mama Jean pulled Jamal back from the door, clearing the way for me. I stepped through, breathing in the homey bouquet of sunshine, gardenias wafting off Mama Jean, and the pervasive scent of Miranda's skin. The scent moved to my stomach and spread in a comforting warmth.

"My daughter-in-law should be back soon," Mama Jean supplied. "Take a seat and I'll make you something to eat."

"Oh you don't have to—"

"Sit, young man." She pointed to the worn wooden chair at their table.

She was definitely used to being obeyed, and I didn't want to be disrespectful.

"What's the gift?" Jamal asked again even as I followed the older woman's orders.

Putting the medium sized box on the floor by my feet, I met Jamal's eager look. "Well, if I stay, I better open it so he can stretch his legs."

Jamal's eyes turned as round as two eggs. "*He?*"

The box shuffled even as I fully opened the box flaps.

The squeal of delight from Jamal was ear piercing. "A dog! Oh my gosh, G-Ma, it's a dog."

Indeed, inside the box was a mixed mutt of every varying shade of color and breed, making for a medium small animal, who looked up at Jamal with mismatched blue and brown eyes, tongue hanging out the side of his mouth. His one ear stood erect while the other flopped endearingly to the side. One look at his bright, mischievous eyes, and you knew he wasn't an ordinary dog.

The mutt didn't appear to be a puppy, or particularly old either. Though I suppose age wouldn't really apply to this creature anymore, considering where I stole him— err —got him from.

"You think it's appropriate to show up at someone's house with a pet as a present?" Mama Jean said from where she stood by the sink even as the dog leapt out of the box and earnestly licked at Jamal's face.

"I wouldn't know what's appropriate," I said honestly.

She crossed her arms and shook her head, even as her eyes softened when they landed on the dog who now had Jamal on his back to get a better angle to lick the boy's giggling face.

"I don't think my daughter-in-law will appreciate being given another chore."

"I'll take care of him," Jamal rushed to say even as he got back to his knees to pet and hug the dog.

"I haven't given her a chore," I said, defensively, setting my hand on the table. "The dog is well trained." She had no idea. The supernatural pup wouldn't cause Miranda any problems.

Mama Jean's eyes narrowed. "Are you giving me attitude, young man?"

"Miranda needs to have more fun, and I thought a dog would... help with that." I wasn't about to reveal Miranda's past pain. That was her secret. "You're worried the dog isn't trained? Give it a shot yourself."

Still pinning me with that wary expression a moment longer, Mama Jean shot a command at the dog. "Come."

Immediately, the dog disengaged from Jamal and trotted over to the older woman.

"Sit," she said next. The dog complied instantly, a serene yet intent expression on his face as if recognizing it was auditioning for his role.

Mama Jean rattled off as many commands as she could think of, including play dead and jump, and the dog followed every instruction.

Jamal's eyes settled on me after a while with a knowing look. The kid knew too much, and I could tell he was picking up that the dog might be extra special compared to the canines on the street around here. I ignored his intent gaze.

"Satisfied?" I asked when Mama Jean ran out of things to try with the dog.

"What's his name?" Jamal asked.

The dog met my gaze this time as we entered a silent conversation. "The dog had a name, but that was from his old life. I think he'd like a new one."

Jamal's eyes turned as big as saucer plates this time.

AN HOUR LATER, I was smashing buttons on the handheld controller like my life depended on it alongside Mama Jean while Jamal stroked the dog and coached us from the sidelines.

"No, you've got it in reverse, press the left trigger—left trigger!" Jamal cried at me.

The dog let out a yip of encouragement.

"Ha-ha, you can't catch up now," Mama Jean cackled as her purple car on the television screen peeled away from me.

I gritted my teeth, hit the left trigger and got my virtual car on the track again. I couldn't believe she actually ran me off the road.

"I'm coming for you, old lady," I growled.

"Age before beauty, young man," she shot back, while sticking a tongue out the side of her mouth in concentration. "Know your place."

"What in the hell is going on here?" A voice cut through the din of game play. Mama Jean found the pause button before I did, and we all turned toward the front door.

"Hey Mom," Jamal chirped, as if he didn't notice her stormy expression or the way her hand gripped the door jamb until her knuckles turned a light color. "Xander got us a dog."

Either Miranda was having a stroke, or... well it didn't look like anything else could be happening based on her twitching expression.

Yeah, I was definitely getting stabbed.

CHAPTER 14

THE BEAST

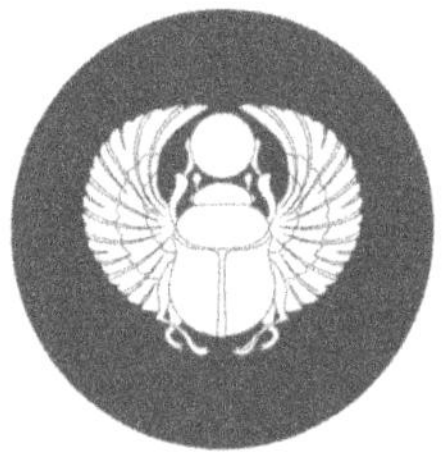

"You—" Miranda pointed at me.

"Me?" I gestured to myself.

Mama Jean shot me a pitying glance before getting to her feet. "I better check on dinner." I automatically reached out a hand to help steady the older woman, but she shooed me away.

"Come here," Miranda said between gritted teeth.

Jamal made an 'oo' sound that gave me the distinct impression he knew I was in trouble.

I dutifully set the controller down on the glass coffee table and crossed the distance to Miranda who yanked me the last foot onto the front stoop, shutting the door behind us.

As we made our way onto the concrete stoop, the intense heat of the sun immediately engulfed us. The angle of the sun's rays seemed to intensify the temperature, almost as if it were purposefully cooking us. The moment our feet touched the stoop, the searing heat penetrated through our shoes and into our skin. It felt as if we were walking on a bed of hot coals.

I was about to ask if we could go back inside, but Miranda's eyes snapped at me with an almost tangible whip of irritation. I shut up and took an involuntary step back.

Normally she had a protective shell around her, but right now it was as if walls shot from the ground to dizzying heights, protecting all parts of her, with a crocodile infested moat to boot.

"What are you doing here?" she asked in a hushed whisper, fist clenched on the doorknob. "We're not supposed to meet for hours at Sinopolis, and I come home to find you ingratiating yourself with my family."

A sharp pang of disappointment pierced through me, a physical ache that lingered. It was like a punch to the gut, realizing that she didn't want me near her family.

Not that I could really blame her. I wasn't exactly a stable, family kind of guy.

I tried to shake off her unwelcome demeanor. "Like Jamal said, I brought a gift."

Miranda opened her mouth but was cut off from whatever she'd been about to say.

"Hey Miranda," a deep voice off from the left interrupted.

"Oh, hey Michael," Miranda replied, suddenly

distracted by the newcomer, giving him a slight wave and half smile.

A man wearing a suit and carrying a briefcase pulled out his keys as if coming home from work to the house next door. He toyed with them as he spoke.

"Whatever you're cooking over there has got me salivating," he said with a low, rich laugh. My eyes narrowed as a hot feeling flared in my body. "You keep cooking like that, and I'll be breaking down your door to get a spoonful of whatever that heaven is."

I waited for her to say if he came through her door, she would kick his teeth in, but it didn't happen.

Instead, Miranda pushed a braid behind her ear and her cheeks grew rosy.

The fuck?

"That's actually my mother-in-law," she explained. "She is an amazing cook. We're very lucky."

"You and your husband are very lucky," Michael the stupid-face neighbor said, his eyes briefly touching on me with disappointment.

My lips curved up in a smug grin as I embraced the idea that he thought I was Miranda's husband.

"Oh, oh no, no, we aren't married," Miranda corrected too quickly. A hand covered her chest. "I'm a widow. Have been for a while now."

Interest flickered in the neighbor's eyes, as if realizing he stood a chance with the goddess next to me.

My hurt was replaced by ire as I took in the man on his front porch next to Miranda's. The human was tall, fit, and what I'm sure most would consider to be attractive. And apparently so did she.

I grabbed Miranda's arm and pulled her closer to my side to show this guy where she really stood.

As soon as my hand encircled her, Miranda let out a sharp cry. Her body stiffened and flinched before she broke away from my grasp.

"What the—" the words flew out of me as she cradled her arm while putting a few steps between us.

Something inside me cracked.

"Hey man, let her go," Michael frowned, stepping off his porch and starting toward us.

"I'm fine, it's fine," Miranda rushed to say, holding up a hand to keep him back. "Michael it was nice to see you, but I have to talk with my… friend."

Now I was the one being grabbed and pulled off, around to the opposite side of the house instead of going inside. Thankfully, we were able to step into a shady area, though it was still over a hundred degrees out here.

Before she could speak, I said, "I hurt you." A part of me was mortified and the other side completely confused. "I didn't mean to. I must have excess power or don't understand my own strength—" I was babbling, my words becoming more panicked and disjointed as I considered that I could accidentally hurt her. I hadn't smashed the game controller? But what if I broke Miranda's bones?

The god-likeness roiled under my skin. The distress was ironically pushing it closer to the forefront despite that being the very last thing I wanted.

Miranda pressed a hand to my mouth, cutting me off midstream. I breathed her in, enjoying the warmth of her palm far too much. "You didn't hurt me," she explained, quietly. "Well, not the first time anyway."

Before I could ask her what she meant, she rolled up her T-shirt sleeve, showing me a bandaged arm where blood spotted and seeped through the white bandage. I reached out to gently hold her undamaged flesh around the bandage.

All emotion bled out from my body, leaving only rage.

"Who did this to you?" I growled, even as my hands remained gentle.

"Little fucker named Bes. He put up a fight but I got him. I got one, Xander." Her eyes gleamed with pride and excitement, overtaking her unhappiness at finding me at her home.

Unfortunately, I couldn't share the same sentiment.

"You went hunting without me?" I asked, my voice flat and cold.

She stepped back, pulling her arm out of my light grasp. "Well, yeah. You were gone, and I had to get a win."

For a minute, I couldn't tell who I was more pissed at. That little chaotic fuck of a god for touching my woman, or Miranda for deliberately going out on her own where she could have gotten killed.

Miranda's blatant disregard for her safety boils my blood to a dangerous degree.

Did she have a death wish, or was she determined to prove she didn't need me? She didn't understand the difference between flexing her independence and being straight up reckless.

I seethed with fury, torn between wanting to protect her and wanting to lash out at her idiocy.

"Had to? You couldn't have waited until this evening when we could have gone together? Do you know how dangerous that was? You should have taken me with you."

Her nostrils flared with defiance. "I handled myself just fine. I was going to tell you I'm taking the night off since..." she trailed off, but I knew.

It was mid-afternoon, and she hadn't slept yet, not even after we practically broke that bed.

Bringing her to the point, I gestured to her arm. "You got hurt. Who knows how much worse it could have been?"

As angry as I was, deep down, all I wanted was for her to be safe.

Still, my body reacted with visceral, primal energy. My brain kicked up a buzzing sound. Tendons and muscles flexed inside me, threatening to elongate and shift for the second time today. I was about to lose my cool and knew I should start working on getting control of myself before I did something I regretted.

"It was fine," she said, her voice like granite.

She was going to drive me insane. I mean, I was still half unhinged, but she was going to send the rest of me careening back over the edge of sanity.

Too furious to form coherent sentences, I took a deep breath and tried to calm the gears grinding against each other in my mind.

"Now explain why you gave my kid a dog," Miranda crossed her arms, fully on the defensive again.

It took everything in me to speak slowly, carefully. "I remembered what you told me about your dog getting hit by a car when you were young." I started.

I knew it affected her deeply when she pushed the words out to me, confessing that one day while she was playing in the yard and didn't want to watch the puppy anymore, she sent it away. That's when it got hit by a car.

Miranda dropped her arms, an unreadable expression coming over her face. Not quite blank, but almost a deer in headlights look.

"So I went to the underworld, tried to find him."

Her entire body tensed. "Find who?"

"Your dog. I didn't find him, but I found... someone else."

"You got me a dog from the underworld?" Miranda's voice seemed to come from a far away place. Like she couldn't comprehend what I was saying.

I wanted her to heal from her grief. To bring back what she lost so she could feel safe enough to let her guard down, to have fun, to love.

But she looked anything but elated.

Starting to grow uncomfortable, I stared past her to the browning grass. "Well, really, the Afterlife. So he's immortal. House trained, low maintenance. I thought it might be... fun?"

The dog rounded the corner at that exact moment. He immediately began to explore his new surroundings, his tail wagging like a flag in a breeze. He sniffed around, then with a sudden burst of energy performed an impossible leap, flipping over in mid-air before landing perfectly on his paws. It was a subtle hint of his otherworldly nature.

He was showing off for his new master.

Jamal's voice broke through as he rounded the corner. "Hey Mom, dinner is ready. Can we go get Heinz some dog food right after?"

"Heinz?" Miranda asked.

"He's like that Heinz 57 sauce," Jamal patiently explained, "where there are fifty-seven ingredients. He's all different kinds of dogs in one."

"I don't think that sauce really has fifty-seven ingredients," she said hesitantly.

Personally, that sounded like too many ingredients for anything, but the kid should do what he wanted.

Jamal shrugged. "He seems to like his name, dontcha Heinz?"

The dog barked in a clear affirmative.

Meanwhile, Miranda watched, her expression still an unmovable mask.

"We can keep him, right Mom?"

"I can't believe you did that," Miranda whispered the words, almost to herself. At the root of her words, I found accusation and disbelief.

It hit me then. I'd fucked up. I completely missed the mark. I thought this would be a welcome, thoughtful gift.

Of course, I knew it could go wrong, but I'd followed my gut.

The air hung thick between me and the woman next to me. I could practically hear Miranda's thoughts, her doubts, her fears. And worst of all, her disappointment in me. I had wanted to make things right, to bring some semblance of happiness into her life, but instead, I had only added to her burden.

"I'm sorry," I murmured, the words heavy with remorse. "I didn't mean to upset you."

Miranda remained silent, her gaze fixed on the dog—on Heinz—who now sat at her feet, looking up at her with adoring eyes. I could see the conflict in her expression, the war being waged behind those guarded eyes.

As Jamal chattered away about Heinz's tricks, I turned to leave, the weight of my gesture—and its reception—heavy on my heart. "I'll see you tomorrow night for the hunt," I said quietly before slipping away.

CHAPTER 15

THE BADASS

"He got you a puppy yesterday?" Vivien exclaimed from where she stood on a velvet pink pedestal, getting her dress measurements taken. "Oh my gosh, it will be like Cupcake has a cousin! Or a brother. Or a best friend," Vivien spiraled off as if the relation of her invisible reaper puppy to my stolen corporeal underworld mutt were a complex algebra problem.

I was at the Paris hotel with Vivien and Timothy to prepare for the upcoming event.

Bianca, the Oracle goddess, insisted on having her designers dress us for the immortal ball, so we were here, where the place was as Hollywood glam as the goddess herself. Something soft and fruity hung in the air, and everything around me was soft and feminine.

Basically, the opposite of me. Yet I enjoyed the uber girly atmosphere.

Timothy's even toned question cut off Vivien's squeal of excitement. "Did you *want* a dog?"

He sat across from me on a matching plush settee, drinking from a delicate China teacup. When you were rich as gods—literally—this is how you shopped for a dress. One was designed for you.

Or as Vivien called it, we were undergoing a *Pretty Woman*.

The fact neither of us are hookers didn't seem to make her back off that comparison.

I touched an empty spot on the chaise lounge next to me, my hand subconsciously reaching for Bob. I wasn't the only one getting a glow up today. My weapon was whisked away for a shine and sharpen by someone Timothy vouched to be the best of the best. While Bob seemed more than willing to spring for a spa day, it felt like I was missing a limb.

I'd been reluctant to hand him over and had to ask Bob why Bes hadn't been able to take him away from me during the fight yesterday. Xander had disarmed me many times during sparring. Bob explained I didn't give consent, that our bond was protected by my energies. So after a long assessment of the hotel maid who was to take Bob away for care and Timothy's assurances it would be fine, I relented.

Not that Bob would be any comfort in this uncomfortable conversation.

I answered. "No I didn't want a dog, but—"

What Xander tried to do, what he tried to return to me

touched me deeply. It also brought on a tremendous amount of guilt.

Like a whale-sized canopy of guilt.

I had given Xander a partial lie about what happened when I was a child. There was a reason he couldn't find my pet, and the truth was much darker and more painful than he knew.

His gift forced the past to bubble up like hot lava, burning and churning in my gut with a near unbearable fervor.

"Do you not want the puppy?" Vivien asked, her tone carefully tiptoeing around me. Man, I must really seem fragile if Vivien was treating me with kid gloves.

"It is a big responsibility," Timothy added, pouring more tea into his cup. The woman taking Vivien's measurements whisked out of the room, presumably done with that task. I had yet to be poked and prodded.

Needing to do something with my hands, I picked up the flute of champagne from the glass table next to me and took a swallow. I shouldn't be drinking before going out to hunt tonight, but Xander had rattled me... bad. "The dog is pretty self-sufficient, actually. Jamal is instantly in love, as is my mother-in-law. But I just don't know why he would... do that."

"Get you a gift?" Vivien asked.

"To try and secure your affections?" Timothy guessed.

"But why *that*?" Frustration crept into my voice. "Why would he go to the underworld to try and find a pet of mine? Or Afterlife, or whatever." I threw up my hands.

Vivien and Timothy exchanged glances I couldn't read. Timothy put his cup down. "You know he is... fond of you." For a minute he seemed like he was going to choose a different word.

"He's hopelessly, head over heels, dead blind in love with you," Vivien corrected, stepping down to sit on the edge of the dais.

I sighed. "Xander's been trapped underground for so long, he doesn't know what he wants. I'm just the first person to show up who piqued his interest after lifetimes of misery and pain." I paused. "That, or he is super into the fact I stabbed him to death nightly for a while there."

Everyone had a kink. Death was his.

That or playing games with me. Both literally and metaphorically.

I went on. "But he's free of the cage and he's in the world now. He'll find out soon enough that I'm nothing special and figure out where he really belongs."

"Oh."

I glanced up to find Vivien's emerald eyes widening as if filling with some kind of understanding.

I furrowed my brows. "What?"

Timothy studied the tea in his cup a little too hard.

"*What?*" I asked defensively, suddenly on my feet, too agitated to be still a second longer. In fact, I was considering fleeing this place all together.

"You don't think you're good enough for him," Vivien said with a healthy dose of disbelief.

I squirmed in my seat. "That's not what I said."

Timothy set his cup down, his eyes meeting mine. "Miranda, despite my own reservations about your potential together, it's evident that Xander's feelings for you are... profound. His affection seems to stem from something deeper than mere whimsy."

I crossed my arms, uncomfortable with where this was heading. "He doesn't really know me. I get the sense he is a god trying to flex his power—that he just wants to conquer me as something to do."

Liar, liar pants on fire, a voice in my head chanted.

I felt slimy even saying the untruth out loud, but I was desperately trying to wriggle out of Xander's grip. It was slowly closing in around my heart, and I couldn't let it trap me for good.

Vivien chimed in, her tone filled with a fierce conviction. "Come on, Miranda. What if it's more than that? What if *you're* the something real he's never known before? Something he desperately needs? You are as real as it gets."

The truth about the dog situation jerked up into my throat. That story hadn't been entirely real. I swallowed the lump back down.

I'd never shared with anyone about that day. Not even my late husband knew.

"Hey," Vivien said, her face wrenching up in suspicion. "What the hell is this?"

"What the hell is what?" I asked.

"Don't you guys see this?" Vivien stood and backed up, her eyes darting all about her.

"See what?" Timothy asked, his eyes focused on his cup as he sipped more tea.

"The pillows, the pillows!" she cried out, flapping her arms around her. "There's dozens of them. They are all around me. I'm surrounded."

"She's finally cracked," I said to Timothy.

He continued to sip his tea a little too intently, which leads me to believe he might see exactly what Vivien does.

The whites of her eyes nearly swallowed her irises just before her face jerked to the side as if some unforeseen force collided with her face. Then her shoulder snapped back unnaturally.

"Timothy?" I asked.

"Mmm?"

"Did Grim assemble a bunch of ghost pillows to attack Vivien?"

His dark eyes met mine. "Are you suggesting the god of the dead, Anubis himself, would waste his time and energies on creating pillows from the ether just to torment his wife the way she has been doing to him?"

I matched his stare even as Vivien cried out and batted at empty air in futile defense.

Then I picked up my champagne and took another sip. Neither of us were inclined to get in the middle of the great pillow war. That would be the same as trying to stop a dog fight. It would only end in blood. Ours.

As Vivien cried out and tried to escape her relentless invisible attackers, I wondered why I'd shared such an intimate story with Xander.

I don't know what possessed me to even give Xander a small part of that story. It was like I was handing the ugliest part of my soul over on a silver platter to a man who'd lived nearly as long as time.

"Come on guys," Vivien cried out. "Help me."

But at the time, I'd felt a safety I didn't remember ever experiencing. It was like Xander and I could be torn up messes together and it would be okay.

Then he hurt me. And I hurt him when I flirted with my neighbor in front of him.

I was trying to convince both of us this thing between us wouldn't work.

"Argggh!" Vivien lay back on the pedestal, kicking and flapping her hands up in the air in defense. She'd literally been beaten to the ground.

But then Xander went into the motherflipping under-world to find my long-lost pet.

Aw crap.

Vivien was right.

I didn't think I was good enough for him.

Timothy's gaze was thoughtful. "Xander's experiences have been... quite severe. Through that, he might see what truly matters. And it seems, *you* matter to him a great deal."

I countered, my voice tinged with a mix of defensiveness and vulnerability. "But he's immortal. And I'm not. Why would he choose me?"

Vivien swept the champagne glass from my hand and downed it in one gulp. "What the hell guys?" Static-charged hair flew around her flushed face. She batted the strands back down with rage-filled swats.

"This is between you and Grim," I said with an arch of my eyebrow.

Ignoring Vivien entirely, Timothy went on. "That's the point, Miranda. To someone who's lived forever, the raw, genuine nature of mortal life can be irreplaceable. Your mortality doesn't make you less; it could be what he's drawn to."

"So he *only* wants me because of my mortality?"

Vivien's nose wrinkled even as she tried to calm her fly-away hairs. "Damn biatch, you are twisting Timmy's words around to prove that Xander's feelings for you couldn't possibly be real. Are you this cynical and mean to yourself in your head too? 'Cause, well... damn."

Timothy sighed, his expression softening. "You are my friend, Miranda, and you are enough as you are. Whether or not you're with Xander, don't doubt your worth."

My gaze fell to the ground, my heart wrenching at being found out. Timothy's words pierced through my façade, exposing the raw fear that has consumed me for far too long—the fear of never being good enough.

They dredged up all my insecurities, my deep-seated fears, and I could feel the weight of them crushing down on me.

Despite my constant efforts to compensate with hyper-vigilance and outworking those around me, it's never been enough. And lately, it seems to be getting me nowhere but deeper into this pit of self-doubt.

Xander thinks you're enough, my brain spits back.

But Xander doesn't know his own mind. He says he does, but I don't believe him.

"Wait," Vivien held up her hands as if to slow us all down. "Is all this uncertainty and fear coming up because of the immortal ball?" She tapped her lower lip, her hair still a wild mess. "Ball. Balls. It is so weird to say, much less go to one."

For being on the unhinged side, my friend was oddly perceptive. I reached down to re-lace one of my boots that was already perfectly tied.

"Oh, my sweet baby lambs," Vivien shot to her feet. "I'm right!" She did a little dance, shaking her hips.

I rolled my eyes and walked to the opposite side of the room, pretending to be interested in a painting of elegant women in a boat along a flower filled river.

I tried to keep my tone light. "This event is supposed to be a homecoming for Xander. He needs to socially rejoin his kind. He can take possession of one of the hotels, wear a sleek veneer, play twisted games out of sheer boredom, and indulge in ambrosia-fueled orgies."

Sure, Xander said he didn't want to rejoin them, but he couldn't put off going back to where he belonged for long.

A pair of hands found my shoulders and turned me

around. Vivien's emerald eyes bore into mine, her expression serious and sincere. "Xander is *not* like the others. I've met enough of these a-holes to know."

"A-hem," Timothy said loudly and with great offense.

"You don't count, Timmy," she casually shot over her shoulder. Vivien picked my hand up. "It's okay to be scared. Letting someone in, especially someone like Xander, is terrifying. But sometimes, it's the broken souls who love the fiercest. Maybe you're what he needs... and perhaps he's the messiness, the passion you didn't know you were missing."

I lifted my gaze, meeting Vivien's. Inside, I was torn between the safety of my emotional barriers and the terrifying yet enticing prospect of a love that could easily destroy me.

Deep down, I knew my reluctance was about more than just Xander. It was about a lifetime of believing I didn't deserve happiness, not after what happened to my... dog, not after losing my husband, and certainly not after unleashing chaos on the world from the blade. How could I allow myself to enjoy anything when I was responsible for so much pain?

The weight of my past, the guilt—it was a secret burden I carried, always reminding me why I couldn't just relax and be happy. Happiness was a luxury I couldn't afford, not when every moment of joy felt like a betrayal of the memories of those I'd lost. And now with Xander, it felt like walking towards something I had long denied myself—a chance at love, at happiness, which... deep down, I feared I might never truly deserve.

Unaware how intensely I was processing her suggestion, Vivien straightened, her fingers tightening around my shoulders. "But yes, this event is going to be wall to wall with bloodthirsty sycophants who will treat you like the gunk between their toes. And since Xander won't be there to distract the masses with his glorious return, we had better arm you."

"She's right," another soft lilting voice added. Bianca strode into the room.

The goddess might have invited me here, but I hadn't forgotten that she'd begged me to stay away from Xander when I killed him nightly for weeks on end. She knew something terrible would come from it.

But I hadn't listened.

And we were all in danger now.

CHAPTER 16

THE BADASS

Bianca's blonde hair was arranged in perfect curls. The Oracle's dress was a dreamy, white, form fitting number that showed off her curves.

If only I had believed her predictions, it might have stopped me from falling for Xander, from bringing him back, from unleashing all the evil from the blade.

Or it might not have.

Nerves and guilt had me rolling my shoulders back and straightening my spine in the goddess's presence. She had every right to despise me, and I deserved it.

Instead of voicing that, I said, "I'm not sure how the

immortals will feel about me casually toting around the blade known as the 'god killer' at the party."

"There is more to me than just killing," Bob sniffed haughtily.

The maid from earlier rushed in and presented me with Bob, still in his sheath. I slid him out enough to see gleaming steel.

"Oh my gods, Miranda. I think I am in love. The blacksmith, her hands. I've never felt so cherished. The way she washed my blade."

I wanted to cut him off, but considering how many times Bob kept his mouth shut about witnessing my intimate moments with Xander, I didn't have a step to stand on.

Bianca glided across the room, her crystalline baby blues meeting mine. It was like staring into a cloudless sky, and my mood shifted into a lighter state. In that one look, she communicated more than should have been possible.

A brief flash of disappointment over how things turned out, deep empathy for me over Xander's death and now for the burden I carried.

Not sympathy, *empathy*.

It was like she cupped her hands gently to my heart with a loving aura that soothed my sins.

My lip trembled as the forgiveness flowed through me. Her divinity was like touching the softest ray of sunshine.

Her power over me ebbed as she wrapped her slender fingers around my shoulders, leading me to the platform Vivien was just on. Bianca nudged me to step up onto the riser and look at myself. "Vivien didn't mean arm you with lethal weapons. The gods will view you as weak simply because you are a mortal. When you walk into that ballroom, you need to be dressed in a different kind of armor. One that will teach them exactly who you are. A warrior. One worthy to protect us all. And rest assured, we can help with that." Her lips curled up in a mischievous smile even as Timothy and Vivien came up from behind me on the other side, a knowing glint in their eyes.

Viven added, "Oh, we guarantee you will knock 'em dead tomorrow night."

A spike of fear shot through me, but I was surrounded.

AFTER THE DRESS FITTING, I was exhausted from the pushing, pulling, and sheer number of decisions that needed to be made. I had to pull Vivien back from her wild ideas until I curbed the design to something that would reflect me. Thankfully, Bianca was the voice of reason, keeping things from getting too out of hand.

Despite feeling like an irate pin cushion, I dragged my ass to the gym to get in a workout while I could.

As I reached for the free weights, I focused on the burn in my muscles, each lift a step toward becoming stronger and more capable. The wounds on my arm still burned and ached, a vivid reminder of Bes's attack, but I pushed through the pain. I needed to be prepared for what lay ahead. I killed one god, but I had countless others to go.

Sweat dripped down my face as I pushed through another set of shoulder presses. The clinking of weights and the buzz of gym equipment filled my ears, but a familiar voice cut through the noise.

"Working hard, I see."

I turned to find my neighbor Michael standing there with a towel around his neck, his gym attire accentuating his muscular physique. His presence was unexpected, yet not entirely unwelcome.

"So, you've joined my gym now?" I asked, setting the weights down.

Michael flashed a casual smile. "Seems like it. I've been looking for a good place to work out, and this one's close by. It's a bonus getting to run into you. Need a spotter?"

I hesitated for a moment, then nodded. "Why not?"

A little company couldn't hurt. Besides, I really did need a spotter.

There was something about Michael that was intriguing, a kind of gentle strength that was hard to ignore. His presence was comforting, a stark contrast to the chaos of the last couple days.

As I settled onto my back to do some heavy chest presses, he chatted about his life as a financial consultant, and joked about rising his way to the top where he would inevitably rule the world. He laughed low and hit a timbre that resonated through my bones with unexpected warmth.

He was everything that should appeal to me—handsome, stable, normal. Yet, as much as I recognized this, my mind kept drifting back to Xander. His wild, untamed nature, the way my body responded to his mere presence with a burning intensity I couldn't deny.

I went harder on the weights, trying to push out the confusion and desire swirling within me.

Michael was clearly interested in me and was the sensible choice—a man who could offer stability and maybe even normalcy. But my heart, my very soul, seemed entwined with Xander's chaotic essence. The thought of him ignited a fire in my belly, a yearning so visceral that it scared me. It wasn't just attraction—it was a profound connection that defied logic.

Michael and I worked out, side by side, while he politely kept the conversation light. Still, I could feel his eyes on me, appraising yet not intrusive.

Night was fast approaching, and with it the inevitability of facing Xander again. It sent a thrill mixed with dread through me.

Finishing my last set, I sat up, catching my breath. Michael handed me a water bottle, his touch lingering just a moment longer than necessary.

"You're quite impressive, Miranda," he said, his voice low and earnest. "Not just your strength, but your resilience."

I offered a weak smile, the weight of his words sinking in. "Thanks, Michael. I'm always just trying to get a little stronger every day."

He chuckled softly. "I have a feeling you're more than just a *little* strong."

I stood up, wiping the sweat from my brow. "I should get going."

Michael nodded, understanding in his eyes. "Well, if you ever need a break, or someone to talk to, I'm right next door."

I thanked him, grabbed Bob from my secure locker, and left the gym, my mind a whirlwind of emotions. As I walked away, I couldn't shake the feeling that there was more to Michael than met the eye.

But right now, it was time to focus on the hunt, on Xander, and on the next god I was going to kill.

Now if only we could keep our hands off each other.

CHAPTER 17

THE BEAST

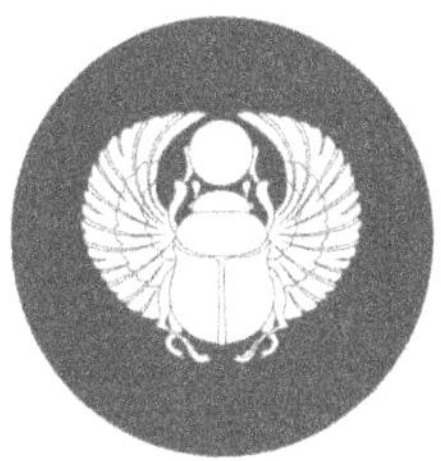

The Vegas Strip, with its neon-lit allure, stretched out around us like a carnival of the bizarre and colorful. As we maneuvered through the crowd, I couldn't keep my eyes off my hunting partner.

Miranda was a stark contrast to the glitz. I'd become convinced there was nothing more real than her. She moved with lethal grace, her eyes sweeping through the darkness, missing nothing. It was like watching a panther stalk through a flock of peacocks. My chest tightened, watching her. Every instinct in me wanted to draw her closer, to bridge the gap that stretched between us, yet I knew better.

I fucked up. Somewhere between her slimy neighbor and my gift, I'd made a number of missteps. All these years, I'd thought living in mind melting pain day in and day out was the hardest existence. I'd forgotten just how hard living was.

The uncertainty, the complexity. After all these years it felt like trying to speak a language everyone else knew that I barely mastered simple commands in.

"I still can't believe you got me a dog," Miranda said suddenly, her voice cutting through the noise of the Strip.

Something in her tone told me maybe I wasn't quite the massive screw up I'd been beating myself up for being.

"Yeah, well," I started, rubbing the back of my neck, "I figured you could use something less stabby in your life." I glanced at her, trying to gauge her reaction.

Miranda smirked, that dangerous little curve of her lips that always sent my thoughts into overdrive. "Less stabby, more fluffy. Got it."

"I thought you would like a canine companion. You know, someone to play with, to cuddle with when I'm not around..." I was pushing my luck, but I couldn't help it with her. I never could.

Her lips tightened as if she were trying to suppress a smile.

Maybe my gift wasn't totally off the mark.

"I did want to thank you properly, Xander," Miranda continued, her voice softer now, "But there's something I didn't tell you about my... dog. The real reason you couldn't find him in the underworld."

Her confession hung between us, poised on the edge of a knife. I could feel the shift in the air, a moment teetering on the brink of something important. Every fiber of my being leaned in, craving her truth.

Just as she opened her mouth to go on, her damn phone rang, shattering the moment like glass. Miranda's expression switched instantly from vulnerable to all business as she checked the screen before answering. "It's Echo."

I watched her, a mix of frustration and concern churning within me. The ringing phone was an intruder robbing me of the confession she meant to share.

As Miranda listened, her face hardened with urgency, and I knew her mind was back on the mission.

"What do you mean, scorpions?" she asked sharply, her body tensing like a coiled spring. "Which hotel?"

As she listened to Echo's response, I got the familiar itch of anticipation. Maybe I'd get to work out some of my extra frustration tonight, one way or another.

Miranda ended the call, her gaze meeting mine. "A goddess named Serqet has unleashed her scorpions in Fallon's hotel. He can't control her. We need to go. Now."

We raced toward the hotel, the city's cacophony fading into the background. As we approached, the scale of the chaos became apparent. People streamed out of the building in a panicked exodus, their screams and shouts filling the air. We pushed through the crowd, making our way inside.

The opulent lobby was in disarray, with scorpions swarming across the marble floors, their venomous tails raised threateningly.

Miranda's eyes flared wide and wild, her body recoiling. "I hate bugs," Miranda confessed.

"Technically, they are arachnids, like spiders."

The look she shot at me could have killed.

Okay, maybe not the time for a lesson.

"I got you," I assured her with a cocky grin. Walking

straight toward them, they split for me, leaving the perfect trail for us to walk through. "Stay close," I told her.

Miranda was practically plastered to my back, her breath on my neck, causing goosebumps to rise. Despite needing to be on guard, part of me reveled in her closeness.

As Miranda and I edged closer to the epicenter of chaos, I couldn't help but marvel at the scene before us. "You know, for a goddess of scorpions, she's really got a flair for the dramatic," I quipped, eyeing the swarming arachnids with a mixture of disgust and fascination.

Miranda gave me a sidelong glance. "Dramatic? She's turned the hotel into a death trap."

"Oh, come on. You have to admit, it's kind of impressive, in a terrifying *we might not make it out alive* kind of way," I said, trying to lighten the mood.

I'd never let that happen to Miranda though. The goddess wouldn't lay a finger on my angel of death.

I led us to the main lobby where people stood like statues surrounding the massive obelisk at the center that glowed with purple energy. The humans' eyes were glazed as they murmured praises to their new master.

A towering figure of dark majesty loomed in the center of the chaos. Serqet was tall, her presence commanding the room like a queen of shadows. Her dress, a flowing garment that seemed woven from scorpion shells dripping in ichor, clung to her form, accentuating her menacing grace. On her head, a scorpion-shaped crown glinted in the dim light, each segment of its tail articulated, moving with a life of its own. Her eyes were a merciless cold, a black void.

Around her, the scorpions swarmed as if drawn by some invisible force, a testament to her control over the creatures of darkness. The air crackled with malignant energy, the power of the obelisk amplifying her already formidable abilities.

I glanced at Miranda, a sense of foreboding tightening in my chest. "Be careful," I warned her, my voice low. "Serqet doesn't just control scorpions. She gets inside your head, dredges up your deepest fears and darkest thoughts. She'll twist your mind if you let her."

Miranda's jaw set firmly, her grip on the Blade of Bane tightening. "Bob will protect me."

I could only assume the talking blade only she could hear had assured her of this.

Strangely, a stab of jealousy went through me at her having secret conversations with an inanimate object. For the millionth time in the last several weeks, I was reminded I was an outsider in this world in every respect. But I shoved off the self-deprecating bullshit for later when I'd inevitably brood alone.

"That obelisk," I nodded towards the towering structure in the center of the lobby, "It's not just a fancy decoration. It's a conduit for power, amplifying whatever energy it's fed. She's using it to bolster her control."

Miranda's eyes narrowed as she assessed the situation. "Great, so we're not just fighting a goddess, we're fighting a supercharged goddess."

Serqet's voice, cold and haughty, cut through the commotion. "Bow before me, mortals. Witness the resurgence of a goddess scorned. This city, this world, shall know the might of Serqet."

As she said those words, an ether of life force emerged from her followers, fueling the obelisk. She was going to drain them to death.

"Hey, goth scorpion lady," Miranda called out. "Let

everyone go and maybe I won't stab you into your old prison."

Clever girl. We had no element of surprise here, and we needed to distract Serqet before she killed these people.

Serqet's gaze snapped to Miranda, her lips curling into a sneer. "A mortal wishes to challenge me? You are but a tool for my divinity."

With a flick of her hand, a wave of psychic energy surged towards Miranda, intent on ensnaring her mind. But the blade in Miranda's hand glowed, creating a barrier that repelled the attack.

"Thanks Bob," Miranda said quietly. "Pretty sure *you* are the tool," Miranda shot back at Serqet.

Tension coiled in my body, a mix of admiration for Miranda's bravery and a gnawing fear for her safety.

Amidst the chaos, I caught sight of a Black man laying slumped against a pillar. Fallon. His dark suit was rumpled and neither his blue nor his brown eye opened or so much as twitched. A wound oozed a purple liquid from his neck, a clear sign of Serqet's poisonous touch.

"You think you can defy me?" Serqet hissed, her form growing more imposing as she tapped into the obelisk's power. "I will crush you."

It was my turn. "Hey there, sis. I may have been underground for the last several thousand years, but I know a couple things you don't. We don't reveal ourselves to humans, we don't take followers anymore, and we sure as fuck don't throw tantrums for the glory of what, your ego?"

I held her attention as Miranda crept around to the side.

Serqet's sinister laughter filled the air as she raised her hands, the scorpions on the floor surging towards us like a living tide. Within moments, we were surrounded, the venomous creatures forming a barrier that held us in place.

I couldn't make them part to get to Miranda.

Fuck.

There came a knocking on my mind. Like the deep sonorous poundings against a massive castle door.

Serqet was trying to get in my head.

Panic rose within me as the walls of my mind shook under the strain of her power.

Serqet's eyes gleamed with malice as she turned her venomous gaze toward me. "Oh, Nun, once a mighty god, now nothing more than a deranged shadow, trembling on the brink of madness," she sneered, her voice a razor slicing into my mind like a scalpel.

My fists clenched involuntarily, and a cold sweat broke out across my skin. I told Miranda I would protect her, but Serqet was pulling my mind apart like a child with a pile of blocks. It had been a mistake for me to come. My mind was too weak, and I put Miranda in danger.

"Look at you," Serqet continued, her tone dripping with disdain. "Pathetic. Clinging to a mortal for some semblance of balance. Do you think she can save you from the chaos raging inside your head? She's a mere human, Nun. She cannot anchor a mind as fractured as yours."

Her words echoed my darkest insecurities—the fear that I was too far gone, beyond saving, beyond redemption. The fear that if I gave into my inner beast, I would never regain control, that I could not protect Miranda, the one person who had pierced the darkness of my existence.

"You're a ticking time bomb, Nun." Serqet's voice turned hushed. Her eyes locked onto mine, reading my turmoil. "One wrong move, and you'll unleash destruction upon those you claim to care for. How long before you turn on her, I wonder?"

Serqet prodded at the nightmare that haunted me—

losing control and harming Miranda. That thought alone was unbearable. Whether I turned into the mindless monster I was, or simply crushed her fragile, precious heart, there were too many ways I could cause her pain and all of them felt inevitable.

"And you," Serqet turned her scornful attention to Miranda, "Do you realize the danger you're in? Aligning yourself with a god whose mind is a tempest of madness? How pitiful that you find strength in someone so broken and unstable."

Miranda's jaw tightened. "Xander, don't listen to her. She's wrong. You are in control, not her." Miranda's voice was firm, commanding. She was my lighthouse in this storm, but even her pull couldn't dispel the shadows clawing their way out.

Serqet's laughter echoed through the lobby, mixing with the hiss of her scorpions. "Let's see how long your resolve lasts. The broken god and his mortal crutch—what a tragic tale you both weave."

Serqet's hisses echoed in my head. "Feel the chaos clawing at your mind. Let it loose, Nun. Show your true self to your precious mortal."

The words were a relentless drumbeat, pushing me towards the edge. I could feel my darkness stirring.

It whispered at the back of my mind, a reminder of the depth and tempest of the powers I possess. *Let go,* it hissed, *Show them the might of Nun.* I clenched my fists, nails digging into my palms, a futile attempt to anchor myself to my humanity.

The monstrous part of my godhood that I had fought so hard to control threatened to break free. It was tempting, so tempting, to let go and unleash the fury and power that churned within.

A desperate laugh bubbled up from my throat, the sound more akin to a growl. *Is this it?* I wondered. *Is this the moment I become the monster?* But even as the thought crossed my mind, I knew I'd do anything, become anything, to protect Miranda.

There would be no telling what chaos or damage I would inflict if I gave into the monster inside. Not even Miranda would be safe.

In the reflection of the obelisk, I caught a glimpse of my eyes—no longer human, but deep pools of the abyss, swirling with unbound power and madness. The sight was both terrifying and exhilarating.

I would *not* be a monster to her. I would be a man.

Even as I insisted this to myself, the world narrowed down to those hissing whispers, each word a strike against the fragile dam holding back my madness.

A torrent of ancient power stirred within me, fighting against the chains I'd wrapped so tightly around it. My skin itched with the need to shift, to unleash the roiling sea trapped within my soul.

The air around me crackled with tension, thick with the impending release of chaos. My grasp on reality slipped, my thoughts fragmenting under the weight of her words.

Suddenly Serqet's words came from inside the cavern of my own mind.

"You are not a man. You are a monster, you always will be. Give in, Nun, to your nature. Give in to your chaos."

My control cracked, and bright blue ravines of power lit up at my fingers, traveling up my hands and forearms.

Power surged through me like a tidal wave, unstoppable and all-consuming. My bones shifted, my skin stretched, and for a moment, I was suspended between man and deity—a creature of water and wrath about to crash down on those who dared threaten what I held dear.

THE BEAST

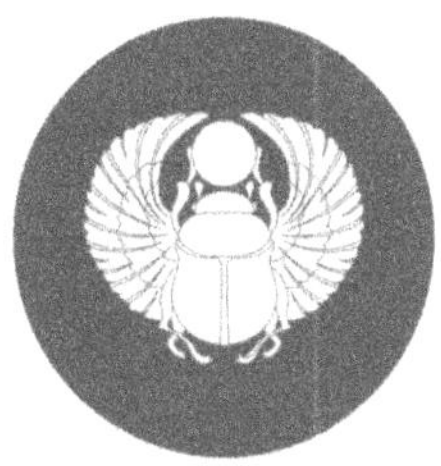

Electric blue sizzled off my skin with near atomic power that made all the cells in my body vibrate violently.

Taming the storm within me wasn't graceful. It was like trying to put a leash on a hurricane. Every attempt to calm down just ticked off the beast more. The power inside me was wild, gnashing and roaring for release. For a moment, it felt good letting it take the wheel, but then I caught Miranda's determined look.

"Xander, listen to me," Miranda called out, her voice a sharp blade cutting through the fog in my mind. "This bitch *does not* know you. Not like I do. And nobody can make you do anything you don't want. Not even burn those hideous Hawaiian shirts." The corner of her lips lifted, even as she pinned me with her intense stare, tethering me to her.

Don't you dare give up on me now, her eyes seemed to say. It was enough to make me wrestle back control. Hell, if Miranda thought I could do it, maybe I wasn't totally lost.

I met Miranda's gaze, finding an anchor in the storm. Her eyes were so clear, so trusting, so knowing. As if she had zero doubt I would pull myself together.

A reminder that I had something—someone—to fight for. That even in my darkest moments, when I felt most alienated from myself, there was a part of me that remained untainted, capable of resisting the descent into madness.

The wild, unbridled power that had been a breath away from overtaking me began to wane, my skin cooling and my thoughts sharpening into focus once again.

In that moment, something shifted between us. A bond, already strong, forged in fights, deaths, and the quiet moments in between, grew even tighter. It wasn't just about calming me down and pulling me out from my own destruction. It was about knowing each other's strengths and vulnerabilities and choosing to stand together regardless.

Serqet let out a furious hiss. "Listen to me, Nun. Your madness will consume you!"

But her words, once so potent, now seemed to lose their edge, blunted by Miranda's unwavering support.

What the hell had I done to earn it?

That didn't matter right now. What mattered was kicking this goddess' ass.

Serqet's face twisted into a snarl. "Insolent mortal! You're nothing but a plaything to the gods!" She extended her hand, a wave of dark energy pulsing towards us.

Again, the force of her power hit me, smashing against my mind, trying to unleash that which I kept caged.

With a roar, I pushed against Serqet's influence, the effort sending ripples of pain through my head.

"I'm more than just my madness," I growled, breaking free of her. Shooting a hand toward the wall fountain, I grabbed hold of my power and the water exploded from the pipes and into the room, sweeping the scorpions away and clearing a path.

Miranda lunged forward, her blade cutting through the air with deadly precision. Serqet countered with a burst of dark energy, throwing Miranda back.

"You are nothing but a speck to me, mortal!" Serqet spat, turning her attention to Miranda. She reached out, trying to ensnare Miranda's mind with her psychic power.

But the Blade of Bane in Miranda's grasp glowed brighter, repelling the attack. "Not today." Miranda charged again.

Together, we closed in around Serqet from different sides.

I threw myself at Serqet again and again, my fists meeting with her chin, her gut. Serqet absorbed my blows as quickly as I landed them.

A scorpion, larger than the rest, lunged at Miranda from the side. She rolled away, blade slicing through its body in a swift, clean motion, her focus never wavering from Serqet.

She had been training in my absence.

"You dare defy a goddess?" Serqet roared, her form growing larger as she drew power from the obelisk.

Something shifted from under the back of her dress and a massive scorpion tail emerged. The lethal stinger snapped forward like a whip to pierce me. I dodged, rolled, and dodged again.

That's right, you bitch, come after me.

The thrill of the fight coursed through my veins, but my heart raced with fear. One wrong move and the results for Miranda would be fatal.

Serqet whipped around, her tail aiming directly at her. Miranda ducked, the stinger grazing her hair, a breath away from a lethal blow.

With a burst of speed, I closed in on Serqet, my fists slamming into a barrier of dark energy she conjured. The impact sent shockwaves through my arms, but I didn't relent.

"Miranda, now!"

In that moment of distraction, Miranda found her opening. She leapt forward again, the Blade of Bane flashing in the dark purple light of Serqet's energy.

Miranda let out a fierce cry as she plunged the blade into Serqet's back. The blade cut through until the metal tip emerged out the front of her chest, dripping with thick, black blood. The goddess's scream echoed through the lobby, a sound of defeat and disbelief. Her form shuddered, then began to dissolve into shadows, her power ebbing away as her skin turned gray and flaked away into ash. The scorpions still scuttling on the edges followed suit.

Exhausted, Miranda stumbled back, her breath coming in ragged gasps. I rushed to her side, my own body aching from the fight.

"That's one less god causing havoc," Miranda said, her voice laced with fatigue but victorious.

I couldn't contain my admiration. "You are incredible," I breathed, my emotions raw and unguarded.

In a surge of impulse, I grabbed her and crushed her lips to mine in a fierce, fiery kiss. She tasted like adrenaline, citrus, and victory. She smiled into my mouth and the perfect moment imprinted on my ravaged and damned essence.

The remnants of Serqet's followers began to stir, their trance breaking.

Just as quickly as the passion flared, reality crashed back into focus.

"We need to wake Fallon," Miranda said. "He'll calm everyone down and use his power to wipe their minds, so they won't remember what happened here."

I didn't want to wake Fallon.

I wanted to throw Miranda over my shoulder and take her to my lair like a caveman with only carnal desires in mind. She was glorious, and the bastard I was, I wanted to drag her away and keep her all to myself.

Instead of saying any of that aloud, I only nodded.

FALLON WOKE up cranky as fuck. Not only because Serqet got the drop on him, but he now had a passel of people to brain wipe.

Then Bianca flew in on the scene in a particularly binding pink dress, her hair falling in beautiful, curled waves. Despite her looking put together, Bianca was practically frantic. She fussed over him like he was a baby.

Fallon's glower remained, but it softened as she tended to him, asking him if he felt dizzy or needed to lie down, or if she should use some of her healing powers on him. The imposing god only requested a stiff drink and a quiet place to relax after he dealt with wiping the minds of the human witnesses.

Miranda and I snuck out even as Bianca was trying to

convince him it would do him good to let her run a healing bubble bath for him, using some of her tinctures.

Last I saw those two together, which was when we all lived among the pyramids in Egypt, they were at each other's throats over something stupid, like a differing interpretation of a prophecy or vision they both experienced. Now, the moon-eyed god could barely contain his raging affection for one of the most kind-hearted goddesses among us.

Heh, sucker.

My blood still rushed with adrenaline and I wasn't ready to call it a night. Judging by the glassy sparkle in Miranda's dark, cat-shaped eyes, she was of the same mind.

"We should celebrate," I pitched, practically bouncing on the balls of my feet.

Her grin spread wide. "I don't hate that idea." The smile faltered. "Though it might be wise to keep hunting. There are more threats on these streets."

I turned her shoulders to me. "You've killed not one, but two gods this week. At what point do you take a damn break, so you can celebrate your victory?"

"Our victory," she corrected quietly. Looking into her eyes, I expected resentment to swim there. She was so staunchly independent, and she made it clear on countless occasions that she didn't want my help. Instead, I found begrudging gratitude. We'd worked as a team.

"Fine," she consented.

It was like fireworks went off inside my chest. "I know the perfect place."

We started off toward my secret destination, but we'd only been walking for ten minutes when Miranda grabbed my hand, squeezing it hard as she tugged me in a different direction.

"Let's, uh, take a quick detour."

I raised an eyebrow at her. Miranda's eyes were wide, glassy, and she couldn't stop licking her lips.

Electricity zipped and danced along my skin as I felt her arousal, a palpable energy in the air.

I could only nod my consent with a lopsided smile. The truth was she could ask me anything and I'd agree. Pressure built up as she pulled me to a darkened storefront, the neon sign that read, *Arcadia Ba*r flickering sporadically, like a beacon calling us into the night.

"A little help?" she asked with a dare in her eyes, jiggling the locked door handle.

Someone was feeling naughty.

With a flick of my wrist and a murmur under my breath, the lock clicked open—a simple trick, but effective.

Miranda's grin was all the thanks I needed as we slipped inside. She closed and locked the door behind us before leading me into the darkness of the empty arcade bar. The air was thick with the scent of spilled beer, disinfectant cleaner, and the ghost of laughter, but now it was our playground.

The arcade machines stood silent, their screens dark, waiting for the touch of eager players. But tonight, they had an audience of two.

Miranda's hand found mine in the dark, her touch electric. "This is insane," she whispered, but I could hear the thrill in her voice, the excitement that mirrored my own.

Our bodies met, and the world narrowed to the space between us. I captured her lips with mine, the kiss deep and hungry, fueled by the adrenaline of our earlier battle.

Hands roamed, exploring, as we made our way down the rows of arcade machines, our moans mingling in the quiet bar. I backed her up to a pinball machine, the cold glass pressing against her back. Her legs wrapped around my waist as our kiss deepened, desperate and consuming.

The flickering neon lights painted us in surreal colors, casting long shadows that danced around us as I battled her hot, sweet mouth for dominance. Miranda clawed my shirt off like an unhinged animal. The sensation of being filled and engorged with desire was overwhelming. My arousal grew until it was almost painfully hard and throbbing in anticipation.

She bit and nipped at my lips, only stopping when I yanked her top off. Taking advantage, I dropped my mouth to bite and suck at her puckered nipples. The distinct taste of her skin filled my senses, ripping a groan from my throat.

Miranda cursed and moaned, her movements more desperate by the second. She shoved me away to kick off her boots and rip off her tight pants while I hurriedly tore mine off, so we were both naked. She only paused to gingerly place Bob behind the bar, as if he needed to be out of sight.

"I've seen these machines on movies and television, but I'm not really sure how they work," I confessed. I was doing anything I could to distract myself from the blood rushing south. My control was slipping fast, and I didn't want to scare her off.

"I can show you how to play," she said, her voice husky. With that, she pushed me back then dropped to her knees. She engulfed my cock in her hot mouth. My arm shot out to grip the counter of the bar.

"Oh fuck me," I groaned, panting. "You better stop or this is going to be over quick."

Her lips curved around my dick that felt more like a heartbeat about to explode. Deft fingers reached up and began to stroke my balls as she took me all the way down her throat. She let out a low sultry hum in her throat that vibrated up into my balls.

Oh fucking hell.

My abs flexed at the way she sucked me into the tight hot heaven of her mouth. A coil of heat and tension tied a string together from my spine to my testicles and drew upward too fast. My mind clouded.

I was going to lose it.

When I tried to pull away, she sunk her fingers into the meat of my ass, keeping me in place.

Control freak.

Fuck, she was dominating and playful and I loved every godsdamn second.

"Fuck sweetheart, I'm going to—"

Her nails dug harder into my ass, unrelenting in her wet sucking, taking me all the way in over and over.

I threw my head back. White sparks exploded in my body as I came down her throat. Miranda didn't stop, swallowing every last drop of my desire. My head was far too light and fuzzy, and nothing made sense except the woman on her knees in front of me.

"Oh shit," I breathed.

Miranda's nails grazed down the front of my bare thighs, and she looked up at me with a sultry gleam in those cat-like eyes. For a minute, I forgot she was mortal. Naked, on her knees before me, she was a seductive, other-worldly creature that I didn't deserve, but fucking hell if I wasn't going to take her.

The way her skin gleamed, so soft, over taut, long muscles made my fingertips prickle, and those seductive eyes and full lips had my chest wrenching in a vise.

She may be on her knees, but I worshiped this woman and always would. Eternity meant a very real thing to immortals, and as a god, I'd easily pledge it all away to her.

Pulling her to her feet, I teased and kissed her full lips and tasted myself, which sent twinges of desire pulsating back through my cock.

Her grip on me grew desperate.

Where I was floating, she was in need. And I sure as hell planned to provide.

My eye caught on an arcade game nearby and something absolutely wicked came to me.

"Do you trust me, my little badass?" I asked. My fingers swept up her slit. Fuck, she was so wet.

"No," she scoffed even as her eyes rolled back in pleasure.

I laughed darkly, and whispered into her ear, "Good."

That's when I picked her up and carried her over to a nearby game console. "Open up for me, sweetheart, so we can play a new game."

She barely understood what I meant before I lowered her slowly onto the joystick of the game. It penetrated her swollen slick folds, disappearing into her body.

Miranda's eyes flew wide, and she let out a sound of protest that she bit off into a moan of confusion and arousal.

CHAPTER 19
THE BADASS

"Oh fuck," I groaned even as I bit down on my lip, feeling so exposed, strange, and way too turned on at being penetrated by a literal joystick.

I'd pulled us into the arcade bar because I couldn't wait another minute to attack Xander to work off my excited energy. Maybe it had been the subconscious relation I had to our playing games that had me acting so recklessly when I saw the dark sign of Arcadia.

But I hadn't expected this.

"Oh fuck, sweetheart," Xander echoed my words with breathy awe. He firmly held my hips even as he dropped to his knees before me. The game was low enough that it put him at the perfect height.

His tongue darted against my clit in a way that made me want to both push him away and pull him closer at the same time. He snaked a hand down and shifted the joystick inside me, and I couldn't help but arch my back and ride it out.

A half-cry escaped me. The object didn't go deep enough, but it was hard and shocking to my system.

"This is so wrong," I groaned.

"You fucking love it," he growled into me, continuing to lick and suckle at my sensitive bud, sending lightning strikes through my veins.

In the dark, I still saw the outline of his face between my legs. His eyes closed in concentration as his tongue moved intricately and insistently against my center.

The muscles in his arms flexed as he held me down, his entire body focused on giving me pleasure.

His hands rocked my hips on the joystick this way and that. My head fell back as unhinged, wild sounds escaped me.

So, so fucking wrong.

With the skill of a true gamer, he manipulated all the right buttons and triggers to drive me to the peak of pleasure.

His tongue pressed more insistently against my center. My body twisted and writhed beneath him as he built a vortex inside me. Swirling chaos swept away my thoughts until I was unable to comprehend anything other than the intensity of the sensations coursing through my body.

"Game over, sweetheart." His husky rasp barely cut through the noise in my mind. "Come for me."

Shudders wracked me and I broke into a thousand

pieces, thighs shaking, gripping the sides of the machine for dear life.

When my body calmed, Xander stood, licking his lips like a wolf. "And here I was worried I wouldn't know how to play any of these games, but I think I just got the high score."

I swatted him even as he picked me up and carried me again, laying me down on the air hockey table.

"We both know you won that game." He playfully grinned, standing at the edge of the table, stroking his hard length in one hand.

I pushed myself onto my forearms. "Never thought I'd see the day when I'd be spread-eagled over an arcade game, let alone a fucking air hockey table," I panted, my voice slightly hoarse.

Xander's gaze landed on something beneath the table, and his eyes sparkled with excitement.

He reached for a small, red plastic puck and placed it between my slick, exposed folds. It was cold. The dark gleam in his eyes matched the evil smile on his lips.

"You having fun?" I asked, trying for my best scowl.

"Oh yeah," he breathed, continuing to stroke himself as he ran the cold, thin object down my sensitive swollen lower lips. He looked more sinfully sexual than was right, playing with me and the little object he picked up.

Something about him was so curious, so childish, but I guess that came with becoming reacquainted with a world he'd hadn't interacted with for so long.

"I fucking love seeing you like this," he growled, his voice low and thrumming with lust. "So hot, so wet, so ready for me."

I tried to act unaffected, but his words coupled with the puck pressed into me, sent a shudder of delight through me. My muscles clenched around the edge of the object.

"Give me that," I commanded in a huskier voice than I planned, while opening my hand. He handed it over then slid his naked body until it was settled between my spread legs.

Without warning, Xander surged forward, driving himself into me with a violent and unrelenting thrust. My body convulsed in pain and pleasure as I cried out, my hand clenching the puck so hard it felt like it might break, while the other dug into the edges of the air hockey table, struggling to hold on as it rocked violently under the force of his relentless pounding.

I was so full, I couldn't think. He reached places that turned my mouth dry and my mind inside out.

He pressed his lips against mine, and I could taste the lingering musky sweetness of my arousal on his tongue. I moaned softly as our tongues danced together, the warmth spreading through my body.

Sweat slicked our bodies as we writhed and fucked in long, hard thrusts.

Then I made my move, pushing the slickened air hockey puck into his mouth before I grabbed his hair, jerking his head back. He groaned either at the feel or the taste. I was below him but in complete control.

Xander surged forward, hitting me with a deep, powerful thrust, groaning, teeth gritted on the puck. He gripped my hips, pulling me closer as he slammed into me. Our bodies slapped together, the sounds of our fucking echoed in the arcade, punctuated by Xander's grunts and my breathy moans.

Xander's face was a picture of fierce concentration. His eyes, hooded and heavy-lidded with need, locked on mine as he continued to drive me higher. He turned his head and spat out the puck. He pushed my hands over my head, trapping them there.

"You're going to fucking come for me, Miranda."

"You'll have to work for it," I managed to choke out.

A devilish grin spread across his handsome face, his eyes never leaving mine. "It's always a fight with you, isn't it?" He leaned down, his breath hot and heavy in my ear, "And it's another challenge I'm willing to accept."

With that, he moved faster, his hips pounding into me with a fierce intensity that was both exhilarating and terrifying. I was being taken on a wild ride, one that I had no control over and yet, strangely enough, loved.

The hum of a machine turned on and air shot out of the table's tiny holes, penetrating my overheated body.

"What the hell?" I muttered.

"You got me too worked up," he rasped.

My brain was foggy with lust, but I realized Xander triggered the machine with his power. Whether consciously or not, I wasn't sure.

As his rhythm increased, my body responded. My muscles clenched around him, my breathing becoming ragged and erratic. I arched my back, trying to meet his every thrust, desperate for more.

The pressure in my core, the sensation building to a crescendo, threatened to consume me whole. I was close, so close, and I wanted him inside me when I came.

"Yes, Xander, yes!" I cried out, my voice hoarse with need. The intensity of his gaze bore into me, and I was swept away by his power over me.

The god's body shuddered with pleasure as he thrust hard and deep into me. His muscles tightened under my hands, and I knew he was close as well.

With one final surge, Xander's body convulsed, and he cried out as he came inside me, filling me with his warmth.

We lay there on the air hockey table, our bodies entwined in post-coital bliss. Only the hum of the engine and our loud pants filled the air.

"Did you turn it on, on purpose?" I asked, still trying to catch my breath.

He laughed slightly as he shook his head. "Nope, you're the only one I wanted to turn on."

The cool air of the table was a welcome feeling, cutting through the cloying heat we'd generated in the dark gaming bar.

My hands covered my face. "Oh my god, I can't believe we just did that. So much of that was so wrong." Feelings of horror and shock began to cut through the salacious things we just did.

He tugged my arm down so I'd look at him. "Can we not overthink this for once? Or at least, until tomorrow. I still have somewhere I want to take you. I promise you can regret all of this tomorrow, but not yet."

"We're a mess and look like we just had the kind of depraved sex we just had. We should probably clean up first, and definitely clean up in here. 'Cause if I didn't think about this being an adult hotspot, I'd say we need to get the place condemned."

Xander's thumb covered my lips. "Can you just be here with me for a little while longer? A complete and utter mess together?"

Something in his voice cut me to my core. It was the diverging point between us. My need to control and keep things in order and his inability to do so. A loneliness wavered in his eyes that told me if I didn't do this, he would be more alone than ever.

I took a deep breath and nodded. I could try.

Then Xander's face broke into a smile that made my heart skip and tumble all over itself in my chest.

I realized I couldn't deny him anything.

And for once, that didn't feel as scary as it should have.

THE BEAST

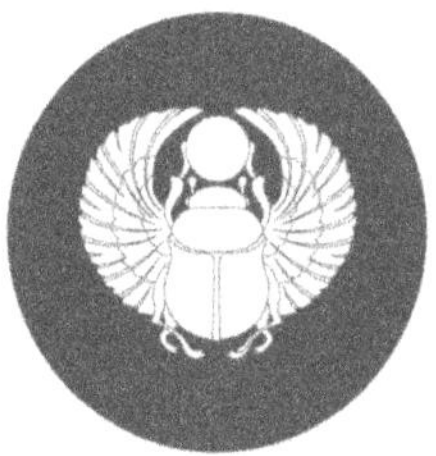

We cleaned ourselves and the bar as best we could, then less than ten minutes later, we walked down the steps to my favorite bar, the Rusty Nail.

Stepping into the dive bar felt like entering another world, one far removed from the supernatural chaos that had become our daily routine.

The air was thick with the scent of aged whiskey and stale cigarette smoke, but the air conditioning from the loud, overworked A/C unit provided a stark contrast to the sweltering desert night. Neon lights buzzed overhead, casting a warm, inviting glow over the well-worn pool tables and battered bar stools. Classic rock hummed softly from a jukebox in the corner, the tunes a comforting backdrop.

Miranda moved beside me, her presence a constant pull on my senses. The way the dim light danced in her dark eyes, the confident measure of her walk, all drew me in like a moth to flame.

Even after fucking each other like the world was ending, the pulse of desire for her beat under my skin. She was everything, and the fact she didn't know it was frankly fucking insulting.

True to her word, she'd tabled all her reservations as we got dressed so I could bring her here.

"You... uh, like this place?" Miranda asked, giving the place a skeptical once over. "And don't worry about hepatitis?" She murmured that last bit, and I pretended not to hear.

I grinned at her. "It's completely off grid from the other immortals. This is an old-fashioned humans-only bar." There were only about ten other people milling about at the bar and at the high-top tables, making for a subdued environment as Chuck Berry crooned in the background.

The reservation on her face told me she didn't care for this as much as I did, so I proceeded to take her on a tour of the place. "See there are pool tables, and have you used one of these? It's a jukebox. I'd heard of them, but never got to use one until recently. And the drinks are..."

"Cheap and watered down," the bartender interrupted me.

A short man with gelled hair and olive green eyes, wearing a striped shirt smiled even as I leaned over to shake his hand.

"Nice to see you again, Xander. Can I get you the usual?"

"Yes, and whatever the lady would like."

"I'm Lester," the man introduced himself as he reached over and shook Miranda's hand. "What'll it be, madame?"

"Miranda." Then she asked me, "The usual?"

"Shirley Temple," I said, grinning. "Have you tried one?"

She shot a glance to the bartender who gave her a shrug. "You come here to *not* drink?"

I didn't exactly go into how drinking wouldn't help my mental stability so I told her the other half of the truth. "I'm here for the ambiance."

"I'll take whatever beer is good on tap," she said to Lester.

He clutched a cleaning rag over his chest. "A woman after my own heart."

"Be careful there, Lester," I laughed, though it was strained in my own ears.

"Don't put off my new boyfriend," Miranda mock accused me with a daring look, and set her hand on the countertop. Lester covered her hand with his own, playing into her antics.

"Yeah, can't you see we're in love?"

Miranda's eyes sparkled with mischief. "Yeah, we'll be getting married soon."

A possessive streak, dark and powerful swirled in me, making me want to yank his hand off hers, pull her against me and show her who she should be in love with. But I also rarely saw this relaxed playful side of Miranda. Tonight's win really lightened her mood, and I didn't want to ruin that. So I clenched my fists at my sides and gave a tight smile of warning.

"Which is why all our drinks will be on the house," she finished.

Lester removed his hand at that. "Sorry sweetheart, I think we should see other people."

Miranda laughed, in a full belly relaxed way I'd never seen. "Drats! Well, it was worth a try."

I grabbed her free hand and dragged her over to the pool table, knowing Lester would bring our drinks over. The way her hand felt in mine sent hot shocks up my palm and into my bones. Fuck, it felt so right to be near her.

Reluctantly, I let her hand go and picked up a couple pool cues. "Would you play with me?"

Lester silently dropped off our drinks with a wink before taking off again, leaving us to our private corner of the bar.

"Another game? I thought we'd had enough of those for one night."

I shrugged, hoping against hope. Just when I thought she'd shut it all down and walk out, she picked up one of the sticks. "Prepare to have your ass kicked, god of none."

"I don't care how you touch my ass, as long as you're doing it," I breathed, shooting her a leering smile. Miranda shook her head, even as she bent over to pull the ball rack out. My stomach jumped up into my throat before falling as her perfect rear was put on display for my view.

Memories of plowing into her tight body on that medieval bed in that theater came back in slow-mo technicolor, making my throat dry and my shorts instantly tighter. "How about we make things more interesting?" I asked, my voice a dry rasp.

Miranda lifted that perfectly arched eyebrow as she racked the balls.

"A little game called truth or dare. Every time you sink a ball, you get to pose a truth or dare to the other person."

Maybe I was pushing my luck too far. Miranda didn't

want me poking around in her head, and as much as I didn't want my brain poked either, I was desperate to get past all those defenses.

Miranda licked her lips in a slow, torturous movement that made me want to capture those swollen petals into a kiss so hot her clothes would melt off. Instead, I gripped the pool cue with all my strength, doing my best not to crack it.

"Deal," she finally said.

There was something in her eyes that told me I might have made a massive mistake.

She leaned over, thrust the stick until the crack of balls broke the air and two solids disappeared into a corner pocket.

"Tell me about Aten, and how we can kill him."

Well, fuck, that turned on me fast.

CHAPTER 21

THE BADASS

Xander's relaxed grin twisted into a snarl, shoulders tensing and flexing. "You won't be going anywhere near Aten."

I resisted the urge to fight him. I knew by now that both of us were equally stubborn. If I wanted information, I'd have to take a different tactic.

"Fine," I lied. "But I still want to know. If I'm to be blamed for bringing back the biggest, baddest god of them all, what exactly has everyone shaking in their boots?"

Xander circled the pool table, examining the lineup of balls, his face still arranged in a grim expression. "He's not the biggest or baddest, he's just..."

He trailed off, and I mentally filled in for him, "*...the one who killed me.*"

That did put me on guard. The thought of Xander burning under Aten's power made me queasy anytime I thought about it.

"You should listen to him," Bob advised. He was fastened back to my hip and thankfully hadn't said anything about our detour.

I spoke to him with my mind. *It's my duty, my responsibility to put the cat—er, the sun god—back in the bag. No matter what either of you think, it is what it is.*

Xander picked up where he left off, "He's a sadistic bastard. Greedy, twisted, and I wouldn't let him within a thousand-foot radius of you if I could help it."

"So how was he killed?" I asked again, bringing my point back around even as I took another shot at a solid-colored ball. It sunk into the corner pocket. A smug grin curved up on one side of my face. I batted my eyelashes at him expectantly.

Xander shook his head, the unkempt hair swinging over his eyes with the movement. "I don't know. When I emerged from the cradle, I was out of my mind for I don't know how long. Grim and Timothy were able to sequester me for a time, but eventually they realized I was too close to the seas to be trusted. Egypt suffered floods and storms unlike any other until they moved to a place far from any open body of water."

"You're the reason all the gods are in Nevada?" I completed for him, the awe in my voice evident to my own ears. Xander was the very reason everyone had to pack up and move to a desert in North America.

I lined up another shot but missed. To realize the beast the Grim Reaper kept in the basement of his hotel all these years was the reason the gods resided in Las Vegas now was mind-blowing. From what I understood, most of the gods were not aware of what Grim had kept locked away, or rather *who*. They simply knew the portal to the Afterlife and the hub of all human souls was here, so they had to be here as well.

Osiris forbade them all from taking worshippers a long time ago because gods had become too powerful, domineering, and cruel. They could only stay powerful if they were near the well of souls that Grim reaped from this world.

I doubted Grim would love that I knew all this, but give Vivien a moisturizing face mask, some sliced cucumbers for her eyes, and two dozen pink frosted cupcakes at girls' night and she would spill anything.

Xander nodded. "Eventually, I came somewhat to my senses and Grim explained that because of my sacrifice the other gods were moved to action, and they took Aten out. But not without great cost. Many were slain and sent back to the cradle of life. And of those, I believe few, if any, have reemerged." He bent over and his stick met the white ball with a loud crack. Three striped balls fell into two separate pockets.

"I still get another truth," I pointed out before he got ahead of himself.

That sly grin returned, making my heart flutter. It was that, or maybe the way his ass looked as he bent over to take his shot.

Xander shook his head. "Nuh, uh. You asked if I'm why the gods are in Vegas. That's your second truth. And if you keep pouting like that—" He slid closer to me, eyes still coolly scanning the pool table, though I could feel the heat of his body seep into my side. "—I'm going to kiss and lick that expression right of your gorgeous fucking face."

His words hit my spine like an electric shock, and I forgot to breathe. Sweat broke out between my breasts as my skin tingled and ached in anticipation.

I picked up my beer and took a generous swallow, trying to cool down.

"Truth or dare, sweetheart," he posed casually, rubbing the chalk on the end of his stick.

I never knew what a loaded question that could be until this moment.

"Dare," I said, trying to be nonchalant, but my insides quaked. I set my hip against the pool table, pretending to be unaffected. Pretending I wasn't anticipating him taking advantage of me.

How did he do that? A moment ago I was all consumed with pumping him for information, and now I wanted him to pump me in other ways. Again.

Xander took my pool cue and set both of them aside, turning to face me. "I dare you to close your eyes and not open them again until I tell you."

I frowned.

A spark glimmered in his eyes in response. "Ah, I knew you wouldn't do it."

My frown only deepened. I thought he was going to dare me to kiss him or something. Instantly, my hackles rose at the suggestion. We were in a crowded bar, well, semi-crowded. I wasn't super familiar with my surroundings, and it felt wrong to submit to Xander's dare.

He tilted his head. "I can almost see the smoke coming out of your ears from overthinking this."

I thought he meant it as a dig, but Xander merely

studied my expression with open fascination. As if I were the most interesting person in the world.

"What do you think will happen?" he asked in a low husky voice. "Do you fear the second you close your eyes, one of these guys is going to spring upon us with a knife? That a god will pop out of nowhere and attack? That you won't be in complete control of your environment?"

I hated, absolutely fucking hated that exact scenario had run through my mind already.

"And you think I'd let anything or anyone remotely near you?" One of his brows arched in question. He wasn't touching me, but he stood so close I continued to breathe in his heat.

I narrowed my eyes at him, letting him know I wasn't happy with this before letting my lids flutter close.

"Now what?" I asked, deliberately sounding annoyed.

"Now..." he trailed off, and I could sense him watching me. I wasn't sure if it made me more nervous, or if I just felt stupid with my eyes shut in the middle of the bar. "Now you wait."

"I can't believe you're wasting a dare on this," I snorted. My skin prickled with unease. The sounds of clinking glasses, low chatter, and the jukebox in the background were all too indistinct and too acute at the same time.

While Xander stood in front of me, my back felt unprotected and exposed. I shrugged my shoulders a couple of times, feeling stupider and more vulnerable by the minute.

When he spoke again it was even lower than before. "You are perfectly safe."

I snorted.

My doubt did nothing to ruffle his quiet, even tone. "I would never let anything happen to you, Miranda. If you want, you can relax your shoulders."

"They're fine the way they are," I argued, feeling saltier by the minute.

Why didn't he just kiss me and get this over with?

"Okay," he replied smoothly, as if completely unphased by my thorniness. "Then keep them tense if that makes you feel better."

I hated how that immediately made them fall a couple inches.

His voice, rich and soothing, continued to flow over me. "But just know, you don't always have to be on guard. Not with me. I've got you."

There was a pause, a breath of silence that seemed to stretch between us, filled with the unspoken.

The memory of him after I brought him back from the blade slammed into my brain as it had done so many times in the last month, making my stomach tense and my throat to start to close.

A mask of betrayal and seething hatred twisted his features. I was sure it was for me. Even though Xander told me at the time he'd only been thinking of Aten, I didn't believe him. I deserved his scorn, his disappointment.

My throat closed up even more.

"Miranda," he murmured, and I could almost picture the gentle tilt of his head, the way his eyes would soften when he looked at me. "Whatever you're thinking right now, it's just a thought. It's not real. Whatever attack you are making on yourself, you don't have to."

I was about to open my mouth and tell him off for telling me what to do, but then he said, "But if you want to keep fighting yourself I'll just stand right here with you, and remind you to feel the floor under your feet, the way your clothes wrap around your body. Focus on the sound of my voice."

The angry, self-loathing thoughts began to slip away. Was I being hypnotized again? Had he been hanging out with Max and Alfonso, picking up tips?

I felt or maybe heard him shift his stance, though he came no closer.

"Trust is a hard thing to give, especially when you've been through what you have. But I want you to know you can trust me. I'm here, right in front of you, and I'm not going anywhere."

I bit my lip, the knot of tension in my stomach loosening slightly at his words. It was ridiculous how just a few sentences from him could start to chip away at the walls I'd meticulously built around myself.

"You can let go, even if it's just for now. Let yourself feel, Miranda. It's okay." His voice was almost a whisper now, a caress against the tension that held my body rigid.

And so, I tried. I consciously relaxed my shoulders, letting the tension seep out with a long exhale. The sounds of the bar seemed to fade into the background along with my wariness, leaving only Xander's voice, steady and sure.

"Good," he praised, and I could hear the smile in his voice. "How do you feel?"

"Vulnerable," I admitted, but the word didn't hold the usual weight of fear. It felt different this time—safer, somehow.

"That's okay. Vulnerability isn't a weakness, especially not with me. It's strength, Miranda. The strength to show your true self, to let someone in."

"And you? What does this make you feel?"

He chuckled, a sound that vibrated through the space between us. "Honored to be near. Fiercely protective. And... incredibly drawn to you."

The air between us seemed to spark with his admission, sending a thrill down my spine.

"Can I open my eyes now?" I asked. "You've used up a dare and a truth." He asked me how I was feeling. I was counting that against him. Even though he could do the same thing since I asked the question back.

"Not yet," he said, and I could hear him moving closer. "I've got one more. Truth or dare, Miranda?" A shiver ran up my spine at the way he said my name.

Seeing how he'd used the dare against me in ways I couldn't have anticipated, I knew what to choose this time. My breath hitched. "Truth."

"Do you love me?"

I opened my eyes though he didn't tell me I could. The world had somehow narrowed down to just him. Xander gazed down at me from under his long hair, eyes somehow piercing and vulnerable at the same time. His hand was on the pool table next to my body, but not touching me. He was as close as he could get to me without crossing any real line.

"Dare." There was no fucking way I was answering that.

A wry smile twitched at the corner of his lips. "I dare you to let me in."

He'd backed me into a corner. I either answered if I loved him or let him in. I didn't want to do either.

Though right now, in my relaxed state it felt almost too easy to do both.

He broke into a chuckle, taking a step back while shoving his hands in his pockets. My heart plunged into the space between us and it was like falling off a cliff.

His tone turned light and teasing. "You already owe me a date, but maybe I should use my dare to force you to pick the place and time."

The tension broke. As if he knew he'd crossed a line and went too far, he gave me space and room to breathe. Half of me was grateful. The other half of me wanted him to push me, force me to do what I wouldn't allow myself to.

"I'll take that dare," I said, quickly finishing my beer. "Tomorrow night, eight PM, the Florence hotel."

Xander's face shut down, all his emotions bleeding away from view. "The god's ball." The words came out flat and cold.

"Yes," I said, suddenly aware I was on unsteady ground. "Why?"

He didn't just ask why, the betrayal stamped in his eyes asked *why would you dare bring this up?*

Tell him. Tell him he gives you strength.

Tell him part of you is afraid to face the hatred of all the immortals and wear your shame like a large red painted letter.

That he gives you strength, and you are starting to learn to love that.

That you're starting to learn to lov—

"Because I think you need it. It would be good for you,"I blurted before I could finish the thought in my idiotic head.

Coward.

"Good for me?" he scoffed, picking up his pool cue again. He leaned over and took another shot at the balls. They clacked around the green felt but none of them found a pocket.

"You are one of them, Xander. You act... you act like you're alone, but you're not. You are one of the gods." A laugh of disbelief bubbled out of me. "I know it will take time to get used to this new world, but instead of taking your place above ground, you've retreated to another underground cave." I opened my arms indicating the dive bar. "You're hiding from what you are. From who you are and could be. Timothy told me you have the right to a hotel on the Strip, with wealth beyond imagining at your fingertips. And here you are, down in the muck, buying cheap Hawaiian shirts and acting like you're just another face in the crowd. But you're not."

His body tensed with every word, his emotionless face somehow becoming more distant and foreboding.

"You're telling me to join the ranks of my kind? What about you, Miranda?" He closed the distance between us again. Though he spoke softly in my ear, it felt as if he was yelling the words. "You either think you are invincible, or are willing to be a sacrifice because you deserve to be punished. And or what?"

I squeezed my eyes shut as his accusations hit me like physical blows. He didn't understand because I hadn't told him.

It wasn't a dog who died because I fucked up.

It was worse. So much worse. I never deserved to be forgiven for it.

"But let me tell you, sweetheart, I was the sacrifice for my kind. I warned them of Aten, and they didn't listen.

"Do you know when I asked for help, when I tried to warn everyone, they did everything from spit on me to kick sand in my face? They were more interested in fucking and feasting than helping me do what must be done. I gave up my life trying to stop him, and only *after* did anyone do anything about it. Do you think during the thousands of years I spent in the bowels of this desert—in agony, in unrelenting pain and imprisonment—I thought those arrogant narcissists were worth my life, my pain?"

So that would be a no.

"I'm not returning to the fold. I like being another face in the crowd. I like cheap T-shirts. I like spending my time with a human, which is something they would also sneer and spit on me for. Fuck them. Fuck that life. The only thing I want is you. I guarantee the second they think I intend on being with you without turning you into my sekhor, they will do everything they can to stop me or change you themselves."

I reared back. It was as if he slapped me, his confession snatching the breath from my lungs. "I would never choose to be a vampire."

His gaze dropped to my mouth with a cruel, knowing smile. I realized I was baring my teeth at him in challenge.

"You think I don't know that? That you would never abandon your child, your family to choose a life amongst the immortals?"

Something akin to grief or resignation glimmered in his eyes before it disappeared in his rage.

"Those assholes can burn for all I care."

With that, he turned and left the bar. He only stopped to throw some bills on the counter for our drinks. Lester barely looked up as he grabbed the green, knowing damn well how to mind his business.

I clutched the edge of the pool table, most of my weight supported by my arms as my legs felt like shaky noodles.

I didn't tell him I would be going tomorrow. That I would face them all alone. And that's how I felt now. Utterly and totally alone, and for once I didn't want that.

I wanted Xander by my side. Which didn't make any sense because this was messy and we were both fucked up and this would never work.

So why did my heart beat so hard, so painfully, pounding out his name over and over in my chest all the way home?

CHAPTER 22

THE BADASS

I've been sleeping less and less. I can't tell if it's due to the insufferable heat that grows more intense by the day, or because Xander is knocking around inside my head.

Still splayed out on my bed above the covers, I rub my hands over my face. Jamal is at school and Mama Jean is out with her friends for lunch.

The bed shifts under the weight of someone new. A warm, fuzzy head drops on my stomach. I look down into big beautiful puppy dog eyes that seem to feel all of my pain, confusion, and uncertainty. The warm weight on my stomach instantly grounds me, and I feel my anxiety drop a couple notches. Which is confusing as hell considering Xander is the one who gave me Heinz.

Another wave of gut gnawing guilt plowed into me.

I still can't believe what happened yesterday. From killing a god, to the absolutely depraved things we did in that arcade, to Xander's sudden outburst and exit from the bar.

It feels like I'm living another life at night. Like I'm another person. But which one is the real me?

"Maybe both are you?"

I huffed. "Bob, could you pretend you aren't there and able to hear my every thought?"

"I could," he said carefully, "but I think you've been alone with your thoughts long enough."

"You're right," I said, sitting up. "I should head to the gym if I can't sleep."

Heinz sat up with me and firmly pressed his paws into my chest, forcing me back down.

"Heinz and I agree," Bob went on. "You need to be more forgiving of yourself."

My hand automatically went to Heinz's soft head, which was especially absurd because the dog just bullied me back down.

"What?" I asked. "You and the dog are conspiring against me now too?"

"Yes, but only in the most loving, supportive way."

"I liked it better when you were mute," I grumbled.

"Now we both know that's not true. Though I can't say I'm thrilled to be in the world, sucking down the blood of others. Blech."

Heinz let out a yip.

"Care to translate?" I said, dryly.

"Heinz thinks you should tell Xander the truth about your past."

Okay, I hadn't actually expected him to translate. I'd been joking.

"And the dog knows everything too? You been having a lot of time to spill the tea together?" I couldn't deny the sharp slice of betrayal that Bob told the dog about my past. Then I couldn't deny that this entire situation was fucking bonkers.

Bob sighed. "The dog is from the afterlife. Just assume he probably knows more than even me."

"And now he's a house pet, dining on kibble and named after a condiment."

"Heinz quite likes his name and when Xander went looking for your lost loved one, Heinz volunteered to come back to be with you and Jamal."

Emotion swelled in my chest though I couldn't name it. Grief, gratitude, guilt? Definitely one of the Big Gs.

"That's it," I said, lifting the dog with both hands before gently putting him on the ground and getting to my feet. "Enough therapy from supernatural creatures and objects today."

Despite my irritation with Bob, I took him into the kitchen with me. I put the kettle on, though I didn't really feel like having any tea. Heinz followed closely at my heels Apparently he felt he needed to be heard.

"This is crazy," I muttered.

"Of course it is," Bob said, though I really hadn't been looking for his input. "But what's making it more difficult is you aren't allowing it to be what it is."

"What does that mean?" I asked with a frustrated sigh, pulling at my braids.

I really should be resting. Tonight was the immortal ball and I would basically be put on trial in front of everyone. A piece of bait in a shark pit. I should be preparing my mind to be strong. Instead, I was unraveling faster and faster.

"It means you aren't just one thing. You try to put everything into neat little boxes, and you put the ugliest things in boxes, burying them six feet under and never pulling them out again. Xander is making you feel and be everything at once and it's confusing. Let it be confusing. You are not any one thing:mother, warrior, sinner, lover—"

"Have you been listening to Meredith Brooks?" I asked, cocking a hand on my hip with suspicion.

The sentient blade went on as if he didn't hear me. "You are all things at one time. It's messy, Miranda. Being human is messy."

I made a retching sound of disgust.

Heinz dropped onto my feet, looking up at me again with those big doleful eyes as if to say, *You should really listen to him. We both feel this way.*

"Xander is your equal opposite. He cannot control himself."

"That's not true," I snapped. "Serqet almost pushed him past the edge, and he came back to himself before he lost it." Not that I knew what that looked like anymore.

I suspected it had to do with him turning into his god-likeness, a monster of epic proportions that was out of its mind with pain and power. But Xander was divested of his excess of power.

"You pulled him from the brink, just as he pushes you out of your little tidy boxes that are slowly rotting and decaying in the ground."

The kettle whistled until I lifted it off the burner, making no move to make tea.

"Have you always been so keen to get a word in on your wielder's behavior, or am I just lucky?" I asked, suddenly feeling tired.

"I've never been wielded by a mortal before," Bob confessed quietly. "And I must say, it has been the best experience I've ever had by far."

I swallowed hard, the room suddenly feeling too quiet, too hot and heavy.

"Why's that?" I didn't really want to ask, but I knew he'd hear the question in my mind.

"I have been a weapon of destruction for thousands of years," Bob said solemnly. "But in your hands, I have found purpose beyond bloodshed. You are a wielder of compassion and strength, Miranda. It brings me solace to serve someone who values more than just power." Heinz nudged my leg with his nose, as if in agreement with Bob's words.

I leaned against the kitchen counter, feeling the weight of Bob's words settling around me like a heavy cloak.

"It's also why Heinz came along. He recognized Xander was looking for something in the afterlife, and once he learned of you, the pup realized he wanted to be with you."

My hand dropped to scratch Heinz's head, causing his tail to wag enthusiastically.

The reality of my situation—preparing for the Immortal Ball, navigating the complexities of my relationships, and coming to terms with my own identity—seemed even more daunting now. But a warmth spread from the center of my chest at Bob's words.

Suddenly being human didn't seem as bad as it had a moment ago.

I jerked when my phone buzzed on the counter. Grabbing it, I answered as soon as I saw who it was.

"Hey Timothy—" I started.

"I know we are to meet much later to prepare for the evening's events," he rambled in a hurried rush. "But there is a situation I feel you may be suited to—"

"Spit it out," I commanded.

He sighed on the other side of the line. "It's Xander."

CHAPTER 23

THE BADASS

Xander was where Timothy said, standing in the Menaggio fountains. The god was completely naked, in the middle of the jets of water rocketing into the sky in time with music and lights.

The crowd surrounded the edges, entirely focused on the man standing waist deep in the water. Phone cameras were out documenting the crazy guy yelling and splashing in the water.

As I approached the edge of the fountain, Grim and Timothy stood side by side, their expressions a blend of concern and impatience. Grim, drenched from head to toe, appeared particularly irritable, water dripping from his soaked clothes onto the pavement, casting a dour shadow.

Steering clear of the pissed off and wet god of the dead, I sidled up next to Timothy. He was furiously tapping on his tablet. "What is Xander doing?"

Grim growled from the other side of Timothy.

Timothy paused, raising his head. "Losing his mind and making a scene I'll have to clean up."

A delivery man, uniform slightly askew and pushing a heavily laden cart, maneuvered through the crowd towards us. He locked eyes with Grim, an air of determination in his stride.

"Excuse me, sir?" he called out, pulling a small, oddly shaped package from his cart. "I have a delivery that requires your signature."

Grim glanced at Timothy with a raised eyebrow before turning back to the man with the cart. "This isn't a good time."

The courier shrugged as he chewed his gum in loud, open mouth smacks. The guy had no idea he'd chosen to face off with a god who could rip his soul from his body. "I can't leave until you sign and take your delivery, and I've got at least fifty more stops. The longer you take, the more people you'll be denying their important packages."

Grim snorted like a bulldog but acquiesced, stepping forward to meet the postman. He quickly scribbled his signature on the electronic pad, eager to dismiss the interruption and return his focus to the unfolding drama at the fountains.

However, as soon as Grim's signature completed the transaction, the delivery man, with a practiced motion that suggested he'd done this more times than one would expect, swung the small package directly into Grim's face.

The package burst open upon impact to reveal it was, in fact, a pillow—a very soft, very non-threatening pillow.

The exchange was so out of context, it left me blinking in confusion.

The crowd that had gathered, initially tense with the anticipation of conflict, erupted into a mixture of laughter and applause at the absurdity of the situation. Grim, momentarily stunned, touched his face where the pillow had made contact, then looked at the courier with a mix of disbelief and outrage.

Completely nonplussed and shrugging as if this was just another day on the job, the man muttered, "My job gets weirder every day," before turning on his heel and walking away. He left Grim holding the pillow, a physical reminder of the unpredictability of his marriage.

"As if it isn't enough, I've been nearly drowned today." Grim shook his head as he turned his attention back to the fountain.

Determined not to get caught up in Grim and Vivien's ludicrous war, or newfound love language, I turned back to the person making a far bigger scene.

"Xander isn't doing anything godly that would draw suspicion," I pointed out. "He just looks like some crazy guy having a mental breakdown." Despite my dismissal, something inside me felt off kilter. As if my senses were telling me there was something very wrong that shouldn't be laughed off here.

"Oh?" Timothy raised an eyebrow as he pursed his lips. "What if I were to tell you those fountains aren't supposed to go off for another twenty minutes?"

I did a double take. "*He's* doing that?"

A jet exploded into the air like a geyser, far past what

the Menaggio fountains were capable of. "Why don't you go in and get him?"

Grim flapped his hands at his own body with wet slaps as if to show he had tried.

Timothy snorted. "Oh we tried. *His majesty* blasts anyone who comes within striking distance of the edge. I'm working on getting a special tranquilizer gun delivered for our friend here."

"I'm going to lock his ass back up in the cage and put a collar on him this time," Grim muttered, more to himself.

I licked my lips, my heart pounding against my ribs, knowing what I was about to do. Slipping off my coat, I walked toward the edge of the fountain.

"Miranda, what are you doing?" Timothy called out in a panic.

I set my coat over the lip of the pool and shot back, "This is what you called me for. He won't hurt me." Throwing first one leg over, then the other, I dropped into the chest-high water.

"You don't know that," Timothy countered.

He won't.

"Miranda, think this through," Grim shouted after me.

Ignoring Timothy's and Grim's attempts to intervene, I knew it was up to me to reach Xander. As bizarre as the pillow attack was, it reminded me that sometimes the unexpected could break through the chaos. Maybe, just maybe, I could be Xander's unexpected moment of clarity.

Meanwhile, on the other side, more hotel security attempted to get into the fountain to pull the crazy naked man out. A strange cackling laugh, halfway to a hysterical hyena came out of Xander as he slammed his hands on the water. Shoots of water plowed through the men, hurling them back twenty feet until they crashed into the crowd of people watching. Screams and cries filled the air, but it was all background noise as I made my way toward Xander and keyed in on his strange chatter.

"It's no good, it's no good captain. This isn't your boat. You have no ship. You are lost at sea."

The strange cadence of his words reminded me of when he'd been in the cage, trapped and driven mad by his own power. My brows furrowed as something tightened in my chest. The madness he's exhibited should have been long gone after his rebirth from the blade.

The god turned as if sensing my approach. The crowd sucked in a collective gasp as if expecting him to blow me away next.

"Xander," I called out, wading my way slowly but surely toward him.

Turquoise eyes had turned stormy and unfocused, and for a moment he didn't recognize me. Xander's mouth moved as if he were still talking to himself in a jumble of nonsense.

My skin prickled with the realization Timothy could be right and Xander might view me as an enemy.

"What did I tell you about a shirt and shoes?" I called out in a taunt, hoping to snap him out of it. "And now you can't even be bothered with pants?"

Xander's eyes narrowed as he focused on me with all the attention of a predator, assessing if another being was adversary or prey. I stood my ground, unafraid.

"Miranda," he said my name with a growl, finally recognizing me. "You shouldn't be here."

My heart leapt in my chest upon hearing his voice, but it wasn't the warm, tender tones he would use when we were together. It was cold, distant, and filled with suspicion.

"Taking up the hobby of streaking?" I kept talking, keeping his attention on me. "Or is this another one of your ill-begotten attempts to seduce me?"

Xander's lips twisted into a smirk. "I don't need to seduce you, Miranda. You're already mine." His words were laced with a possessiveness that sent a shiver down my spine.

I forced myself to remain calm even as my heart raced in my chest. "I belong to no one, Xander. You know that."

"Do I?" His voice was low and dangerous. "You're always finding your way back to me, no matter how hard you try to resist."

I swallowed hard.

"Xander, you need to come with me," I said firmly, still wading toward him. "You're scaring the guests and causing a scene."

He laughed, the sound manic and unhinged. "I'm not going anywhere, Miranda. Not until I've found what I'm looking for."

"And what's that?" I asked, treading carefully.

"My place." Xander suddenly looked stricken as he parted the water with his hands, looking down into the liquid as if he could find what he sought there.

"Your place?" I asked, stopping a few feet away from him.

"Yes, yes," he mumbled. "I've lost it. I belong nowhere. I've been lost in time and space, and I lost it, lost my place."

My lips parted as my heart cracked a little. "Xander," I said softly. In that moment, I wished I knew where he'd been staying. I didn't know where he was sleeping after being confined to an underground prison for so long. He needed something tangible—an address, something.

"You belong. I know you've been gone from the world a while, but you'll adapt. I promise."

Xander's agitation grew as he tunneled through the water more insistently. "No, no, no, no." Then his eyes squeezed shut as he clenched his fists shut. "It's not here. *I'm* not here. I can't find my place."

Those fists rose then slammed back into the water, causing a geyser to blast off. For a moment, I thought a bomb hit me. My hands clapped over my ears. I barely heard the screams and cries of the bystanders.

"Xander," I yelled. "You have to stop."

Cracking an eye open I found Xander's face contorted and mouth open in agony as the water continued to flow and explode all around us, but he never blasted me out. I wanted to cling to him, ground him in safety. So I did just that. Stumbling forward in water that was now only knee deep, I threw myself at him.

More water bombs went off.

"Xander," I yelled, plastered to his body. "It's okay, I'm here. You have a place with me. You're safe, everything is okay."

Underneath me, his body shuddered as if explosions similar to the water around us were taking place in his cells.

My hand gripped the hair at the nape of his neck, holding him to me, trying to ground him.

The silence that followed was deafening after the cacophony. Two strong arms wrapped me up and Xander held me to him until only my tip toes touched the ground.

In that moment, with Xander's form trembling against mine, a realization struck me like a bolt. He was a powerful god who commanded the elements, yes, but beneath that, he was achingly vulnerable. Here he was, lost and seeking a place in a world that had moved on without him. My throat tightened at the thought and a wave of tenderness washed over me.

His confession, raw and honest, sliced through the barriers I'd built around my heart. "I think I'm lost," he murmured, his voice a mix of despair and desperation.

Sharp pricks jabbed at the back of my eyes, emotion clogging my throat. "You aren't lost. I've got you." My voice was steady despite the turmoil churning inside me. Here, in the midst of the chaos he'd unintentionally wrought, I found a truth I'd been reluctant to admit—even to myself. I cared for Xander, not just as a god, or a fighting partner, but as the complex, fractured soul he was.

"I'm so sorry, Miranda. I'm sorry for everything." He clung to me like a lifeline, like his salvation.

The moisture in my eyes formed a tear, sliding over my cheek. I couldn't say it back, but I was sorry too. I wasn't even sure what for. For him? For me? For the pain he was in, for the mistakes I'd made?

That his apology was unnecessary because I found his flaws as lovable as his strength?

As we stood there, his arms wrapped tightly around me, I realized that his strength wasn't just in his godly powers, but in his willingness to show his vulnerabilities. In that vulnerability, I understood him more deeply than I had anyone else. And it scared me—how much I wanted to do the same. To let him see me as completely as he showed himself. Though it terrified me to my core.

After a long moment, when I was sure my heart wouldn'texplode in my chest, I said, "We need to get out of here." Side eyeing the crowd that had massively thinned out, I could see there were still phones held out, capturing our incredibly private moment. We needed to be anywhere but here.

Meeting Timothy's eye, he gave me a grave nod.

"Where do I go?" Xander's voice broke on the question.

"Where do you want to go?" I countered, letting him make the choice to find his own anchor.

"To where it's safe," he said, a note of hopelessness in his tone that clawed at my insides.

"Where is that?" I asked, my heart in my throat.

Was he about to tell me where he'd been for so many weeks after I resurrected him?

His eyes met mine, and in them, I saw a reflection of my own longing for acceptance, for a place to call safe. "Where we first met," he said, and the simplicity of his answer—the longing for a connection to a moment in time when things were less complicated, less burdened by the weight of the world—broke me.

CHAPTER 24
THE BEAST

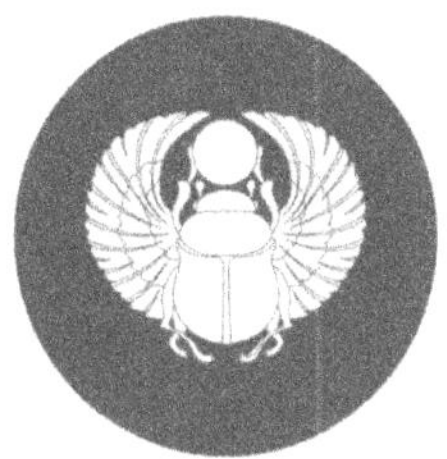

"Close the door, please," I asked, my voice hoarse. Bees and gnats still buzzed around my head.

Miranda pulled the massive cage door shut, but she closed it behind her, shutting herself in with me. I'd put some pants on that Timothy had at the ready when Miranda led me out of the fountains.

Instantly, the clank of my cage allowed me a sense of safety and assurance.

"You don't need to stay," I said more gruffly than I needed to.

Make her stay.

Make her leave.

Tell her to go away, not to look upon you like this.
Go drown in the ocean, drown,
drown,
drown.

"Hey," she said, snapping my attention to her. "Stay with me. I'm not going anywhere right now."

I grabbed my hair and yanked as I bent over, emotions and feelings drowning me in a confusing chaos, topped by a massive dose of shame. The sensation of fracturing from within is a constant companion, a reminder that I'm a mosaic of broken pieces, sharp and jagged, dangerous to the touch, even to myself.

"Xander, what's happening, talk to me," Miranda said quietly.

With every erratic beat of my heart, a new crack splinters through my psyche, widening the gaps where madness seeps in, whispering seductive lies of endless despair.

"I'm broken, sweetheart." That unhinged titter of laughter escaped me. "I tried... I tried to hide it. I tried to heal it. I tried to make it go away for you, you, you."

I blinked and found myself across the room, though I didn't remember moving. Miranda studied me intently and her gaze felt like razor blades slicing through my flesh.

It reminded me of all the times she killed me with the blade on her hip.

I wanted to taste it right now. It would silence my mind. I needed silence so badly. I needed to prove to her I could be still, be whole.

"I thought your powers weren't out of control anymore," she said quietly.

There's a hollowness echoing within me, each pulse a reminder of the chasm between who I am and who I yearn to be, a gulf filled with the debris of shattered dreams and unattainable peace.

Another hyena laugh tipped out of me. "It's not my power."

And even though I was still ancient and primal, and my mind was still racing with thoughts of the outside world, I knew in this moment, I was exactly where I belonged.

I paced to the far end of my cage and back again. Again and again. I did it for years. I'd continue to do it for years.

"It's not my power, it's my brain. It's broken. I'm broken. I didn't want you to see." A sob lodged itself in my throat, and I refused to let it out. If I did, an ocean would rush out behind it.

I wasn't making sense.

I'm never making any godsdamn sense.

"You thought I hated you. I could never hate you. That would be like hating oxygen. But I didn't deserve oxygen." Or was I supposed to say I didn't deserve her? "I tried to hide it from you. I didn't want you to see. So I hid away. I tried to be like you. I tried to control it. I tried to be steady. I tried to be what you needed, but I'm not."

My hands wrapped around the bars as I confessed all my dirty little secrets to her. "Outside of here, this world is too big. It's too bright. There are too many people. I don't understand what anyone is saying. They type on tiny devices and they don't look up. The lights up there are so bright they burn. The sounds of slot machines are machine guns against my brain. I can't, I can't, I can't be calm!" I was yelling now. Not at her. Never at her.

I was yelling over the pain and confusion in my brain as my stomach and chest constricted so tightly, I thought my organs would collapse inside me. But they wouldn't, they never did.

"But I practiced. I practiced so hard. Be normal, Xander. Be steady, Nun. Calm the waters inside, she needs calm waters. And I tried to calm them until I could come out. Come out to you."

When I turned to look at her, Miranda was still there. For some reason I expected her to be gone. My voice dropped to a whisper. I desperately didn't want to yell anymore.

"You have a name for this now," I said with another hysterical titter of laughter. "Crazy. I am crazy, Miranda. Things burn inside my brain, but I don't want to burn you." I slowly made my way toward her. She didn't move but her shoulders tensed.

"So, I come here and lock in all of my crazy." I needed her to understand. I failed, but I tried so hard, so very hard to be better, to be what she needed. I dropped to my knees before her.

Every attempt to tame my own traitorous brain was a battle lost before it began. My insides churned with a maelstrom of emotions, each one a sharp reminder of the fractured existence I couldn't escape. Miranda's presence here, in this space that represented my failures and fears, only amplified the turmoil. I'd spent countless moments, hidden in the shadows, trying to piece myself back together, to be someone worthy of standing by her side. The irony wasn't lost on me that in seeking to protect her from my chaos, I've only drawn her deeper into my storm.

The pressure to be what Miranda needs—a pillar of strength in her world of uncertainties—felt like chains around my chest, tightening with every breath. I wanted to come back to her, whole, healed, a beacon of stability in the tumultuous sea of her life. Yet, here I am, disintegrating before her eyes, a testament to my inadequacies.

The realization hit like a physical blow, leaving me gasping for air in the suffocating space between who I am and who I desperately want to be. For her. When my voice fractured the silence, it carried the weight of my brokenness as I confessed my deepest fears and failures in a raw outpouring I couldn't contain.

"I tried to be a man for you, but I'm not. I'm not a man. I'm not a god. I'm just pieces smushed together."

My arms wrapped around her strong legs as I buried my face in her stomach. I kept my hold light, as if she was as fragile as glass.

Fingers stroked the top of my head and I shuddered under her touch.

"I'm so sorry. I'm so sorry, Miranda." I needed her forgiveness so desperately, but I didn't deserve it. Yet I begged for it anyway.

"Shh," she hushed, continuing to stroke the hair on my head in a soothing manner until I sagged against her.

I didn't want to look at her face. I was too afraid to see what was there, and even more ashamed that I couldn't bring myself to face her.

She pulled at my arm after I quieted, bringing me to my feet, but I still couldn't bring myself to look at her face.

Thankfully, she didn't ask me. Instead, she drew me toward the back of my cage to where the light disappeared, and a hidden door lay. She pushed it open and led me down the stone steps into the rest of my enclosure.

I'd been to a zoo now, and I knew that's exactly what this was. An enclosure like the humans had for dangerous animals.

The humid air wrapped around me like a blanket as the reflection of my stone pools shimmered off the walls. The light was low down here and my shoulders lowered as my stomach stopped clenching. My senses calmed being away from the neon lights set at the front of my cage.

She guided me over to the largest pool and stopped us before yanking her own top off.

I was still turning my head away to keep from looking at Miranda, or maybe to keep her from looking at me.

She continued to undress, then reached for my pants. They dropped to my feet.

Strong, elegant fingers slipped between mine and my hand automatically gripped as if she were my only lifeline. With a tug, she backed into the pool, drawing me along.

The feel of the water along my skin made me catch my breath. It wasn't just any water; it was from the Red Sea. Imported from the shores of Egypt, from home. A place I wasn't allowed to be near again. Not when I made them boil.

Miranda had seen me do that before but this time the water remained blissfully calm. Another shuddering sigh escaped me as I crouched down with her, the water lapping against my neck.

"Look at me," Miranda murmured.

Despite the comfort of this place, I couldn't swallow around the lump still lodged in my throat.

Her hands found my face, forcing me to do what she said.

My heart pounded so hard against my ribs, my bones ached. When I looked into her eyes I saw a deep, cutting sadness that matched my own. Tears streaked down her cheeks.

Did she pity me? Was she sad I broke any chances of being the man she needed? My mind raced to fill in the space.

"I am so sorry," she said, her voice thick with emotion.

Of all the things I expected her to say, I hadn't expected that. I reached for her waist, pulling her over to me. Her legs wrapped around my waist, but she didn't release my face from her grip.

"I'm so sorry you felt you had to hide all the broken parts of yourself from me. I'm so sorry you felt you weren't good enough. The world is often too much for me, and I've been living in it all this time. I can't imagine what you must be going through."

My fingers dug into her sides as her words hit me almost physically.

I managed a small, pained smile, but the lump in my throat still wouldn't budge. "You don't know what you've done for me, Miranda. Without you, I wouldn't have made it this far. You didn't just give me a place to hide, you gave me sanity amidst the chaos." My voice wavered but I pressed on, trying to convey my gratitude.

"I made you feel you weren't enough," she rasped. I shook my head, but her fingers tunneled into my hair, forcing me to stop the motion. "You couldn't allow yourself to be broken with me, because I refused to allow myself to lose control around you."

"You've lost control around me," I countered, though it felt inappropriate to bring up our various sexual trysts. Even the thought of the bed on that stage, her writhing on that arcade game, the way her eyes turned glassy when she came apart under my touch, made my cock harden in the water. I couldn't help it.

Miranda nodded. "I did. I have. And it felt fucking incredible. Terrifying but incredible."

I gathered her closer to me. "I don't want to terrify you."

"I've been terrified of myself. Someone recently told me I should be forgiving of myself, let myself be all the things.

Xander, you are *all the things*. The god, the man, you are steady when I need you to be, you are a mess when you have to be, and we need to stop punishing ourselves for all the messy parts."

She pulled back slightly, bringing her lips close to my ear. "And I'm here for you, Xander. I'm here to help you find your way back to yourself. If that means I have to stay in here with you when you need it, then so be it."

With that, her lips brushed against my neck and a jolt of electricity coursed through me. Her warmth seeped into every pore. The tension in my muscles began to dissipate as we held each other.

As we floated there, the darkness around us morphing into a million shades of blue, the sudden surge of relief that flooded through me was so intense and pure. I never knew such an emotion could exist within me.

"Miranda," I whispered her name, but it echoed gently in the cavern. "I love you."

Her response was a sharp inhale, and I wondered if I just undid everything all over again.

THE BADASS

My heart stalled in my chest, the beat replaced by a deafening silence as Xander's words sank in. He wasn't just confessing his feelings, he was handing over his soul to me, bloody pulp that it was, and in this place the declaration was so sacred, tears stung the backs of my eyes again.

Xander went on in a rough voice, "I don't need you to say it back, I just need you to know that in my entire existence I've never felt more alive, more anchored, more terrified, or had more fucking fun than when I'm with you."

My arms tightened around his neck.

"I need to tell you something," I forced through my

constricted throat. It felt as though my body was physically trying to hold back the words that were begging to be released.

"The story I told you, about my dog, how I begged my parents for a dog because I would love it and take care of it? There is a reason you couldn't find him in the afterlife."

Self-hatred rose up inside me. My entire being recoiled at being forced to confront this deepest, darkest secret of my past. Every dark, twisted part of my soul curled up tighter at the prospect of being exposed.

To his credit, he didn't ask any questions, just gave me all the runway and space I needed to get the words out.

"It was a sibling I wanted. I wanted a little sister or brother. On my birthday they announced my mom was pregnant and gave me a picture to prove it. I was getting my wish... a little brother. I was more excited about being a big sister than anything and helped take care of him, but after a couple years, he started to get on my nerves and I started to push him away."

The guilt and shame washed over me like a hot wave, threatening to consume me. Knots twisted my stomach until bile rose in my throat. I could barely speak through the lump in my throat as I confessed to Xander. "I was supposed to watch him in the backyard, but I was annoyed and wanted to do my own thing. I wanted to *play*." I said the next part quickly. "He walked out into the street and was hit and killed by a car."

Admitting this truth to Xander felt like standing at the edge of an abyss, the ground crumbling beneath my feet, threatening to swallow me whole. Every word I uttered felt like I was excavating parts of my soul I had kept buried under layers of self-recrimination and denial. The weight of the confession pressed down on me, a tangible force that squeezed the very air from my lungs.

It's not just a secret I was revealing; it was a scar, deep and raw, a wound that never fully healed. No matter where I am, or what I'm doing, that moment always roils at the base of my every move, my every thought.

The silence that followed my confession was suffocating. It was everything about myself I tried to deny and outrun, but my mistake wasn't simply something I did. It was part of me. The vulnerability of this moment overwhelmed me as I laid bare the most broken parts of myself to the one person whose opinion mattered most.

"You were a child," Xander said quietly.

I shook my head, feeling like I had sliced my guts open and they were now floating in the water with us. "That doesn't matter. If I had watched him, if I did what I said I would… if I had been a good big sister, watched over him instead of playing, he would still be alive. He wasn't even three years old."

My parents did their best to keep what happened under wraps, saying they didn't blame me. But I knew the truth. At a young age, I knew my parents would always resent me on some level. It's why we kept in touch mainly via Christmas cards and a bi-yearly update call or email.

"Miranda," Xander's hands lifted from the water, dripping as they clasped my face, forcing me to look at him. "Where were your parents? What was the driver doing? You were a child. Of course you wanted to play."

I shook my head with a crooked smile. "I've tried telling myself all those things, but all I know, in the deepest parts of my soul, is that I wasn't vigilant and when I allowed myself to play, he died. Since then, I've known that every time I've given into that side of myself, the selfish side of myself, something bad would happen."

Shame coils tightly around my heart, a constant reminder of the irrevocable mistake of my past. It's a shadow that's followed me, growing longer with each passing year, a dark specter I could never outrun.

He let out a deep sigh. "When you brought me back, something bad happened."

I nodded. The shame burrowed into my heart, like worms eating their way through an apple.

"I love you, Xander."

He sucked in a breath as if pained, but I knew he was overcome with emotion.

"But I have to confess, I don't know how this works. I don't know how to do this even if I want to. Not to mention the whole other part."

The part I hadn't even allowed myself to entertain because I couldn't get past the first barrier much less the second.

"What other part?"

"You're a god and I'm a mortal."

His face wrenched up as if experiencing physical pain.

"You know I won't turn into a vampire. I have my son, who I love. I don't want to live forever. I want to grow old like Mama Jean. I want to see lines of age on my face. One day, I want to rest in the Afterlife."

Xander's nostrils flared, hands gripping me so hard to him though we both knew it wouldn't be enough to keep us together.

"I know," he said, his voice rough with emotion.

"I don't know how this can work," I repeated in a whisper.

Then he said something that made me feel like I wasn't

alone for the first time in I don't even know how long. He ripped the walls down around me, clinging to me, and confessed, "I don't know either."

I wasn't alone, but being with someone I loved didn't keep me from feeling the deepest pits of sadness. So we clung to each other, unsure of what to do next. Or how to be better.

WE MOVED from the pool to his massive bed, clinging to each other, kissing and touching even as our hearts broke together. As my emotional walls and Xander's big secret dissipated in that pool of water around us, I would have thought nothing could hold us back from each other, but it only seemed to solidify the hopelessness of our situation.

Xander eventually fell asleep, no doubt exhausted from fighting himself. I continued to lie there next to him, combing his hair back as his chest rose and fell steadily. Then I dropped a kiss to Xander's forehead, feeling my heart squeeze so intensely I feared it might implode. I stayed as long as I could before I quietly dressed, gathered my things, and slipped out.

I tried to remind myself there were still gods to hunt and Xander would be by my side as I did so. Instead of putting him off, I'd let him help me. But where would we go from here, him a god and me a mortal? It couldn't last forever. And unfortunately, I needed that certainty.

Xander had my whole heart, but sometimes love wasn't enough. I saw the two paths. One way led to me giving in and becoming a vampire. Vivien would no doubt help me. I'd bond to Xander as his sekhor and drink his blood for all eternity. But I'd resent him. I'd feel robbed of getting to grow old, of the promise of death.

Jamal would get older, he would graduate high school, then college, maybe get married. But as events continued on, I would eventually have to pull away from his life as age refused to show on me. I wanted to hold grandbabies in my arms, stay part of his life the way Mama Jean did with us.

Then there was the thought of outliving my own son, which sent ice cold fear flooding through my veins. No parent should have to outlive their child. Would I hate myself and eventually Xander for choosing a man over my family and how I wanted to live the rest of my life?

Then there was the second route. Xander and I kept things as is, we hunted gods together until I put all of them back into the blade. Even if I completed what seemed like an absolutely impossible task, I knew Xander would stay with me. But how would he feel watching me grow old? The thought of not being able to keep up with him, engage him with my youth and vitality, brought pain too. And one day, he'd be alone. Did that make it my responsibility to try and spend my days trying to nurse his mental state back to health so he could go on after me? Should I encourage him to rejoin the other gods? Help him open up to the possibility of loving someone else?

Selfishness curled sourly in my stomach. I didn't want him to love someone else. I was tired of playing the martyr, but maybe this was the only answer.

Everything in my body felt heavier on the drive home, as if I'd gained twenty pounds of emotional weight.

Pushing open Jamal's door, I found him sprawled on his bed, surrounded by textbooks and scribbling away in his notebook. It helped to know Mama Jean was there when he got home, but I realized I'd been distant lately for a number of reasons. But the kid never seemed to begrudge me for it.

The sight of him so focused and determined sent a wave of love crashing over me, grounding me in the present. Heinz was dutifully resting next to Jamal, receiving the occasional soft pet from my son.

"Hey, buddy," I said, keeping my voice soft as I crossed the room to sit beside him on the bed. "How's homework going?"

Jamal looked up, his expression lighting up in a way that eased the tightness in my chest. "Okay, I guess. Math's a bit tough today."

I glanced at the problems on the page. "Want some help?" I offered, knowing that these moments were the building blocks of our relationship, precious and fleeting.

"Yeah, actually," he said.

As we worked through the problems together, I was struck by the realization of how much I cherished these quiet, ordinary moments. They were a stark contrast to the chaos and danger of my nights, a reminder of what I fought for, what I lived for.

Jamal's laughter filled the room as we cracked a particularly tough problem, and in that laughter, I heard the echoes of a future I longed to be part of. A future where I could watch him grow, celebrate his victories, and support him through his defeats. A future where I could grow old with grace, surrounded by the family I loved.

The thought of becoming immortal, of stepping outside the natural cycle of life and watching from the sidelines as Jamal lived his life without me, was a cold, unfathomable prospect. No amount of time with Xander could compensate for the loss of these simple, human experiences.

My heart was going to break either way.

"You okay, Mom?" Jamal asked.

"Yeah, I'm good, why?"

"You seem sad."

I swallowed over the lump in my throat. My son, eleven going on forty.

"Is it because of Xander?"

"What makes you say that?"

"You were upset when he gave you Heinz." Even as Jamal said the words, his fingers curled protectively into the dog's soft scruff. As if thinking I might try to get rid of the dog. "You like him, but you don't want to."

I reached over and pet the mutt who lifted his head, closing his eyes under the ministrations. "I think Heinz is pretty great too." A little bit too much in my business, but Bob was worse. Until this moment I hadn't realized how the immortal dog made me feel like my son was safer with him nearby.

Jamal shook his head. "I don't mean Heinz, I mean Xander. You *like*, like him."

I tried to keep my shoulders from stiffening but it couldn't be helped. I couldn't reconcile the two worlds, my two selves with Jamal on one side and Xander on the other.

I didn't know what to say.

"Jamal," I began, my voice softer than I intended. "Liking someone... it's complicated. Especially when you're grown up. There are things to consider, decisions that don't just affect me, but us—our little family."

He set his pencil down and turned to face me fully, his young face etched with a seriousness beyond his years. "But isn't Xander nice? He saved me. And you smile more after you've been around him."

The mention of Xander's selfless act tugged at my heartstrings.

"He is nice, and yes, he makes me smile. A lot." I conceded, unable to mask the warmth that thought brought. "But being with someone like Xander... it's not just about the good times. It's about making choices that could change everything."

Jamal considered this, his brow furrowing in thought. "But don't you always say we should do what makes us happy? That life's too short to be scared?"

His words, a mirror of my own often-spoken advice, struck a chord. Here I was, wrestling with the fear of immortality, of a love that spanned the impossible, while my son distilled it all into a simple pursuit of happiness.

"I do say that," I admitted. "And I believe it. It's just... with Xander, it's not about not wanting to be with him. It's about figuring out how we can be together when we want such different things for our futures."

Jamal nodded, a maturity in his acceptance that made me wonder who was the parent in this conversation. "Maybe you don't have to figure it all out right now, Mom. Maybe just being happy together for a while is enough."

His insight, so pure and unburdened by the *what-ifs* and *buts* that plagued my thoughts, offered the clarity I'd been seeking.

As Jamal turned his attention back to his homework I leaned against his headboard, allowing myself a moment to just be.

Between the soft scratch of Jamal's pencil and the comforting presence of his room, life didn't feel so complicated.

That being said, the future did hold a weighty event I couldn't put off anymore. I kissed Jamal and reminded him of his bedtime before I headed out.

After the quick drive to the Strip, I stepped onto the

elevator and hit the white button that led to the top of Sinopolis.

The sun set a half hour ago, so I wasn't surprised to find Vivien standing there waiting for me when the doors slid open. Timothy was there, handing her a massive frozen coffee piled high with whipped cream. As soon as he saw me he turned toward me, stretching out an arm with a large cup. An americano that was more espresso than water.

"I figured you ladies could use some fighting fuel for tonight."

Viven smiled at me. "Ready to get balls to the walls, pretty?"

I breathed in deep. "Ready as I'll ever be."

"Release the hounds," Vivien announced.

CHAPTER 26

THE BADASS

Vivien did not mean literal hounds. She was announcing the unleashing of the hair, makeup, and dress stylists.

While Vivien groaned and complained the whole way through even as they dressed her in an extravagant red and black ball gown, I quietly submitted to whatever they wanted to do to me.

"How can you just sit there and take it?" she asked me with a scowl.

"I trust professionals to do their job."

Vivien blew a raspberry at me.

Out came my box braids, while creams were applied to

moisturize and soften my face. They plucked and pulled at me the same as Vivien, until the job was done.

The room was filled with a weighty silence as I stood before the full-length mirror, my reflection a stranger adorned for war as much as for splendor. Timothy, Vivien, and Bianca had outdone themselves, weaving elements of the divine and the warrior into every thread that now clung to my form.

Hair cascaded around my shoulders in a torrent of loose curls that caught the light with a rebellious shimmer. The ensemble they'd chosen for me was an echo of the ideas we'd discussed, a perfect amalgamation that spoke of power and grace.

The top piece molded to my torso was a masterpiece of dark, burnished gold, sculpted to resemble the intricate carapace of a scarab, a symbol of eternal life which seemed almost a mockery considering the blade I bore.

A skirt of layered fabric, dark as the midnight sea, split along my thigh, offering freedom of movement and an unspoken promise of danger. It was trimmed in gold and dotted with blue accents that caught the light like the surface of water kissed by the sun. My arms were embraced by bands of gold climbing from wrist to elbow, a delicate balance of adornment and readiness.

As I turned, the light danced across the metal and fabric, casting a glow that seemed to ignite the very air around me. The effect was not lost on me—I was the only mortal who would stand among gods this night, the only one with the power to unmake them.

Timothy handed me a headpiece, a circlet that dripped jewels onto my forehead, the centerpiece being a scarab.

"The scarab is a sacred symbol to us," Bianca explained. "Just as the scarab rolls the sun across the sky, your actions can determine the fate of gods and mortals alike. You have been touched by the divine and are an agent of influence, pushing against the boundaries of your mortal existence to affect the divine realm."

I felt the weight of my own legend settling upon my shoulders. Tonight, I wasn't just Miranda. I was the mortal who held the Blade of Bane, the woman who had unlocked the gods' prison and who now walked willingly into their midst.

My hands itched for the familiar hilt of my blade but Bob was concealed, hidden beneath the folds of my skirt and strapped to my outer thigh.

In the mirror, I saw them standing behind me—my friends, my allies. And in their eyes, I saw what they had wrought—a warrior queen, fierce and unyielding. I would enter the Immortal Ball with my head held high, not just for myself, but also for Xander who couldn't bring himself to be there.

AFTER A STRANGE TRIP on a gondola down the canal of the Florence Hotel, our party ended up at an underground secret entrance. Vivien and Grim went in first, followed by Timothy, and then me.

As I entered, the hum of conversation and the soft melody of a live orchestra enveloped me. Everywhere I looked, there were wonders beyond imagining—jeweled goblets that filled themselves with ambrosia, mirrors that showed glimpses of alternate realities, and water canals that spanned the length of the football field sized ballroom. The ceiling itself was a mesmerizing display of shifting constellations, twinkling and dancing in harmony with the live orchestra's music.

The sheer opulence of the ballroom was like something out of a fever dream. Floating chandeliers? Check. Live egrets? Double check.

The smell of sugar and something lightly floral filled my senses. I scanned the room, taking in the glittering assembly of gods and other immortals.

One god wore a cloak made of shimmering starlight, its edges trailing along the ground like a comet's tail. His eyes glowed with an otherworldly power as he regarded me.

I had to admit there was something about a god in starlight couture that made my heart do a little flip. Not that I'd ever tell him. The last thing his ego needed was a mortal's approval. But seriously, if you're going to wear the cosmos, at least coordinate with your deity date. Clashing constellations are a fashion faux pas.

A goddess adorned in a crown of intertwining vines and precious jewels floated effortlessly across the marble dance floor with her stunning partner. Each step she took left behind a trail of blooming flowers, their petals swirling in an elegant dance with the music.

I felt out of place amidst this grandeur, the weight of the Blade of Bane at my hip a constant reminder of my mission. A mission that had turned me into a pariah in their eyes.

As I navigated the outskirts of the crowd I could feel their gazes upon me—eyes filled with a blend of curiosity and disdain. It wasn't long before a group closed in, their intentions thinly veiled behind polite, vicious smiles. They'd as soon slit my throat as smile upon me.

Bob chose that moment to interject. "If they lay a finger

on you, I'll... Well, I suppose I'll give them a very stern talking to. With lots of sharp, pointy words."

A goddess draped in gossamer fabrics with eyes like twin sapphires stepped forward. "Miranda West, isn't it? The mortal who dared to unleash Aten. How... brave of you," she said, her voice dripping with sarcasm.

I squared my shoulders, meeting her gaze. "It was a mistake. One I intend to fix."

A chuckle came from my right where a god with skin the color of the night sky and eyes like molten gold stood. "A mistake? You've endangered us all, human. Aten's return could be the end of us," he said, his tone laced with barely contained fury.

"I'm aware of the consequences," I replied, doing my best not to reach for Bob. If I did so they might see it as a move to attack them. "And I'm here to face them."

Timothy caught my eye from across the room for a moment. His expression was tight with concern and I knew he wanted to intervene.

When we'd been getting ready, Timothy and Vivien had vowed to be by my side all night to make sure this exact thing wouldn't happen, but I ordered them in no uncertain terms not to interfere. If I were to be put on the chopping block I would handle it myself. I didn't need these immortals to like me, but I needed them to respect me, and hiding under the power of someone else would only make me look weak.

Despite Timothy and Vivien's protests, Grim agreed with me.

Their circle tightened around me, a suffocating ring of divine judgment.

"You don't belong here mortal."

"You should be scrubbed from the earth for what you've done. Damned to Amit's belly."

An icy drip of fear started in my belly. Maybe I'd been wrong. Maybe they would try to kill me right here, out in the open. No one besides my few allies would do anything to stop it from happening either.

"I'd stop them," Bob said encouragingly, followed by, "Well, I'd at least make a very cutting remark. But don't worry, I've got your back. Metaphorically speaking."

A hush rolled over the room. The atmosphere shifted. The gods paused their verbal smackdown to see what was the cause.

Xander strode in.

He was near the grand staircase, his presence unmistakable and overwhelming. The unkempt, wild man I knew was replaced by a figure of poise and power. His hair, usually a wild mane, was now neatly swept back, framing a face that radiated an unearthly aura. Dressed in a blue suit that seemed woven from a stormy ocean of silk, he was every bit the deity of deep waters.

"Is that who I think it is?" a goddess whispered from nearby.

"It can't be. No one has seen him for thousands of years."

"I heard he was dead."

"I heard he'd lost his mind."

More murmurs and interest raced through the room, a live wire.

So everyone knew I released Aten, but they didn't know why it came about. I imagined I had Grim and Timothy to thank for their discretion. I was suddenly as grateful to them for keeping those details private as I was for Xander drawing all the attention away from me.

Despite getting cleaned up, Xander lacked a refinement everyone else in the room possessed. It was as if an ancient savagery clung to him, pulsating in his muscles, the tightness in his jaw, in his shoulders.

I could only imagine everyone else felt it too.

A true god amongst house trained pussy cats.

Our eyes locked and a jolt of electricity shot through me. The room, with all its splendor, faded into an inconsequential blur. I was unprepared for the intensity of my reaction—Xander's appearance not only stunned me but set flame to that deep, raw attraction only he inspired.

I was acutely aware of my mortality, of the blood rushing through my veins and the beating of my heart.

As he neared, the immortals closest to me murmured, "He's coming this way."

"I heard he'd gone crazy."

Another god nudged them hard in the ribs. "Shut your mouth. He is one of the first gods among us."

Only in that moment did I realize how much the gods craved to bring Xander back in the fold. They revered him. Like some past savior coming to life, the gods around me gaped, some even misting at the eyes.

And I knew he absolutely fucking hated it.

Xander would rather be wearing a barely buttoned Hawaiian shirt while sipping a Shirley Temple in that dirty dive bar than be here in this glittering realm of sophistication and power.

As Xander neared, I couldn't help but notice the transformation was not just in his appearance—there was a newfound purpose in his stride, a sense of belonging. He was a god who could orchestrate the vastness of the oceans, yet all his attention was fixed on me.

Xander studiously kept from meeting the gaze of

anyone else, his entire being locked on me. His presence transformed me from a soldier on a mission to a woman acutely aware of her own desires and vulnerabilities.

"Do you think he's coming to ask me to dance?"

"Dream on, Jocita."

The murmurs grew louder as Xander sauntered through the crowd, a mix of surprise and speculation rippling through the gods and goddesses.

A goddess draped in shimmering silver with a midnight-blue cascade of hair eyed Xander with open interest. Even her outfit complemented his.

"Nun, the elusive god of primordial waters," she cooed, stepping into his path. "Your absence has been... noted. What tempts you back to our midst?"

Xander's lips curved in a half-smirk, not slowing his stride. "It's a *crazy* story." He emphasized the word crazy, an inside joke between us. I hated how that warmed me by several degrees. "Let's just say I'm here for the view," he replied, his voice laced with a hint of mockery. His gaze remained fixed on me, as if the goddess was no more than a fleeting shadow.

Undeterred, a god with the sheen of polished bronze on his skin stepped forward, offering a hand. "Xander, perhaps you seek new alliances? Or new... conquests?" His eyes flicked up and down Xander's body, suggesting an unspoken offer.

Xander's reaction was immediate and dismissive. He sidestepped the offered hand, his eyes rolling slightly. "Alliances? Conquests? Don't you have anything better to do?" he asked, his tone dripping with disdain.

A murmur of laughter and whispers broke out among the immortals, their intrigue piqued by Xander's blatant disregard.

The god's face tightened, a mix of embarrassment and annoyance flashing in his eyes.

Then, with the ease of a predator ignoring lesser beasts, Xander closed the distance between us. His eyes were alight with a mischievous spark, the kind that told me he was fully aware of the stir he was causing.

"Ms. West," Xander's voice cut through the tension. "May I have this dance?"

Shocked expressions turned toward me, as if trying to gauge if this was a joke.

At first I'd been relieved he'd shown up. He'd become the focus of everyone's attention but just like that, he threw the bullseye back on me.

Damn him.

His presence radiated confidence and power, the very essence of the god he was. But I didn't need his rescue.

"That isn't necessary, *Nun*," I said in a cold, clipped tone, making sure to let him know this was very much a professional setting for me.

He smirked, but his eyes flickered with something when I used his ancient god name.

"Not necessary, but a pleasure," he practically purred. "Can you blame a guy for wanting a dance with the most intriguing and powerful woman in the room?"

More immortals bristled around me, as if his asking me to dance over any of them was a direct insult.

In for a penny, in for a pound.

Despite myself, a tight-lipped smile tugged at my lips. "Just one dance," I conceded, slipping my fingers into his large, warm palm.

As we moved to the dance floor I felt the eyes of everyone on us, their whispers growing louder.

But in Xander's arms I found an unexpected comfort.

His steps were sure, his hold firm yet gentle. For a moment, I allowed myself to lean into his strength.

From the corner of my eye, I saw Vivien giving me the thumbs up next to Grim, who firmly had an arm around her waist.

"You shouldn't have done that," I said in a low voice, somehow keeping up with his lead, though I'd rarely danced.

"Why not?" his low voice grated against my skin in a far too seductive manner.

"Because I need to show them I can, and will, stand on my own."

He scoffed. "Whose genius plan was that?" He went on before I could answer. "You should never truly be alone or at the mercy of others." His tone was so bitter, so angry.

"Xander." His name came out with all the emotion built up in my stomach.

"You should be surrounded by those who would back you up, so no one even thinks they can touch you."

"Hurt me?" I corrected.

"That either."

I chewed on my lower lip to keep from smiling or laughing. "No one wants me like that."

"That's not true."

The solemnity in his words hit me at my core, and I found myself drowning in his intense gaze until I couldn't feel my feet.

"Even your neighbor can't seem to resist you."

"You're jealous." It was a statement. I knew it, but he hadn't said it before.

The side of his mouth kicked up though it didn't reach his eyes. "Of course I am, sweetheart."

I didn't know what to say to that. Casting a look

around, I found varying expressions of shock, awe, and disgust peppered the room.

"I didn't realize how much they all missed you."

Xander's jaw tightened.

"They think a lot of you, for what you gave up for them. They treat you like their savior."

His lips peeled back from his teeth. "They're all idiots."

"But you did save them."

"In symbol alone. I died, Miranda. I didn't beat Aten. He killed me. And even after death he managed to contort my existence into a personal hell. They think I can save them again, but what does that mean? I need to die for them to get off their asses and do whatever it was they did the last time to put him away?"

The dance ended and I stepped back, putting distance between us. "Thank you, Xander, but I need to show them all I can stand on my own. I need you to keep your distance." That last part was hard to get out because I didn't want that at all. The deepest parts of me wanted him glued to my side, touching some part of me to share his strength. But this was how it needed to be.

He nodded, a complex emotion crossing his face. "Understood. But just know I'm here if you need me." Then he couldn't help but add with a smirk, "Sweetheart."

"Thank you for coming," I whispered.

He turned and stalked away but not without a little wink.

The gods gave me a considerable berth after that, only a few bold enough to pass by me to drop a scathing insult and even fewer who would stop to ask me a genuine question. Even the hostess of the party, Isis, approached me. The wife of Osiris and the matron of the gods. A goddess who appeared to be in her forties, she wore a pearlescent dress and exuded energy in a way that tingled my skin like a thousand raindrops.

I barely remembered anything of our interchange, other than she blessed me with luck in my endeavors.

Xander sipped on something that suspiciously looked like a Shirly Temple as a crowd of gods hung around him, flapping their mouths and fawning all over him. Even from across the room I could see something in him I'd never seen before—his eyes were cold and dead.

I thought if... when he rejoined the ranks he would feel like he belonged and he would allow himself out of his self-imposed shackles to embrace his new life, but my heart cracked like a rock under too much pressure as I saw him dying in front of me.

I wanted to go to him. I wanted to save him, but I knew I would cause more problems than I would solve. Instead, I explored until I found a set of stairs to a balcony that over-looked the ballroom.

This ballroom made Buckingham Palace look like a budget motel. If I weren't so busy being so in awe of its beauty, I'd be calculating how many lifetimes it would take to dust this place.

Note to self: *if reincarnation is real, do not come back as an immortal housekeeper.*

"So this is where our guest of honor is hiding," a male voice came from behind me.

I turned to find myself facing a god I didn't know. He was tall and imposing with piercing pale eyes that seemed to see right through me. There was an air of arrogance about him, a sense of superiority that made my skin crawl.

His silver hair cascaded down his back in intricate braids and his cloak shimmered with a strange purple iridescence.

"I don't hide," I replied, trying to keep my voice steady despite the unease creeping up my spine. "I simply wanted a new view of things."

The god's lip curled in a smirk and my blood ran cold. "A brave mortal, aren't you? To speak so boldly to a god." His voice was like velvet over steel, smooth yet dangerous. I resisted the urge to step back, holding my ground even though every instinct told me to flee.

He took a step closer, his presence overwhelming. "Do you think it's wise to be alone up here? Where no one can protect you?"

Danger flashed in my mind like a big neon sign.

I was feeling very out of my depth. But if he pushed me, I'd do what I had to. "I don't need anyone to protect me," I assured him.

"And she's not alone," another voice answered.

CHAPTER 27
THE BEAST

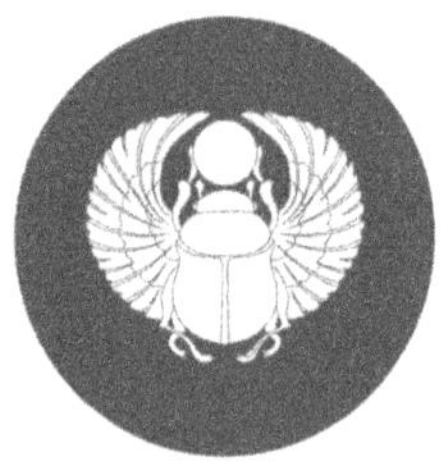

I came upon Miranda cornered by the god Min and every part of me wanted to rip him into shreds once I saw his threatening body language.

The god's face eased into a smile. "Nun, so glad you are back. Now you can help me teach a lesson to this dirty little mortal."

Lifetimes ago we had been friends. We drank, we partied, we even got involved in some sexual exploits that were worth their weight in gold. But I wasn't the same god Min knew. And he'd fucked with the wrong human.

"Don't... don't talk about her like that." My tone was

airy, a half-smile pulling at my lips as a finger wagged in the air. One of those hysterical yelping laughs vibrated at the base of my spine, threatening to bubble up. If it arose and popped, so would the thin hold on my self-control.

The god laughed, his head turning back and forth between me and Miranda, as if he's in on a joke I'm telling.

He didn't understand what I was fighting to keep down. If I let it out, it was definitely going to ruin the party mood.

"You're joking right, Nun? This worthless human thinks she's special because she carries a big toy."

A long groan rolled out from my chest as I rubbed my chin. "Ah, but is that any different from you?"

Min's eyes clouded with confusion before my gaze darted to the place between his legs.

Miranda stiffened, watching me carefully. This god didn't know me, but she did. All of me is dangling off the cliff except for the one hand hold I had on the sanity and decorum these events called for.

The god's brows furrowed, his upper lip pulling back in a sneer. "Oh, I see. Your brain has softened to shit after all these years. What a pity." He sniffed. "You were as formidable as Anubis once. And now you're just a broken little demi, who found a safe little toy to play with." He jerked his head in Miranda's direction.

Before I could react, his face blanched. The tip of Miranda's sword tapped at his balls. "You got a thing about toys, don't you?" she asked, with cool assessment. "Maybe I should take yours away. After all, you're a god, right? It'll grow back. Give you a chance to think with your head instead of your little sensitive prick, since it's clearly turning you into a dick."

The god's eyes bulged as his Adam's apple did a

dramatic rise and fall down his throat. He stupidly looked to me for help.

I shrugged as my lips split into a sly smile. "You shouldn't mess with a girl who carries lethal weapons."

"Or any self-respect," Miranda added with an absolutely vicious grin.

My chest swelled with warmth and pride.

That's my little badass.

Miranda stepped closer to him, hissing in his ear. "I've never chopped off anyone's bits with the Blade of Bane before. As it truly takes the life of an immortal, I wonder if it would permanently claim your balls as well."

A human cut his ego down to size and it awoke a hungry ferocity in me for her. She was so alive and amazing. I wanted to run my tongue along her skin to taste the electricity I saw sizzle in her eyes.

The god's face twisted and flexed. He wanted to say something but knew better than to open his trap while in such a precarious position.

"But as long as you don't fuck with me, I won't investigate that particular feature of my *toy*." Miranda turned on her heel and was out the door, leaving an imperious air in her wake as if he wasn't worth another moment of her time.

The god made to leave, pulling me from my thoughts, but I clamped a hand down on his shoulder, and yanked him back before he could get out of reach.

"Whoa there, hold on just a minute," I said, my voice dripping with delight and malice. "We're not done here."

A flicker of uncertainty crossed his face, and for a brief moment I saw glimpses of the arrogant façade crumbling away. The tables had turned and now it was his turn to feel the weight of someone else's dominance.

With a swift motion, I released him from my grasp. The god stumbled. He glared at me with wariness.

"You don't speak like that to her ever again, do you understand?" Then I laughed lightly as my hand clamped on his shoulder again, crushing the bone underneath.

He cried out and fell to a knee, his face turning a mottled red. I paid his reactions no mind and instead thoughtfully added, "Actually, you don't speak to her at all. You don't even look at her."

The false levity dropped like a hammer as I drilled into him with what I knew must look like the eyes of a demon. The crazy clawed at the side of my brain, begging me to paint the walls with his blood for being too close to Miranda.

"You don't even think of her, do you understand? If you do, I will make what she threatened to do look like a day in the park compared to what I'll do to you. Because I've had an eternity to know what pain really is and how the true torture is never knowing when it will end or *if* it will end at all. And I'd be happy to share my life lessons with you."

Blood gushed from where my fingers brutally penetrated his flesh like a strip of flattened bread dough. His cries and groans for me to stop drowned out my words. I shook his shoulder forcing a shriek of pain to escape him. "I fear you aren't listening. Are you listening?"

"Yes, yes," Min practically yelped. "I'm listening. I'll never look at her or think of her again." With a final wicked grin, I released him. The god fell backward, crumpling into a protective ball. I lifted my hand and licked my blood covered fingers. "Add a little more salt to your diet while you're at it. You taste a little bland."

I strolled out of the room.

• • •

THE NIGHT PROCEEDED and Miranda continued to mingle with those who despised her, though I watched her make a few allies who mentioned her unique bravery and success over Bes and Serqet.

I noted their names and faces for later. As much as the other gods tried to draw me out, I dodged their attempts to be drawn into conversation or dance. I eventually caught Miranda's eye and jerked my head in the direction of an adjoining room. Understanding my motion, she excused herself.

Casting an eye about to make sure no one was watching, I closed the library doors behind me.

"What is it?" Miranda asked. "Are you okay?" Worry etched lines between her eyes.

"No, I'm not okay." I closed the distance between us and cupped the back of her neck, pulling her against me and kissing those irresistibly full lips. A mix between a sigh and a groan escaped me. "Do you know how fucking hard it is to keep my distance? To not kiss you, touch you? When you look like this? You are the most dangerously beautiful creature alive, and I can't fucking stand not touching you a moment longer."

"We have to get back out there," Miranda said, even as her hands clawed at my suit and her tongue invaded my mouth with a hot slick lick.

My dick hardened painfully. "Five minutes. Please, fuck, give me five minutes, Miranda. If you don't, I'll fucking die."

The woman was irresistible. Her dress had been made to kill me. All her strength and softness was on display in equal measure and I had to have her, had to claim her.

The need to bite into her flesh and leave marks behind so everyone knew whose she was, possessed me with a vengeance.

But I could control myself. I was a man, not a monster. And I'd show her I could be trusted with her body, her heart, and her soul.

Her lips curved into a smile under mine before I continued to trail kisses down the column of her dark golden brown throat. Miranda's unique scent and taste filled my senses.

"What if I need longer than five minutes?" she countered, breathlessly.

My lips and tongue traced over the swells of her breasts, pushed up by the carved golden armor molded to her torso. "Oh, you won't need more than ninety seconds."

That's right sweetheart, let me have control for a little while. You can enchant the others, but let me amaze you.

She scoffed. "Well don't you think you're hot shit?"

I lifted my head, licking my lips. "Do you doubt it?"

That eyebrow arched.

"Challenge accepted," I said. I picked her up by the backs of her thighs and carried her over to the tufted settee. I sat down, placing her on top. "If I win, I want the date I've already won to be at your house for a family dinner and I want *you* to cook."

Warning, or maybe fear, flashed in her eyes.

"And if you win..." I prompted.

"You owe me Perkatory drinks for a month."

It was weak, but it would do. I nodded quickly.

I walked over to a counter with a jug of water.

"What are you doing?"

"Making good on my word," I said, throwing a wink at her. Bringing the jug, I hovered over where she sat. "Do you trust me?"

"No," she said, eyeing the jug fearfully. "And if you fuck up my hair, I'll stab you with Bob."

"Don't worry, sweetheart. I would never."

Then I poured it out. Miranda recoiled, anticipating the fall of the water to hit her. It took her a moment to realize the water hovered over her, mid-air. Only when her eyes opened, did I allow a few droplets to hit the tops of her breasts.

She gasped.

I smirked. She had no idea what was coming.

But she *would be* coming, in less than ninety seconds.

Water droplets rolled down, disappearing beneath her armor. They sluiced over the tips of her breasts, and through my connection to the water as they circled the dark tips there, I could feel them harden.

Oh, fuck I wanted to wrap my lips around those pretty buds and suckle her into a frenzy, but I wanted her to experience the lighter side of my power for once.

Some of the water diverted from the frozen mass hanging in the air and dropped to her bare thighs. Instead of following gravity downward, they streaked upward, under her skirts and armor.

Ten seconds.

"What are you —" Her words cut off as the water beads found her center.

With a flick of my wrist, the droplets multiplied, coating her in a fine mist. Each droplet danced along her skin like a thousand tiny hands, massaging her sensitive nerve endings. She let out a low moan, her eyes fluttering shut.

Twenty seconds.

My finger twitched and the mist of water intensified, some of the droplets joining together to form a single, powerful stream. It cascaded between her legs, parting the armor as it went, revealing her throbbing core. She gasped, her hands flying to her chest as the stream filled her, causing her to thrash beneath me.

I smiled. "How does that feel, Miranda? My power caressing you like this?"

I focused my power, urging the remaining droplets to increase their intensity. No longer did they simply graze her skin, but now they swirled and twirled, each one a surge of cool, electric pleasure. The warmth between her legs built as her climax approached.

Forty seconds.

I created a small concentric circle to surround her clit as another small wave of water rolled up and down her slit. Then I increased the pressure and speed slowly but steadily.

Right now, I felt every ounce the god I was and Miranda was my plaything. Perhaps claiming my abilities wasn't so bad?

"How are you doing this?" she whimpered, her voice hoarse from the tremors that had taken hold of her body. But I couldn't resist any longer. I needed to see her crumble before me, to know the power I held over her.

Because she owned me unequivocally. It made me desperate to prove my worth to her. To show her that there could be advantages to being with an unhinged, mentally unwell god who put her pleasure on a pedestal.

Sixty seconds.

As the water continued to stimulate her, her breaths became ragged, her moans echoing through the empty library. She was close. I had her on the edge.

It was time to give her the final push, with a few seconds to spare.

The water surged and vibrated in triple time against her.

Miranda's eyes rolled back as her body convulsed, her hips bucking against the settee. A cry of pure ecstasy escaped her lips as the apex of her release washed over her.

Aw fuck yes, that's my little badass.

Pride swelled in me. She'd seen me fractured, lost, and broken, but now she knew I could control myself too. I'd fought hard for it, for her.

Her aftershocks were slow to subside. Face flushed and breathing ragged, her eyes were alive with desire. At the same time, I pulled the water away, wicking it off her skin and directing it back into the water jug before setting it aside. Miranda frowned and cursed.

I couldn't help but laugh. "When are you going to learn to stop taking bets against a god? That was only a minute."

"Shut up and fuck me, Xander."

That sobered me. "Whatever you say, sweetheart."

My demonstration of control was over, and I'd gladly hand the reigns over to her.

I pinned her to the couch. Our tongues tangled while our hips bucked at each other with the intense need to interlock. In no time, she had me seated, my pants unzipped so the air could hit my hard cock. Miranda lowered onto me, pushing her panties to the side, and I slid home.

We both made a strangled sound. Miranda rode me steadily, driving me to madness.

"Your trick is cool and all, but I think I prefer this," she said in a breathy tone.

"You and me both," I agreed, my hips surging up into her tight wet heat. She bucked and fucked me like a goddess, and all I could do was let her lead.

My warrior. My goddess. My everything.

She wasn't afraid to face the immortals out there though I'd been terrified. I shamelessly borrowed strength from her, but I planned to give it back to her tenfold.

We had to return to the ballroom, but right now I couldn't give a flying fuck. There was only the angel of death, riding my cock like she owned me, which she did.

Miranda arched her back, her nails digging into the flesh of my arms as she reached her climax. The second she let go, her inner walls clenching and milking me, my release overtook me.

I drew her to me, burying my face in her breasts, covering up the groans of pleasure as I emptied myself in her.

"Can we not agree that you technically keep winning our bets too?" I said, breathing heavily as if I'd run halfway around the globe.

"No, we cannot," she said, standing. "Even if it's true," she muttered.

It didn't take long for us to clean up and take turns exiting the library room to return to the party.

I tried to keep the smug smile from forming on my face, but it seemed damn near impossible. But I'd barely been able to enjoy my post-coital bliss when a male voice boomed through the ballroom.

"Well, well, well, did you all miss me?"

"Ah, fuck," a woman next to me muttered.

I turned to find Vivien standing next to me, her face a dark stormy cloud, her fangs elongating in response to the newcomer.

A man with deeply tanned skin and silver streaked hair, wearing several gold chains against an expensive, white snakeskin suit, waltzed in with a martini dangling in one hand.

"Who is it?" I asked, though I had a suspicion even after not seeing my brethren for so many years. I remembered only one who had such a hold on his own slimy charismatic nature to foster his own massive fucking ego.

"Seth," Vivien said through gritted fangs.

CHAPTER 28

THE BEAST

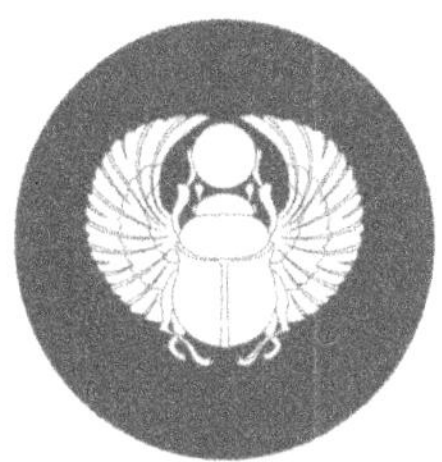

Yep, that's the fucker I thought it was. Seth, or Set. Brother of Osiris. At one time, he tried his hand at usurping Osiris to become top god.

He was also one of the gods who'd been released from the Blade of Bane.

I glanced across the room, finding Miranda slipping backward into the crowd while surreptitiously pulling Bob out.

Well, the party was fun while it lasted.

"What? You aren't all happy to see me again?" Seth asked at the top of the stairs.

Vivien growled next to me. A dark mass was suddenly

there at her back, steadying her with hands on her shoulders. Grim.

"Can I get the cliff notes of his most recent crimes?" I murmured when Timothy sidled up to my other side.

Recorder that he was, Timothy rattled them off. "Conspiracy to incite another uprising, this time against Anubis. Captured and held a god against their will. To say the least."

"You are saying the least," Vivien growled again.

Grim spoke to her in low warning. "Most gods have committed sins and returned to join the ranks after a time. If he'd gone to the cradle instead of the blade, we would have had to deal with him eventually."

"Too soon," Vivien muttered. "*Way* too soon."

"Regardless," Grim ground out as if he didn't like it either, "If he wishes to play nice, he gets to stay."

"Oh look," Seth announced drolly, with a wave of his martini. "It's Grim and his bitch."

"Guess he's not playing nice," I pointed out the obvious while sticking my hands in my pockets and stepping away as all the attention turned toward Grim and Vivien.

"Why are you here?" Grim asked, his voice suddenly as resonant as Seth's in the massive ballroom.

I couldn't shake the feeling that this was all about to go horribly wrong. The tension in the air was a tangible thing, a live wire sparking and ready to ignite. Seth's presence alone was enough to set everyone on edge, but it was the look in his eyes that had me feeling the real danger. It was the look of a predator that had just cornered its prey.

Seth raised his arms and the murmur of the crowd hushed in a crescendo of suspense. "My dear friends," he began, his voice a melodic poison, "I thought it was time for a grand reunion. You've been hiding from the world, wallowing in your own self-pity and fear. It's time to remember who we are!"

As he spoke, the edges of the room darkened, shadows shifting and coiling like living things. A chill ran down my spine as I realized what was about to happen. "Miranda," I breathed, my eyes searching frantically for her in the crowd.

As if summoned by Seth's words, the gods and monsters released from the blade began to appear. They materialized from the shadows, grotesque and terrible, their eyes alight with bloodlust and chaos.

A monster slithered from the shadows with its many heads weaving through the air, each one bearing a crown of venomous fangs. Another creature that could only have spawned from the darkest depths of fear itself, moved on all fours, its body a grotesque amalgamation of wolf and serpent. Its sickly yellow eyes scanned the room with a predator's interest.

Next came a goddess, her beauty terrible to behold. Her eyes burned with a furious light, her gaze alone enough to ignite the very air. Flames danced around her, not providing warmth, but a cold, consuming fire that sought to incinerate all it touched. Her laughter echoed, the sound of delight and destruction, turning blood to ice.

The air became a cacophony of roars and hisses, the elegant ballroom suddenly a stage set for a massacre.

It was an ambush.

I pushed through the crowd, my heart pounding in my chest. "Miranda!" I called out, my voice drowned by the burgeoning chaos. I had to reach her, had to get her out before all hell broke loose.

I spotted her then, moving with a grace that belied the deadly purpose in her stride. She was making her way behind Seth, unnoticed by the preoccupied god. My breath caught in my throat as her hand gripped the hilt of the Blade of Bane as she maneuvered through the throng of deities.

Seth, too caught up in his moment of glory, was blind to the mortal danger approaching him. "We will rise again," he proclaimed, "and under my leadership, we will—"

Miranda lunged, the blade piercing through his back before it split through his front. Seth's eyes widened in shock, the crowd gasping in unison as the god of chaos was skewered by the only mortal in the room.

And then the impossible happened. The tip of Miranda's blade emerged from his chest, and the exit wound caught fire.

Like an ant under a magnifying glass, Seth began to burn.

CHAPTER 29

THE BADASS

The smell of charred flesh assaulted me as Seth burned on Bob like a shish kabob on a barbeque. His chest was a pulsing beacon of light, somehow sucking the air from the ballroom.

Light erupted from Seth's chest in a blinding, pure, brilliant white that seemed to radiate from within him. It shot out in thick beams, hitting each dark god and monster with precision.

It spread out in every direction like a burst of energy. It seemed to target the dark gods and monsters that had surrounded the ballroom. They burst into flames, their screams and cries filling the air as they all burned alongside

Seth. Flames danced and flickered across their writhing bodies.

The smell of burning flesh and hair filled the room, a pungent aroma. The mixture of sulfur and charred meat was suffocating, filling every corner of the ballroom with its putrid stench.

Then the panic exploded amongst the immortal guests in the ballroom. Half of them began to shift into their god-likeness, while the others tried to flee. They turned on each other in the confusion.

As chaos enveloped the ballroom, Vivien leaped into the fray with a ferocity that was both exhilarating and terrifying. She moved like a shadow among the flames, her figure a blur of motion as she dispatched dark gods and monsters. Her laughter, wild and unrestrained, echoed above the turmoil, a testament to her unhinged nature as her fangs gleamed with menace. But when a dark god landed a lucky strike, wounding her, the atmosphere palpably shifted.

Grim's reaction was immediate and visceral. His form blurred, and for a fleeting moment, the fearsome visage of death itself flashed across his face, a skull wreathed in shadows. With a roar of outrage, he extended his hands, telekinetically hurling assailants away from his wife with the force of a tempest. His power, dark and implacable, swept through the room like a scythe, clearing a path to Vivien's side.

Timothy, ever the tactician, didn't leap into physical combat but instead orchestrated a battlefield of his own making. His fingers flew over the surface of his tablet, glyphs and symbols dancing in the air around him. With a few swift taps, barriers of light snapped into place around allies, deflecting attacks and sealing wounds with precision.

Fallon transformed into his monstrous likeness of Horus, his eyes glowing with a fierce, blue light. The transformation was both terrifying and awe-inspiring. With a roar that seemed to shake the very foundations of the ballroom, he positioned himself in front of Bianca, his massive wings unfurling to shield her from the chaos. His sharp talons glinted dangerously, ready to tear apart anyone who dared come near her.

For her part, Bianca stood calm and serene behind Fallon's protective form, her hands glowing with a soft, golden light that pulsed with power.

"Bob?" I asked audibly, shock turning my limbs numb.

"It's not me," he confirmed, his tone filled with revulsion. "Now get me out of here. It's disgusting."

I pulled him out of Seth and stumbled back, only to be caught by a pair of strong hands. I didn't have to look to know it was Xander who held me.

Seth turned even as flames licked the flesh off his body. "You." His raspy voice was monstrous and tortured as he locked eyes with me. "*He's* going to take away what you love most until he is the only one left."

And then with a hideous grin, or maybe his lips were just burned away, Seth collapsed into a pile of broken burning limbs.

"Xander," I said, my voice failing me.

"We need to go, now," he said, then yanked me out of the ballroom before I could protest.

I came to my senses and ran alongside him.

"What's happening?" The wild look of terror and pure rage in his eyes was one I'd never seen before.

"It's Aten," he said.

"What?" Sun god, burning other gods. It somewhat

computed in my brain but it also didn't. "He wasn't in there," I protested.

"He must be close." Xander grabbed my arms and hauled me up for a fierce kiss. "And you are getting out of here."

"The fuck I am. I'm the only one who can kill him." I raised Bob as if to prove my point, though even Bob was shaken into silence.

It was one thing to slice through a god, another to do so before they burst into flames. He already hated blood, and I could tell skewering a burning body was beyond him.

"Listen to me," Xander said carefully. "It's all of the gods against him. I went up against him alone. Together we can subdue him. But I can't focus or help if you are around. I'll be too worried about you. If Aten doesn't get you, surely one of the other gods might take their shot at you. I can't protect you against that many."

"I can protect myself, Xander," I practically snarled at him.

His lips tightened as he looked back in the direction of the ballroom we fled. Screams and shouts kicked up higher. "But can you protect Jamal and your mother-in-law?"

The atoms in my body stilled all at once, and I couldn't hear anything else but his words. "What are you saying?"

Xander's voice lowered, and it suddenly felt like I was under water. My ears were clogged, and everything was moving too slowly, including my mind. "He's going to take what you love most away. Seth was talking about Aten. You need to get home. You need to protect your family."

The water I was under crashed over in a breaking wave and my heart nearly exploded from my chest in violent beats. "No." Even as I denied it, I knew it to be true.

The gods had powers and were already congregated to

fight together, while my very mortal family was at home, alone and unprotected.

I gripped Xander by the back of the neck and kissed him just as hard as he'd done to me, until a coppery taste filled my mouth. I didn't know if it was his blood or mine.

"Don't die," I commanded.

That devil may care grin spread on his face. "Only you are allowed to kill me, sweetheart."

With that, we rushed off in two different directions, and I swore my heart split in two.

As I ran out of the hotel, I managed to unhook my skirts, leaving me in a bodysuit, albeit a very fancy, armored bodysuit. I'd made clear to Bianca and Timothy in no uncertain terms that I didn't want to be bogged down in fabric if something went down.

Maybe I jinxed the whole night by adding that detail.

Driving home, I was like a bat out of hell, and god help anyone who got in my way.

The tires screeched as I pulled up to my house, my heart hammering against my ribs. The street was eerily quiet, the only sound the rapid beat of my own pulse thrumming in my ears. I didn't bother with subtlety, bursting through the front door, Bob gripped tightly in my hand, ready for a fight.

My hand trembled as I reached for the light switch, but no matter how many times I flicked it the room remained shrouded in darkness. Suddenly, my eyes adjusted to the dim light and a scene straight out of a nightmare greeted me. Mama Jean and Jamal were on the living room floor, bound and unconscious with heads lolling lifelessly. In a corner, Heinz lay silent and still.

Waves of panic crashed over me, drowning me in horrifying thoughts. Each one worse than the last.

Am I too late?

Are they dead?

Please don't let them be dead.

Terror constricted my throat, leaving me gasping for air. My mouth went dry and my tongue turned heavy and useless. I was simultaneously sweating and shivering, my stomach churning into knots. My heart thumped rapidly in my throat, threatening to choke me.

Desperation clawed at my chest as I fought back tears. Muscling it all back down, I forced myself to stay calm and keep my cool.

I rushed forward to untie them when the *click* of a firearm shocked me still and a figure emerged from the shadows. "I wouldn't do that just yet."

My heart thundered in my chest, threatening to burst through my ribcage. But I couldn't let panic take over.

"Sunny," I hissed, recognition flaring as I took in the sight of her, her gun not trained on me, but on my kid. Thankfully, I was close enough to spot the slight rise and fall of his chest. Both Jamal and Mama Jean were breathing.

My knees nearly buckled at the knowledge I wasn't too late.

I was finally face to face with the one who tricked Aoiki and me into releasing everything from inside the Blade of Bane.

She was no longer the teenager adorned in a school uniform. Now, the fae girl was all seriousness, her sleek black bob framing a face that was a mask of concentration. Her square features and thin eyes were cold and calculating.

"Seems your family is just as compliant as you are when it comes to my dream weaving," she said, tilting her head to the side.

Sunny had been responsible for my dreamwalking that nearly resulted in me killing my own child. I'd suspected, but she confirmed yet another reason I had to take her down. And I'd do so with extreme prejudice.

"What do you want with my family?" My voice was a low growl, barely containing the fury boiling inside me. Bob felt alive in my grasp, vibrating with a shared desire for retribution.

Sunny turned to face me, a small, mocking smile playing on her lips. "Just ensuring Aten's plan goes smoothly. Don't worry, your family is unharmed. And they can stay that way if you accept *him* into your heart and mind." She pressed a finger into her chest then her temple.

I wanted to shoot back a mouthy retort, but with Jamal in the crosshairs, I couldn't risk it.

"What makes him so great?" I asked instead, trying to draw her attention enough to let her guard down.

She smiled, eyes lighting up as if I'd asked her the only question she ever wanted to be asked.

"What makes him so great?" Sunny repeated. "He is the one true god. He is the one who bathes the rest of us in his warmth and glory. No one has power like him."

I thought of the gods—Grim, Timothy, Bianca, and Vivien—back in that ballroom, fighting Aten. Surely they and Xander could take him out.

I forced my voice to sound genuinely intrigued, suppressing the revulsion bubbling inside me. "Why go through all of this? Why me? Why my family?"

Sunny's eyes gleamed with a fervor that made my skin crawl. "Aten wants *you*, Miranda. He sees your strength, your power. And he admires it. But he also knows you're loyal to those you love." Her gaze flickered to Jamal and Mama Jean, then back to me. "He wants to show you he can protect what's dear to you, make you part of his new world order."

I had to bite the inside of my cheek to keep from lashing out. "And you believe him? That he's going to just let us live peacefully?"

"Of course," she said, her conviction unsettling. "Aten's world is one of order, not chaos. Under his rule, we'll all thrive. You, your family... All under his benevolent gaze."

I took a step closer, feigning interest. "And what about those who oppose him?"

Her grip on the gun tightened. "They'll learn. Or they'll be removed. It's for the greater good, Miranda. You'll see."

At that moment, a floorboard creaked behind Sunny, but her attention was so fixed on me that she didn't notice. A shadow moved, a figure approaching her with silent determination. Someone had come in through the back door, silent and stealthily.

They crept closer, but I never took my eyes off Sunny. I couldn't chance alerting her to the new presence.

"But you are more important than any human, Miranda. You have the power to slay immortals alongside *him*, bring order to the chaos that is these self-involved spoiled gods." She practically spat the words.

The man who crept up behind her now held the rolling pin Mama Jean used for making her famous pies. With a swift, precise movement, he swung it, connecting it with the back of Sunny's head.

The fae girl crumpled to the ground, unconscious before she knew what hit her. The gun clattered harmlessly to the floor.

For a moment I could only stare, a mixture of relief and confusion swirling within me. Michael met my gaze, his expression one of concern and urgency.

It was my neighbor who had come in through the back and to our rescue. His light green eyes were in earnest as he explained, "I heard yelling earlier, and saw her with a gun when I went by the window. Are they okay?" He gestured to Mama Jean and Jamal.

I nodded, still processing the turn of events. "Yeah, thanks to you." My words were sincere.

Moving past him, I went to tie up Sunny before she came to. I didn't know how long it took for fae to recover from injuries. Michael caught my shoulders in his strong hands and kissed me.

What the holy hell?

I wrenched away from him. "What are you doing?"

Why in the fuck nuggets was my near stranger of a neighbor pulling a move when my family had been attacked? It came from left field and made zero sense.

But maybe I'd lost my mind somewhere between Seth burning in fire and my family being in danger.

His hopeful smile faded only slightly. "I guess I'm just glad you are okay."

"Cool, well maybe don't show your gladness with your lips. It's called consent, and you don't have it." My words came out harsher than maybe they should have. Apparently he thought we were something more, but I didn't have time to molly-coddle him. Shit right now was far bigger than his apparent crush.

"Miranda," Michael said, stepping closer, his voice turning husky. "You must know how I feel for you."

I must have entered some kind of twilight zone.

A sun god was attacking my immortal allies, a fae gunwoman lay on my floor, my family was tied up, and my neighbor was trying to make a move on me in the midst of it all.

Everything felt a little too surreal. Like a puzzle with big chunks missing from its picture.

My brain couldn't catch up to some important fact, even though I knew it was in grasping distance.

"Thank you but I need to tie—Shit!" I cried out.

I stepped around Michael and my gaze landed on the spot where Sunny collapsed. It was empty.

I cursed some more.

"Don't worry, I'll protect you if she comes back," Michael announced with far too much certainty. He rubbed my shoulder, but I shrugged him off.

My fury that she'd gotten away because of him simmered like bubbling water on a stove. "That won't be necessary."

Michael's smile faltered as I stepped back, creating distance between us. His eyes, once filled with concern, now sparked with a new intensity. "Miranda," he pressed, his voice carrying an edge that sent a shiver down my spine. "Why can't you see we're meant to be together? I saved them." He gestured towards my family, "For you."

I shook my head, feeling Bob's vibrations as a silent warning in my hand. "Saving my family doesn't give you a claim over me. I don't owe you anything."

Heinz, previously subdued and silent, erupted into a cacophony of barks and growls, his body tensed and hackles raised, directed not at the darkness outside, but at Michael.

My relief that the dog was okay was chased away by his outburst.

"What's gotten into him?" Michael feigned confusion, but the dog's reaction was unnervingly clear.

"Bob?" I whispered in my mind, seeking understanding

from the only creature who could translate the immortal dog's alarm.

"That is no man." Bob's voice was grave. "Heinz can smell his immortality."

Michael's olive eyes narrowed, as if realizing I knew too much.

The air in the room shifted, growing thick and heavy as if charged by a storm. Michael's demeanor changed and the neighborly façade melted away to reveal a being cloaked in blinding light.

His eyes blazed like twin suns, searing into me with an intensity that made my heart race. The air crackled with electricity as he extended his hand towards me, fingers tipped with glowing embers.

His skin shimmered like liquid gold, adorned with intricate patterns of hieroglyphs that seemed to writhe and shift with a life of their own. Beauty and fear melded inside me in an impossible collision of desire and revulsion.

A god stood before me, and everything inside me trembled before him.

"You think you can reject me?" His voice boomed, no longer Michael's but something otherworldly and powerful. "I am the greatest. I am the best. I am Aten."

Heinz's barking crescendoed, a desperate attempt to warn, to protect. But it was too late. Aten's transformation was complete, his figure now a beacon of light that filled the room, casting long, ominous shadows.

The room seemed to shrink in his presence, every corner touched by his incandescent glow. His voice returned to a more natural timber, but it somehow sent a shiver up my spine. "You will learn to worship me, Miranda. Either by choice or by force."

THE BADASS

The air was thick in the charged silence following Aten's reveal and declaration, electric with the tension of a brewing storm. Heinz's barking had subsided into a low warning growl, his body tense and ready. He put himself between Aten and my family, guarding them.

Bob's presence in my mind was a cold comfort, a reminder that I wasn't entirely alone in facing the god before me.

"So you're the big bad," I said, my voice steady despite the adrenaline coursing through me. "The one who has everyone shaking in their boots."

I might be too if I were wearing them, but I wore sandals and a bodysuit, like some kind of ancient gladiator.

"I am more than a god," he replied in a silky voice.

There was a reason I was innately drawn to my neighbor. Divinity was wildly attractive to humans. I should know. I felt it whenever I was around Grim, Timothy, or any other god. I'd been so stupid not to recognize it only a couple feet from my door.

"I am your helpful, handsome, knight in shining armor just next door." He swept a hand out in the direction of his house. "Stable, pleasant, strong, and supportive. Everything you've ever wanted, Miranda."

They were things I'd told myself I wished Xander was, or claimed to have wanted in the past, but aside from that divine glimmer I felt from "Michael," everything fell flat.

"Why waste your time pretending to be my neighbor?" It didn't make any sense.

"Because we were falling in love. I wanted you to love me as a man, not just blindly fall for the brilliant god I am." His lips tilted up in a half smile that screamed, *aw shucks, didn't we just?*

But we didn't, and what an absolutely deluded creep.

"You think a couple interactions would have me falling at your feet?" Disgust filled my words.

His smile slipped and despite his near-blinding glow, his eyes went flat and cold.

"We've barely spoken or interacted. You know nothing about me." I stiffened, my hand anticipating slicing the sword at him.

In less than a blink, Michael—Aten—was right there beside me. "I'd wait to hear what I have to say before you try slashing me down," he cautioned. "If not for the sake of your family, then because there is the very real possibility of you and I talking this out to a reasonable solution."

His warm breath puffed over my skin, and warmth seeped into that side of my face and body. Knowing it was a trick of his power made it easier to compartmentalize now.

"You are special, Miranda. You wield the Blade of Bane. You're a mortal knowingly walking amongst gods, knowing how undeserving and how entitled they are. Whether you realize it or not, we are perfect for each other."

Aten moved to stand behind me, his presence radiating heat that seemed to seep into my bones. It was tempting to give in to the comfort he offered, like a warm blanket on a cold night.

But my disgust for his lies and presumption kept me glued to my senses.

Not to mention, here he was, all shiny and godly, making his pitch while Mama Jean and Jamal were tied up like it was some twisted hostage negotiation.

"Together we can bring order to a world that needs direction and unquestionable leadership."

"You mean a despot," I corrected.

Aten's laughter filled the room, a sound that seemed to vibrate with power. "I prefer to think of myself as a necessary ruler. One who brings order. Humans already ordain so many to manage themselves, from presidents to prime ministers down to managers at the local fast food restaurant. I can effortlessly become part of this natural order to give humans what they need."

I turned to face him, not shying away from the brilliant shine of his eyes. "And what exactly do humans need?"

"To believe in a higher power, to have faith and direction. I can provide both."

"After you kill all the other gods?" My tone was flat and judgmental. "You think I want that?"

"Humans don't always know what is good for them until it's too late," he said with a knowing smirk. It made him more devilishly handsome.

His words hammered at me with both specific and nonspecific guilt. It was as if he took all of my regrets and turned them inward, beating me with hammers until I could barely breathe from the weight of self-loathing and remorse.

"But in my presence, I can melt away the uncertainty," he added. The internal onslaught disappeared, and I sucked in a breath, my body now weightless and free.

"You're quite the salesman. But I've seen infomercials with more subtlety."

Aten's smile didn't falter, but his eyes—they flickered. Not with less power, but with something more human. Annoyance? Frustration?

In case he didn't think I understood, I spelled it out. "You want me because of the weapon I wield."

"Miranda, you misunderstand. This isn't about salesmanship. It's about destiny. Your destiny is to be alongside me."

"Oh, destiny," I ground out between clenched teeth. "That old chestnut. I get it. You're all-powerful, sun-shiny, and apparently, into kidnapping. But you're missing a crucial piece here."

"And what would that be?" he inquired, genuinely curious, or so it seemed. Gods were hard to read.

"Consent. You're missing my yes. And here's a fun fact about me—I don't do well with coercion."

Aten's radiant façade dimmed just a smidge, but it was

enough. "This is about Nun, isn't it?" Before I could answer, he went on. "He always did have a knack for interfering."

I nodded, keeping my stance relaxed though every muscle in my body was coiled tight. "Yeah, what can I say? I got this thing about guys not annihilating their peers or enslaving humanity, and he's weird like that."

Aten chuckled, a sound like warm sunlight. "Nun... Xander... he's always been a thorn in my side. Even back when the world was younger, he opposed me out of principle."

"Principles are pesky things, aren't they?" I nodded. "They can really get in the way of a good dictatorship."

I began to shuffle ever so slightly in the direction of Jamal and Mama Jean. I had to get them out of here.

He leaned closer, forcing me to freeze. Heat radiated off him until it beaded on my skin. "You jest, Miranda, but think of what we could achieve. No more petty squabbles among the gods. A unified world under a single, guiding light."

"What if people—and gods—don't want to be micro-managed by a giant celestial lightbulb? What if they like their free will?"

Aten's smile wavered, and for a moment I thought I'd pushed him too far. But then he sighed, a sound like the wind over the desert sands.

"Miranda, I'm beginning to believe you don't even appreciate my gift," he said, exasperated. "Did you not like my gift?"

"Your gift?" I asked, uncomprehending.

His lips curled up in devilish glee. "Seth was easy to talk into making a move when the rest of the gods were gathered. And he brought the ranks of gods and monsters with him for the coup against the others. I gave you the perfect opportunity to display your power in front of the others, and then took your burden from you."

"My burden?" I whispered.

"You needed to kill all those that you released, correct? I solved your problem in one quick go."

The way Seth burst into flames and then they reached out and set all of his fellow dissenters aflame.

"And the other gods?" If he could burn all the baddies, did he kill Grim, Vivien, and Xander?

My throat went dry as my stomach tightened at the thought.

"They are also enjoying my hospitality." Aten's twisted smile revealed his enjoyment of my suffering, and my heart thudded with fear at what he could do.

My throat constricted as I imagined the fate of Grim, Vivien, and Xander—all imprisoned by Aten and trapped in this hellish realm. The thought alone was enough to make me physically ill.

The realization hit me like a punch to the gut—I was truly alone. No allies, no backup, just me and the cruel god who held all my loved ones captive. The weight of isolation pressed down on me.

"Perhaps in time they will see the wisdom in accepting me as the god of gods, setting a good example for the rest. But Miranda, the more of them I kill, the more I send back to the cradle, the more that will rise again over time and try to defy me again and again. I need your assistance in a more permanent solution."

"The Blade of Bane. That's what you really want." He can't take Bob from me, not without my allowing it.

"No, Miranda, I need *you*. Help me," he urged. "And there will be a place for you, in this new world order. A world without chaos, without needless defiance. A world under one god and his right hand." He held his out to me, an offer.

His plan came into focus. Aten thought he could move in next door and make me fall in love with him. Then I'd either gladly hand over the blade or do his bidding willingly. Except he was a god playing human the way children play with Barbies. He had no true conception of what it was to be a mortal or how to connect with others. In his eyes a human dressed in a suit, went to work, engaged in activities like working out at the gym. Sprinkle in some pleasantries and everything would just fall in line.

What an absolute simpleton. But this simpleton had an insane amount of power at his disposal, which made him even more dangerous.

Xander had been so far removed from the world and yet he had more emotional intelligence in his pinky than this dude had in his entire being.

"And if I refuse?" I asked, already knowing this game had no winner.

Aten's smile turned predatory. "Then I suppose we'll have to see how hot the sun can really get."

I weighed my options, none of them good. Outright defiance wasn't going to cut it, not with Jamal and Mama Jean in the balance. I needed a plan, and I needed it fast. "Give me time to think about it," I said, stalling.

"Time is a luxury, Miranda. But for you, I'll make an exception. You have until tomorrow's sunrise."

Sunrise. How fitting for the sun god to set a deadline.

As Aten vanished as quickly as he had appeared, leaving a trail of warmth in his wake, I exhaled slowly. I had until this evening to come up with a miracle. Or, failing that, a really good plan B.

"Bob? How did you kill Aten the last time?"

He hesitated. "The gods and fae put their differences aside and worked together. Many lives were lost, but there was an opening and my fae wielder took it."

"Well that sounds like a plan to me," I said, realizing exactly what I needed to do next.

CHAPTER 31

THE BEAST

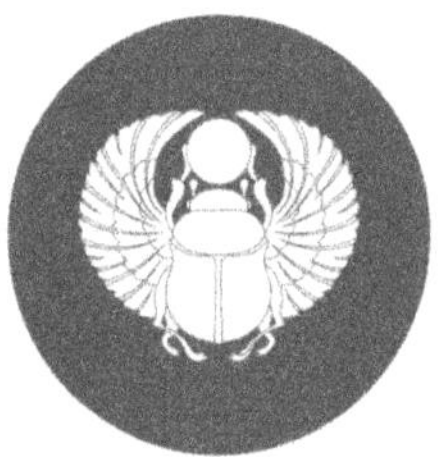

"Didn't take any time to redecorate, did it?" I asked.

The god I'd feared and despised for thousands of years sat on a golden throne. In fact, the entire level now sitting atop the Illusion hotel was bright yellow with gold embellishments. Art of him was everywhere—friezes, paintings, even statues filled the room until my eyes were bursting with the image of Aten.

Even the chains holding me to the wall were a golden hue, but they were made of far stronger materials. Materials that wouldn't melt before my flesh did.

The irony wasn't lost on me—a creature of water, now a prisoner of flames.

Aten cast a look around as if noticing for the first time. "Yes, well I missed that 'at home' feeling and thought some nesting might make me feel more in my element."

"Yeah, it's gaudy and an absolute masturbatory ode to you. Did you put a big picture of your face on the exterior of the hotel as well?"

Aten calmly surveyed his nails.

"I was right?" I couldn't help but break into snorting laughter. "You are such an egocentric asshole, you know that?"

Aten rose from his throne in a sweep of robes. He lifted a hand and my already blackened fingertips lit on fire for the countless time.

Heat blasted my body like a sandstorm from hell. I gritted my teeth and cried out as the searing pain engulfed me.

Even as the flames licked higher, scorching flesh from bone, I clung desperately to my humanity. Because to give in, to let the monster out, would be to lose the very thing that made life worth living—Miranda's love and her acceptance of me not just as a god, but as the flawed man who loved her beyond reason.

Yet part of me yearned to let myself become that ancient wrath.

Miranda's love and belief in me as a man and not a monster, became the only things keeping me from losing myself to the darkness.

Aten released his hold on me and I collapsed, gasping for air as my body trembled from the aftermath of his power. Every breath was a struggle as I tried to regain control and composure after being subjected to such intense pain. But even as I recovered, the fear of feeling that searing pain again lingered in the back of my mind.

The thought of Miranda facing Aten sent spikes of ice through the inferno of my torment. I'd endure a thousand lifetimes of this agony if it meant keeping her safe.

Aten unleashed another wave of torture, and as my body convulsed under the onslaught, a part of me realized the cruel irony—in trying so hard not to become the monster for Miranda's sake, I was enduring a hell few could fathom. Each flame that seared my skin, each bolt of pain that wracked my body, was a testament to my love for her —a love so profound it anchored me to my humanity even as I teetered on the brink of oblivion.

"The people need to know the face of their god and master," Aten said evenly, but the twitch at the corner of his eye and his need to punish me told me I hit him in a sore spot.

"And how is creating a cult going? I've seen some documentaries, and you are no Charles Manson."

Aten cocked his head to the side, his eyes alien and blank.

I landed a good hit, and no one was here to witness it. That's the real tragedy here.

"I'll amass all the followers I need soon enough." He drew a phone from his robes. "Have you learned of these fascinating little devices? People congregate with their minds and astral selves, pouring their energy—all their feelings and attention—into this little... *thing*."

"Can't say I've bothered to pick a provider yet," I said flatly.

He tsked. "You really are missing out. In no time, I've not only created an online church, but so many seeking guidance and a benevolent force to help them have flocked to the church of Aten, where the sun always smiles upon them." He matched the words with a grin that spread too wide on his face yet didn't reach his eyes.

Nausea roiled through my gut.

I couldn't be sure if it was from Aten's ability to gain power and influence so fast, or if it was from the stench of my own charred flesh.

"Sunny." Aten snapped.

A young Asian fae woman with black bobbed hair rushed forward.

"You've been watching Miranda— make sure she doesn't go to ground with anyone. I want her completely alone."

Any teasing humor bled out of me. "What do you want with her?"

Thousands of years have taught me how to endure pain, but the fear of what Aten might do to Miranda carved deeper than any flame.

Panic shot through me. Sunny was going to make sure Miranda was completely alone.

I needed to come up with a plan, and fast. I couldn't let him get to her. But for now, all I could do was grit my teeth and endure the pain as Aten's power once again engulfed me. My body trembled and every breath was a struggle, but I refused to give in.

As Sunny scurried away, bowing backwards, Aten turned an amused look on me.

"I want her to realize how special she is. Don't you?" He quirked an eyebrow.

Absolutely no fucking way will I believe we have the same intentions for Miranda.

"In fact, we have more in common than you think," he said, settling back into his throne. With a flash of his eyes, the soles of my feet began to sizzle and burn. I tried to resist. I rattled in the chains trying to escape the heat, but there was no getting away from it.

"I'm just like you," Aten said, running his fingers back through his golden hair. "I want her to love me."

I struggled to focus on what he was saying as the pain slowly ate away at my senses. Words came out through my clenched teeth. "If there is one thing I know about Miranda, it's that she can't be forced to do anything. She may be mortal, but she has a steel will, more powerful than yours."

Part of me wanted to see her spit on his offer, just to see his face. She asserted her own independence and strength like she wielded Bob. But another part of me feared for her safety, knowing full well the consequences of defying Aten.

He flicked a wrist as if it was of no consequence. "It's not about will. It's about leading her to the only inevitable conclusion."

The fiery burn had traveled from the soles of my feet up my shins and over my kneecaps. Aten was only toying with me.

"What conclusion is that?" I asked, still doing my best to focus on the conversation, and not the agony slowly but surely engulfing me.

"That if there is no one and nothing else for her to love, then she must love me."

The audacity of his statement fanned the flames of my anger, the intensity of my emotions almost as searing as the burn crawling up my legs. The very idea that he could engineer Miranda's love, as if it was something he could isolate and manipulate, repulsed me.

Alarm surged, sharper than any flame.

He wasn't just targeting me. The realization chilled me to my core before a blaze of protectiveness roared to life.

The thought of anyone touching them, hurting them because of me... It turned my stomach, leaving a metallic taste of dread in my mouth.

"Oh, don't worry," he said, noting my response. "It may not come to that. Her family is safe... for now."

The veiled threat, so casually delivered, was meant to unnerve and destabilize.

Instead, it crystallized a resolve within me, a burning need to protect and preserve what was most precious. Not just Miranda, but her family.

In that moment, amidst the searing pain and the struggle against the chains that bound me, a strategy formed, born of desperation.

"You think she'll love you? I've got that woman wrapped around my little pinky. She spends most of her time with me. Who do you think she really cares about?" I forced out, my voice a blend of mockery and defiance, aiming to provoke, to distract Aten from his darker designs. Every word was a battle, a conscious effort to keep talking, keep taunting, despite the agony that threatened to consume me.

Could I really convince him that Miranda loved me more than her own immediate family? Probably not, but fuck all if I wasn't going to try. This vain prick hated any kind of rivalry, and I planned to press every godsdamn button until he forgot about Jamal and Mama Jean.

"And you think she'll want you? Over me?" I snorted. "Please. You may have used your little cheat code with the internet, but we both know I'm older and stronger than you where it counts."

Fire literally flashed in his eyes.

"Soon Miranda and all the world will see how superior I am." That spot under his left eye twitched with annoyance.

I knew what I was about to say would really be a stick in his craw and it would come with a lot of pain, but he needed to forget about going after Miranda's family.

A wheezing laugh escaped me even as the burning blanketed my torso, eating me up like thousands of fire ants. "She won't think you're superior if she finds out your dick is smaller than mine. Not to mention, I've always been the prettier of the two of us."

Aten's nostrils flared, and that spot under his eye twitched double time.

Bullseye. I'd hit my mark.

At that, the rest of me went up in flames. My screams were eaten up by the fire around me until consciousness eventually left me.

WATER. Oh fuck, I needed water, liquid, hydration, anything to replenish my body. The drought inside me was worse than any pain fire could inflict.

Metal clanked, and my sore limbs moved under the heavy, yet shifting chains.

Forcing my eyes open, I gazed upon the most beautiful hallucination I'd ever seen.

"Miranda," I rasped over a bone-dry throat. "I won't let him get them. He'll have to kill me first."

I wanted to say more, but I couldn't speak. I couldn't tell the beautiful mirage that I promised even if Aten sent me back to the cradle, I'd force myself to revive as soon as possible to protect Jamal and her mother-in-law.

"Shh," she hushed, eyes tense with worry as she unshackled me from the wall. I dropped. The beautiful Miranda mirage caught my arm over her shoulder, but the impact knocked all the air from my lungs. My body crunched like a dry husk.

Aman came to my side, catching my other arm. He was short, Mexican, with a thin black mustache over his mouth. His dark brown eyes were serene and serious, as if he'd never heard a joke in his life.

"I've been away so long you got another boyfriend?" I complained to my fantasy woman, my words crackling like my lungs.

"Shut up, beast boy," Miranda said, using her old nickname for me.

It wasn't an illusion. She was really here. She came for me.

She went on, "Be nice to Javier, he's working overtime to help us out. So say thank you and be quiet."

"Thank you, Javier," I repeated dutifully, but meaning it. Then I did as she asked and shut up. Though it was easier to comply when all the energy had been burned from me.

Somewhere between my consciousness wavering in and out I found myself laying on something soft that smelled like potpourri.

Miranda's face and other unfamiliar ones appeared and disappeared over me in blurry halos. When I finally came back to my senses, I was lying on a floral couch in a warehouse where one massive wall was covered in television screens. An IV stuck out of my arm next to a pole with a bag of liquid, and I realized I didn't feel like a dried husk of a being anymore.

Though I desperately needed a dip in the water of my grotto.

"You're awake," Miranda's tense, silky voice said from nearby. My angel of death seated herself next to me on the couch, her warm dry hand covering my forehead as if to check my temperature. I closed my eyes, drinking in her touch. So soft, so perfect, it was like heaven on earth.

Dark circles clung under Miranda's beautiful brown eyes, and I reached out to wipe them away with my thumb. She leaned into my hand, still blackened and a bit on the charred side. She dropped kisses on the abused fingertips. "How do you feel?" she asked softly.

"It probably looks worse than I feel."

A line drew between her brows. "You look like you've been barbecued and then thrown in a fruit dehydrator."

"Oh shit, that's exactly how it feels." I tried to push up onto my arms, panic lacing my voice. "We can't stay here too long. Aten will come for us. For me."

"He won't find you," a brusque voice interrupted. I followed it to the swiveling computer chair that turned around to reveal a rather short, stout woman with a close crop of dark hair, and a wide face. An ethereal glow surrounded her. Some of her essence stretched out in thin bright strings to all of the monitors lining the wall and to the pieces of tech surrounding her. The woman was an immortal, fae if I had to guess.

"I like your muumuu," I said. It had a lot of bright colors on it. Aten long ago incinerated my Hawaiian shirt. Bastard.

Miranda introduced us. "Xander, this is Echo."

Ah yes, the elusive tech support for our hunts. Then what the woman said sunk in. "He can't find us, you say, because of technology or magic?"

Echo's lips thinned so much they disappeared back into her face.

Okaaay, I guess we weren't in a sharing mood.

"I'm glad you are awake," she huffed like a bulldog, which made it difficult to believe her. "This one was a nightmare," Echo jerked her head in Miranda's direction.

"Barking directions and pacing all around you while you slept and healed."

"Aww, you do care, honeybuns," I crooned at Miranda. I was feeling particularly mushy since my rescue.

"Well shnookums, someone had to rescue the damsel in distress," she cooed back though there was a flinty gleam in her eye.

A pretty, teenage girl strode in from an adjoining room wearing an expression that was far too severe for the schoolgirl outfit she wore and the pink pom-poms that held her hair in pigtails.

"She's ready to talk," the girl said grimly.

I looked between the three women. "Who's ready to talk?"

CHAPTER 32

THE BADASS

"Since you love talking about Aten, why don't you tell us a little more about him," I suggested.

Sunny sat bound to a chair in what seemed to be a cleared-out storage room. Aoiki had captured her when Sunny came poking around to find me.

Sunny had planned to kill Aoiki, Echo, and Ryuki to further isolate me. And since she'd previously posed as Aoiki's girlfriend, Sunny knew all the weak points of their warehouse hideout.

But Aoiki and her family counted on that. Sunny walked right into a trap and was now going to answer for her lies and tell us what we needed to know about Aten.

If we knew more about his movements, his plans, we could anticipate them and catch him off guard at just the right moment.

"You should join the church of Aten," Sunny answered, not sticking to her previous role of strong and silent. "You too can feel the glory of his warmth. Feel exalted in his presence."

Aoiki shifted near me. She was playing this off well, but I couldn't imagine how she felt. Sunny had posed as her girlfriend for a hundred years, both of them fae. But Sunny did it only to use Aoiki and her ties to find the blade to free her sun god.

No, that's not true. I could see Aoiki's heartbreak had cost her. It had turned parts of her hard, parts that might never turn soft again.

"Yeah, I'm more spiritual than religious," I said to Sunny. Then I realized. "He made a church?"

"The wonders of the internet," Xander croaked from where he leaned against the wall. My heart still swelled at the sight of him. He'd been broken, burned, and bleeding, but was still alive.

Echo and I hadn't been able to locate where Aten had restrained the other gods, but he had Xander on display in a makeshift throne room at the Illusion hotel he'd commandeered as his own and had been torturing him. It's almost as if he wanted Xander's pain to be on display, as if it were a piece of art for his own sick amusement.

It was hard not to go to Xander even now—to touch him, feel his heartbeat, make sure he was okay.

"It's how he's become so strong and was able to over-power the rest of us," Xander explained. "He'd been elic-iting humans to worship him again, and based off the power I've seen, the church must have gained quite a following."

"The church of Aten is great." Sunny tipped her head and closed her eyes as if she were bathing in his presence right there.

"If I'd known you were such a religious zealot, I would have dumped your ass decades ago," Aoiki snarled. "I should have known you were trash when you kept saying my father didn't know how to brew a proper pot of tea."

She said *what* about Ryuki?

Well, now I wanted to slap her face right off her head.

Aoiki's father was precious beyond all measure and should be protected at all costs. That man was always there with a cup of tea and a kind word.

God, I hoped Jamal could spot the red flags before he ended up with a nightmare of a partner like Sunny.

Whoa Miranda, one trauma at a time.

Sunny straightened, meeting the angry stare from Aoiki. "It wasn't all a lie. You too can join me, Aoiki. We can be together, in his divine light. His love can strengthen ours."

A crazed, almost goggle of her eyes had me wondering if she'd been taking any drugs.

Aoiki's face twisted into a sneer as she crossed her arms tightly across her chest, her fingers digging into her biceps. It was clear she was trying to restrain herself from slapping Sunny across the face.

A dark look passed over Sunny's face, a malevolent spark of darkness in her eyes. "You can't deny him. He will take his place as the rightful god of this realm and remove all false gods." Her hate-filled glare turned on Xander. "And there is nothing you can do to stop him."

I lunged forward and grasped her wrists tightly, the

ropes cutting into my palms. I leaned in close, my face inches from hers, effectively blocking her view of Xander. "We'll see about that. Because Aten won't get his hands on Xander again, and he sure as hell isn't going to make me *love* him." I filled that last remark with as much disgust as I could.

"I love when she gets all territorial over me," Xander tossed lightly to Aoiki.

Instead of wanting to deny or punt his remark, I easily let it stand now. I knew he felt the same for me, and though we may not have our shit figured out, neither Xander nor I would let anyone hurt the other.

With that, I turned on my heel and walked out, Aoiki and Xander behind me.

Back in the warehouse, Ryuki was just setting down a fresh pot of tea and beautiful Japanese tea cups. Echo sat on the floral couch, flanked by her rabbit familiars who were snuggled in.

"Think she'll do it?" Echo asked.

"Oh, she'll do it," I affirmed.

"Do what?" Xander asked, slowly lumbering behind us.

I walked over to a backpack I left on the ground. I pulled out a brand new teal Hawaiin shirt and handed it to him.

"While you were sleeping, we made a plan."

I couldn't tell if he was more shocked by that news or the flowery garment he held between his fingers now.

"What do you mean, a plan?" His expression darkened as he stepped closer. "You should get as far away from him as possible, Miranda. He's coming for you. We need to get your family to safety."

I nodded, keeping myself from running my hands along his carved chest. "I know. Javier took Jamal and Mama Jean out of harm's way." Heinz was with them too. I'd trust my old army buddy with my life, and my family was my life. "But that's why we need to take care of this now."

His jaw flexed. "This isn't a game, Miranda."

Unable to stop myself, I smoothed a hand over a sculpted shoulder. "All the same, I plan to win." A smile quirked the edge of my lips.

Xander blinked.

"*We* plan to win," Aoiki corrected.

"See?" I chirped. "We are all playing on the same side."

"You lose all the time," Xander said.

"As you've pointed out in the past, I usually win in a different way."

From Monopoly to our billiards game, I'd won in a very physical sense. I didn't want to admit it before, but I could now. I threw all the games. For a woman who was fiercely independent, I kept handing over all the power time and time again to the beast in the cage. I'd been too afraid to admit what I was doing to myself, even as Xander teased me about it.

But I wasn't afraid anymore.

And I was wondering what would happen if we played on the same side for once.

He was about to find out.

To PREPARE and get Xander's strength back, we stopped by Sinopolis so he could immerse himself in the pools of his primordial water. He tried to tempt me to join him but I had other plans.

"I want to take you somewhere," I explained, keeping out of his reach and splashing zone.

After he'd thoroughly bathed, he emerged with healed

skin, dripping wet. I had to turn away and focus very hard on the rock formations so as not to be deterred from my plan.

My plan didn't involve licking the droplets of the Red Sea off of his chiseled abs. Not right now anyway.

My grip on his hand was unwavering as I led Xander back through the neon-lit chaos of the Strip. Echo assured me we would be scrubbed from Aten's radar and that we could move freely as long as the god didn't set his eyes directly on us.

My heart pounded until we crossed the grand entrance of the Atlantis hotel and were no longer out in the open.

I wondered if Xander sensed my intentions. His shoulders stiffened and he tugged at the barely buttoned Hawaiian shirt.

The lobby sprawled before us, vast and opulent, yet I didn't pause. I led him to a secluded set of elevators, retrieving a small ring of keys from my pocket. "It closed hours ago, but I used to help with security here so I still have a key," I explained, unlocking the private access to the elevator.

As the doors sealed us from the world outside, I caught Xander's gaze, his breath quickening, mirroring my own racing heart.

"How did you know?" he asked.

"Timothy told me," I said, wondering if Xander would turn volatile. I wouldn't leave him if he did. But this was something he needed to face, needed to own at the very least.

The elevator's chime signaled our arrival and we stepped into a dimly lit corridor that opened up into an awe-inspiring room. The glass walls and ceiling revealed the expansive blue of a vast aquarium. Fish glided overhead, their vibrant hues blurred by the curved glass, bathed in a serene, underwater light that enveloped us in an ethereal ambience.

I carefully studied Xander's reaction. His eyes glazed as his mouth softened and parted in awe. I could feel a soothing thrum over my skin, as if I could get a second hand feel for the way the water seemed to call to him, harmonizing with his soul.

"It's yours if you want it," I pointed out.

"I know," he said airily, eyes still fastened on the giant aquarium surrounding us. His reaction tugged at my heart. Here was Nun, the god of primordial waters, visibly moved by the semblance of his elemental realm.

"I thought you might like it," I murmured, closing the distance between us and slipping my hand into his. Fingers squeezed back around mine. His reaction to the aquatic surroundings confirmed I'd made the right choice. This felt like a rare moment of connection, a bridge to the divine part of him he so often kept guarded.

"If you step up amongst the gods and claim your inheritance you would own this place. You could move out of Grim's basement and live here. Play with the sharks in your downtime."

I expected him to laugh at my joke but the way he stared at the life teaming in liquid told me that might be a very real pastime for him.

When he still didn't answer, I asked, "Why don't you take what's yours?"

Xander turned to face me, his eyes filled with longing. "I have no right to take anything. I have to earn it."

His fingers trailed down my cheek, igniting a fire within me as they traced their way down my neck and over my collarbone. His touch was filled with reverence and longing, leaving me breathless.

Xander wasn't talking about the hotel.

"Have you?" My question came out barely above a whisper. "Earned it?"

He slowly shook his head. "No, but I'm still hoping."

The quiet fell around us like a blanket and there was only the intensity of his gaze. Gratitude, pain, and raw emotion were tangled inside him, and he wore it all out in the open. Whether he could choose it or not didn't matter. For once, I let my defenses down and joined him, letting him see me. The real me.

Reaching up, I traced his jawline, my fingers weaving into his hair, grounding him to this moment, to me. His response was immediate, pulling me closer with a longing that mirrored the depth of the seas surrounding us. Our kiss was a confluence of all the tension and passion that had been building between us.

In that moment, with the gentle glow of the aquarium illuminating us, everything else faded. It was just Xander and I, and the vast, uncharted waters of what lay between us.

Our breathing was harsh in the calm quiet of the empty aquarium. I unbuttoned and pushed Xander's shirt down over his shoulders, revealing the carved muscles. Running my hands over his flexing abs, I could feel them turn to grating washboard.

Finding Xander burnt and bloodied did something to me.

Years of trying to keep my emotions locked away, shielding myself from any romantic attachment, came crashing down when I saw him hanging there.

His incoherent mumblings about saving my family

sliced into my fleshy organ. It made me not want to waste what time I had denying what I already knew I wanted.

Xander's hand wrapped around the back of my neck and his face contorted as if he were in pain. "Do you understand how beautiful you are? How fucking irresistible you are to me?"

"Why?" I shook my head, breaking away. "You're a god."

I should be better than needing his reassurance, but I stopped fighting it. Instead of building a steel box around my insecurities, I handed them over to Xander, trusting him not to crush them in his bare hands.

Xander's grip on my neck tightened, his eyes burning with a fierce intensity. "Because you see me, sweetheart," he whispered, his voice husky with desire. "You see the god *and* the man within me. You don't worship blindly; you challenge and inspire me. That's what makes you irresistible."

His words ignited a need in me, a craving for this man who saw every part of me and accepted it all without hesitation. In that moment I surrendered to him completely, trusting him with my insecurities and vulnerabilities. And as his lips met mine with a fierce passion, I knew I had found my equal—a god who worshiped me just as much as I worshiped him.

Xander's head dipped to kiss down my neck, even as he picked me up. My legs wrapped around his waist, and I notched onto the hardness growing in his cargo shorts.

We both moaned at the contact. My need for more ratcheted upward immediately.

"I need you." The words came out of my mouth before I could stop myself.

CHAPTER 33

THE BEAST

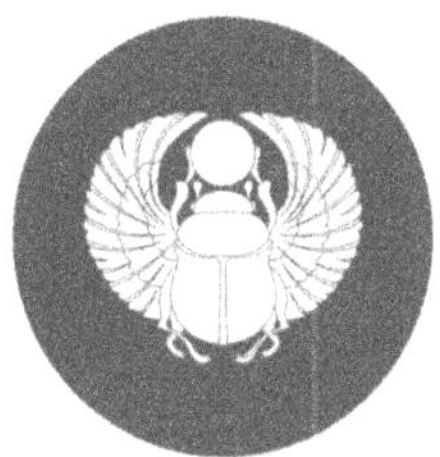

In the serene silence of the aquarium, our ragged breaths were the only sound, a stark contrast to the peaceful environment. As Miranda's fingers worked the buttons of my shirt, exposing my chest, I felt a rush unlike anything else. Her hands traced over my abs, igniting fires deep within me.

This place was sacred, this moment with her was sacred.

When we entered the aquarium I'd forgotten to breathe. The water called to me, sang to me in a voice as old as time, resonating with the very essence of my being. I was

Nun, god of the primordial waters, and this... this felt like coming home.

Miranda's touch was a balm to the chaos that always threatened to engulf me.

The moan that escaped us both was a sound of pure need. Her admission, *I need you*, was a call to every instinct I possessed.

A large, silver shark glided by. Its dark eyes watched us with an almost eerie curiosity before leaving us behind. I set her down gently on the black leather bench and stepped back.

In her eyes, I found a reflection of who I could be—not just a deity bound to creation and destruction, but a man capable of tenderness, of love. This realization, this acceptance, filled me with awe. Here, in the dim, underwater glow of the aquarium, with the serene world of water around us, I felt the divide within me narrow. She didn't just tolerate my complexities; she embraced them and in doing so, showed me that perhaps I could too.

She didn't waste any time removing her clothes. I hurriedly did the same until we were both fully naked and exposed under the glimmering streaks of blue light from the waters.

Miranda reached for me and the heat of our skin pressed against each other in a conversation of hard and soft, want and need.

Her hands moved with purpose and tenderness over my chest and my pulsating heart. Miranda had shown me that to be loved in all my messy, chaotic entirety was not just a possibility, but a reality. In her presence, I was not Nun, the ancient god of primordial waters. I was simply Xander, man and god, loved and loving, wholly accepted. It was beyond anything I had dared to dream, and for that, I was eternally grateful.

Our lips met, a slow and tender kiss that sent shivers down my spine. My body trembled with ecstasy as the heady mix of passion and vulnerability overwhelmed me, leaving me gasping for air and craving more of her intoxicating touch.

As our lips met again and again, I realized that this moment was a departure from every encounter we'd had before. There was no struggle, no attempt to best one another. Instead, there was an unspoken agreement, a mutual surrender to the connection that had always simmered beneath our surface interactions.

She was a woman allowing herself to be seen, to be vulnerable. And in that concession, I saw her strength, her courage to stand as my equal, not just in battle but in love. It was a revelation, a gift of trust that she offered me, laying bare her heart without the armor of sarcasm or the shield of defiance.

As I wrapped my arms around her, feeling her heartbeat against mine, I realized the significance of what we were doing. We weren't just sharing our bodies—we were sharing our scars, our fears, and our dreams. Miranda, in her openness, was teaching me that to love and be loved in return was the greatest power of all.

My hands explored the curves of her body, feeling the soft skin and the warm flesh beneath my fingertips. Her lips parted, inviting me in, and I took advantage of the opportunity, deepening the kiss and angling her head to taste more.

As our kiss deepened, I tasted the sweetness of her lips, the heat of her breath against my mouth. And when my lips trailed down her neck, I tasted the saltiness of her skin mixed with a hint of sweat.

I kissed down her neck, my teeth gently grazing her sensitive skin as I made my way to her breast. I took her nipple into my mouth, sucking gently, eliciting a gasp.

Her body was a masterpiece of curves and contours, her skin glowing in the soft light, beckoning me to explore. Her parted lips were full and inviting, her eyes dark with desire.

Too far gone, words clung to my throat. Unable to speak, my fingers dug into the soft curve of her ass and I hoisted her up. Her legs instantly wrapped around me as I pressed her against the cold glass. She hissed and bucked her hips, grinding into me. The wet heat where our bodies met told me she wanted this as badly as I did. The water glimmered in the soft light and I could see the reflection of our bodies.

I thrust into her slick entrance, her heat wrapping around me. She let out a soft cry, her eyes wide with pleasure. I groaned. Her walls squeezed tight, hugging my hardness to perfection. I wanted to touch every part of her at once.

I thrust deeper, letting her tight heat engulf me.

"Xander," she breathed, her voice hoarse with need.

Her hands gripped my back, pulling me even closer, her nails digging into my skin and leaving small marks that would fade with time. Again and again, I slid into her heat, coming home every time.

I didn't belong in this world. I wasn't right in the head. But I found my home and my sanity right here, safe in Miranda's embrace. With her legs wrapped around my hips as I drove into her, she couldn't possibly know she was actually holding *me* up in every sense.

Our gasps echoed in the glass tunnel as sweat dripped down our faces. Our breaths turned ragged and desperate as our bodies found the rhythm that drove us higher and higher.

Miranda's eyes locked with mine, a mix of ecstasy and vulnerability that took my breath away. I could see her without the defenses, without the walls. It was just Miranda, every messy little imperfectly perfect piece laid bare to me.

As I thrust harder, my body shook. The rush of pleasure and power overwhelmed me. The muscles in my thighs and buttocks tensed, as waves of pure ecstasy threatened to consume me. I was moments from losing it.

Miranda whimpered, her body convulsed around me, shaking violently as she succumbed to the sensations that washed over her. Her body tightened around me, pulling me in deeper.

I groaned, the force of her climax pushing me over the edge. I released myself into her, our bodies shuddering in unison as the orgasm tore through us.

We collapsed back onto a wide viewing bench, our bodies still intertwined, our breaths ragged, hearts beating wildly. I gazed into her eyes, seeing the reflection of our passion and the connection that bound us together.

Then without a word, we dressed and left the tranquil sanctuary of the aquarium, stepping back into the world. The sun was coming up, and we were either going to kill a god or die trying.

CHAPTER 34

THE BADASS

The nights had grown too oppressively hot, and even the pre-dawn light streaked through the sky in red spirals like hellish spikes.

Aten wanted his answer at dawn, and I was ready to give it to him.

Xander's hand held mine with a death grip as we neared KaleidoQuest Experience Center. The wacky museum experience was all the rage, and when we let Sunny go I told her to pass on the message this is where I wanted to meet Aten.

She was to get him exactly where we wanted him.

"I don't want you to go on your own," Xander growled next to me.

I squeezed his hand to reassure him. "I'm a badass, right? I've killed you so many times, this will be a piece of cake."

That didn't mean my insides weren't sloshing around in worry about what could happen.

"Besides, I'll feel better knowing you're nearby," I said as we stopped by the museum entrance. I leaned up and kissed him and Xander pulled me into him, turning a brief kiss into a long, exploratory one that left me dizzy.

Despite his reluctance, he let me go.

We navigated through the fake grocery store with its meticulously placed shelves and plastic produce. Next came the hall of endless selfies, an Instagrammer's paradise with all kinds of floral backgrounds to choose from.

Finally, I came upon the entrance to the maze of mirrors. The walls shimmered and twisted in every direction, reflecting my own image back at me. Taking a deep breath, I positioned myself at the start and prepared for Aten's arrival.

The ceiling stretched impossibly high, adorned with an intricate web of rafters. Later on in the exhibit, visitors would be able to watch others make their way through this same maze of reflections from above. It was like a never-ending funhouse, full of secrets and illusions waiting to be discovered.

I longed for Xander to be up there with me, but he had to remain at a distance. I didn't know where he took up his post, but I was sure he was moments away. His nearness made me feel less alone, less exposed to danger.

After what felt like an eternity—but was really fifteen

minutes later—door opened. My breath cut off halfway on an inhale.

Aten's image filled the mirrors.

The air shimmered around him, particles of light dancing in his wake, casting reflections that dazzled and mesmerized. Every mirror caught and multiplied his image, creating an endless sea of his perfection. The sight was so captivating it almost made me forget the danger he posed.

Almost.

His divine nature had been amplified by the countless prayers funneled through his church.

"Where are you, my god killer?" the sun god asked in an intrigued voice. His new nickname made me cringe. Though I didn't care for being his right arm either.

Aten was at the entrance and he could see my reflection though I was farther in.

Despite the dread pooling in my stomach I steeled myself, forcing my legs to stand firm, my hands to stop shaking.

"You have to come to me," I said evenly.

His love for his own image was evident in the way he paused to admire his reflection, a smile playing on his lips —a god completely enamored with himself.

A strange sense of resolve settled over me as Aten drew closer.

In his eyes, I was nothing but a mortal, a minor inconvenience to be dealt with. As I steadied my breathing, I prepared to face him.

Aten made his way through the maze slowly but steadily. I paid sharp attention to how he navigated, noting that he spent more time looking at his own reflection than focusing on the route to me.

Aten loved his own image, so I gave him as much as I

could of what he loved most. It was already distracting him whether he realized it or not.

I did everything I could not to tense when the heat of his body preceded his entrance into the corridor where I stood.

Finally, he came to stand in front of me. We stood there a moment appraising each other. Thankfully, I'd mastered the poker face long ago, and the sweat sliding down my back and under my breasts could be attributed to the actual heat he cast into the maze.

Aten broke our silence. "Why here?"

"I spoke to Sunny."

"I'm aware," he said, raising an eyebrow.

"She told me about the church, the glory of following you."

"Yes, and…" he drawled expectantly.

"At first, I thought she was full of bullshit, but I wanted to experience it for myself."

He tilted his head and took a step forward, his mouth curving into a lascivious grin. "Experience what exactly?"

"What it was like to be surrounded by you," I said, gesturing to the mirrors around us.

Again, he caught his own eye and couldn't help sending a reciprocal smile to the hundred other Aten's in the room.

It was just distracting enough, just enough to put him off guard, and it was exactly where I wanted him.

If I were Vivien, I'd have something pithy or punchy to say in the moment to let him know the tides were about to turn. But that wasn't my style. I was a woman of action.

Slipping my hand into my pocket, I pressed the little red button.

A massive bin opened overhead. My nostrils burned at the terrible stench that permeated the air. His cry of outrage was garbled as rotting seafood and sticky pancakes came down on him in an unexpected torrent.

Though it happened quickly, time slowed to a crawl for me as I pulled out my sword.

"You bitch," Aten hissed, wading his way through the mountain of trash I'd buried him in with significant help from Echo and Aoiki.

His heat turned white as rage swept over him. My death burned in his eyes. Aten wouldn't suffer humiliation and he would make me pay.

I had seconds before he blasted me into fire and ash.

But taking him down in a specific type of garbage was only half the plan.

A hungry growl resonated in the maze of mirrors. Aten paused.

Then a mass of muscles and fur leapt from the rafters and directly onto Aten. Sheshem and Aten went down with a chorus of hungry snarls and angry yells.

Looking up, I searched the rafters for Xander, but he wasn't there. I wished he'd join us now, but he'd come when he could.

The plan was to lead Sheshem here. Aoiki explained she was great with cats, though I didn't even know what the hell that meant in this case. But she'd delivered.

I did what Xander taught me. I couldn't outmaneuver or use power to defeat Aten. I had to be smarter.

And delegating the fucking up to a massive hungry cat god seemed like a great idea.

Now all I needed to do was find the opening to leap in and run Aten through with Bob and finish this.

The two gods fought but Sheshem had the upper paw so to speak, and was currently trying to gnaw on Aten's head even as the sun god let out a stream of curses.

Just as I saw my opportunity and was about to spring into action, a massive metal hoop fell over Sheshem's head.

"I've got him Max," Alfonso cried.

Oh, no. Oh, *fuck* no.

Why were they here? Or rather *how* were they here?

Xander should have seen them and stopped them.

Max stood behind Alfonso as they both gripped a massive pole attached to the metal loop. They began to tighten it around Sheshem's throat, but the god spawn let out a bloodcurdling roar, shaking his head and backing away from the two idiots.

Before I lost my chance, I lunged between the bucking Sheshem, sword poised to plunge into a bloodied Aten.

A force like a cannonball slammed into my side, knocking me off course.

The moment slipped from my fingers in slow motion as I careened sideways, away from my mark.

The heavy weight of Sunny held me down in a sticky puddle. The sharp edge of a knife bit into my jugular as she stared down at me with a wild gleam in her eye. "You will not hurt my god."

Sheshem let out another displeased roar before knocking directly into a wall of mirrors, pushing it right over. The rest of the maze went down like a line of shattering dominoes in the wake of Sheshem's retreat.

"Hurry Alfonso," Max cried, wasting no time chasing after Sheshem. Max's portly magician friend hurried after him as well.

Shit, my trap hadn't just attracted Sheshem. It'd drawn the attention of Max and Alfonso. The two bumbling idiots had chased off my ace in the hole.

Shock had me by the nuts. If I had nuts.

Did I have nuts?

Control of the situation slipped from my grasp so quickly I didn't know which way was up or what kind of genitalia was attached to me.

Aten lumbered to his feet—a stinking, horrific monster that looked more like a bloody, chewed up piece of bubble gum.

"Get off him," Aoiki screamed. Now that the maze had fallen, I caught sight of Aoiki and Xander fighting off a hoard of people. Their eyes glowed with bright light and they moved stiffly as if zombified.

Aten's followers swarmed the place. Xander and Aoiki were trying not to hurt anyone while keeping them at bay.

"No," I rasped. Everything was spiraling into chaos.

My plan crumbled to ash and there was nothing I could do about it.

"I've got her, Aten," Sunny said, her teeth bared in a vicious grimace.

An incoherent sound gurgled out of Aten's mouth. He reached out toward Sunny, and she instantly grabbed his hand with her free one.

"I'm here, my god! I will serve you however you need."

A blazing inferno erupted from their intertwined hands, engulfing her in scorching flames.

She thrashed and writhed, desperately trying to break free, but Aten's grip was unrelenting.

The flames traveled like a runaway train along her body, melting her. Sunny's screams of agony bounced off the rafters as Aten inhaled the fumes of her essence into his own body.

As his faithful servant burned, Aten regenerated, until not a single hair was out of place on his golden head and Sunny was no more.

Once he'd regained his composure, Aten turned his livid

gaze to me. Bob groaned under the pressure of Aten's magic, and I knew he was trying to take my life force too.

When he realized it wouldn't work, Aten dropped his power.

"You won't help me?" he snarled. "Then I'll do it myself. Sending the rest of my brethren to the cradle will be a massive pain in my ass when they all begin to emerge and challenge me again, but you won't have the blade forever, Miranda. If nothing else, you'll die and the blade will go to someone else. Someone more amenable to my offer."

With that, he disappeared in the direction Sheshem and the two idiot magicians went.

"I got it," Aoiki said, successfully locking the doors against the swarms.

Xander was suddenly there at my side, bleeding profusely. His body was peppered with stab wounds and slices to his skin.

"I tried—I tried to get to you, but they would have killed Aoiki." Even as he said it, I saw the self-hatred raging in his eyes.

I wanted to assure him he did the right thing, that it was what I would have done. But the truth was, she might be in more danger now. We all were.

I ran out the back way without explaining as nasty feeling churned in my guts. Once outside, we found all Aten's worshippers. They all stood before him, still as traffic cones, eyes glowing.

"Give me your love," he announced from atop the building next door.

Now the sun god stood atop his perch, drawing the attention of all of Vegas. They raised their hands up, as if to welcome the warmth and favor of their new god. Aten glowed brighter and brighter under their worship, becoming more powerful with each passing moment.

Then the collective essence flowed out of all of them as Aten inhaled the power of their souls.

Fuck, fuck, fuck.

Xander's fierce expression let me know he also realized we were royally screwed.

With Sheshem gone, my whole plan had fallen apart. I needed that chaotic element to give me the opportunity to strike Aten down. Now he was more powerful than before and definitely pissed.

Wait... a chaotic element.

I had been overlooking the biggest chaotic distraction I had.

"Xander, I need you to give into your god-likeness."

THE BEAST

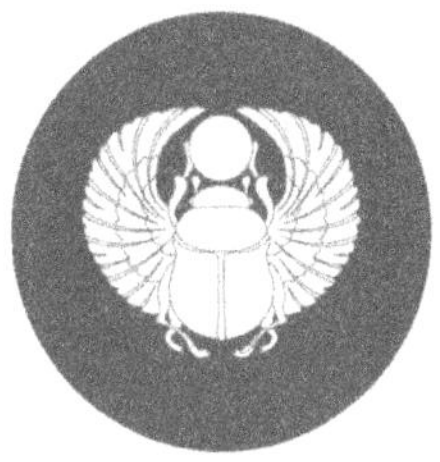

"What?" There's no way she said what I thought she said.

"I need you to change," Miranda reiterated.

She was saying the words, but none of them made any sense.

"I need you to change and distract Aten." She motioned with her hands for me to hurry up.

"I can't do that, Miranda. You don't know what you're asking." I won't risk it. I won't become the monster. With my shattered brain, who knew what I would do if I gave into my power. I hadn't since I was revived, and I had no intention of abandoning Miranda in a critical moment that could get her killed. For crying out loud, I could be the one to hurt her or worse.

The thought alone instantly made me blanch.

"Xander, I trust you." Miranda's pleading eyes bore into me as she asked the impossible.

A dry scoff escaped me. "Well that's a fucking first."

I've asked her a dozen times if she trusted me and the answer had always been no, and that's how it should be.

"Xander." My name snapped out of her mouth as she pleaded with me. "I trust you," she repeated in earnest, taking my hand in hers and squeezing it. "I always have. But I need you to trust yourself. Do it."

I splayed my hands open to show her I couldn't give her this. "Miranda, I don't know what I would do if I let that much power rush into my broken mind."

Something in her face softened and her fingers slid up the side of my jaw. "You'll be perfect. Just as you are. You are perfect."

What she's saying doesn't make any sense. It's all wrong. She can't mean that. I'm the furthest thing from perfect. I'm a mess—a tangle of power, crazy, and usually out of control with lust for her. But there is something in her soft touch that tells me she means every word.

And if there is one thing about Miranda I know for certain, she doesn't bullshit.

I closed my eyes and reached inward to the part of me I'd been holding at bay for weeks, the part that had been trying to claw its way out. There were barriers there, walls I'd fashioned to stay in control after what I observed in Miranda.

It was not with a deafening roar or a battle cry, but with

a sigh that I let them all come down and the inner power flooded me.

My body elongated, the sensation akin to stretching muscles I never knew I had. My skin turned a deep, iridescent blue, reminiscent of the darkest depths of the sea.

As I yielded to the power I had suppressed for so long, the transformation overtook me like a tidal wave crashing over a ship, dragging it down into ocean depths that never end.

Veins of glowing aquamarine light traced across my form, illuminating me from within as if I had become one with the bioluminescent creatures of the deep. My eyes morphed into deep pools of water, swirling with untold power and ancient secrets, reflecting the vastness of the ocean itself.

I was losing myself and I might never come up for air again. A distant, weak cry of fear begged me to come back to my senses—there was something worth remembering. Then it was gone.

A cascade of waterspouts erupted from my back, each one writhing and twisting like a living entity, a manifestation of my tumultuous psyche. The massive, fluid appendages undulated like the tails of whales and the tentacles of a kraken, a testament to the primordial forces that made up my essence. With each movement water seemed to materialize out of thin air, swirling around me in a mesmerizing dance, responding to the call of my reclaimed power. The air crackled with the energy of a storm unleashed, my presence commanding the very essence of all waters in this earthly realm.

The only thing I was aware of was the burning entity before me that threatened everything.

I surged forward, my form colliding with Aten's radiant brilliance in a clash of elemental forces. In that moment of impact, the very fabric of reality seemed to tremble, the clash of our powers unleashing a cataclysmic storm that swept across the celestial expanse. As I grappled with the sun god's divine fury, I felt the primal surge of the ocean driving me.

Each searing beam of light he threw at me felt like a blade of fire slicing through my watery essence. They left behind a trail of blistering wounds that smoldered with searing pain. Yet even as I writhed in agony, the icy depths of my power surged forth, a tidal wave of determination.

We clashed again and again, and slowly but surely, I was wearing off some of his excess power. He burned away my liquid extremities, but we were still evenly matched.

Two ancient, powerful gods, and while he was relatively young compared to me, he was fueled by pure prayer and the undying worship of thousands.

It was just like the last time we battled. Except this time I had a whole can of crazy that just cracked open and now that it was unleashed, it wasn't going back in.

Aten finally broke away, his face contorted in outrage. His light had dimmed and I was just getting started. I'd known nothing but pain thanks to the god across from me.

He may burn me, but I welcomed the end of Miranda's blade for so many nights. I'd died more times than he knew, and I had finally embraced the pain of living.

The world suddenly crystallized as I accepted my own nature. The very thing I'd been keeping at bay was part of what made me whole.

I was still a fucking mental mess, but it all came together in balance as I let all of myself free. I had claimed the beast and now I raged with a power unlike any I'd ever known.

"You think you can stop me?" Aten raged. "You think you can send me back to the cradle? Well perhaps it's best to start this world over from scratch. This world will be good and pure, birthed in my life-giving light, and it will be perfect with me as the only god and being left in this realm."

Aten sounded like a childish brat having a meltdown. I half expected him to fall to the ground and pound his fists on the floor until he got his way.

But as his anger reached a fever pitch, fiery tendrils of energy writhed and twisted around him and coalesced into a swirling vortex of incandescent power. The ground beneath him trembled as though it was unable to withstand the sheer force of his rage.

He wouldn't.

He wouldn't actually attempt to scorch this whole world until he was the only living being left, would he?

Aten's form warped and distorted, the very fabric of his being unraveling at the seams.

Fuck.

This narcissistic piece of shit.

Aten's eyes widened and the veins in his forehead pulsated. A blinding white energy emanated from his body. His muscles tensed and his skin seemed to vibrate with an otherworldly power.

My mind raced for a way to stop him as he began to shrink in stature, but the light around him intensified, almost blindingly so. The only idea that sprang to mind was terrible, reckless, and certified suicide.

With a look at Miranda, the mortal woman who would

give up everything to do what was right, my choice was made for me.

Sinking into the depths of my power, I swelled and expanded until I washed over Aten, engulfing him in the center of my watery being.

The pain.

Oh gods, the *pain*.

I'd known pain and even death, but this was a new level. Aten seared through every fiber of my being as he dissolved me from the inside out. Steam hissed from my melting body as I fought to maintain my form.

"Xander!" Miranda cried out.

My angel of death stood before me. She reached out to touch me, only to hiss and pull her hand back, her fingers an angry red. I was nothing but a volume of boiling water.

It took all my concentration to form coherent sentences.

"I'm sorry to do this to you again, sweetheart. You deserve more. You don't deserve to keep choosing between love and loss."

"No…" She shook her head.

"It's okay," I assured her, the word ending in a pained grunt. "If you didn't know this about me, I've gotten really good at dying."

Ah, that scowl. One of my favorite Miranda expressions because it pushed out that bottom lip.

"Just when I got a good crack at trying to live," I said wryly. "And I was getting kind of good at it too."

I bit off the last word as my head snapped back, and the pain doubled everywhere at once. I was slowing him down, but Aten was going supernova no matter what I did.

"You can't bring me back again," I warned her, my voice raspy and hoarse from holding it together. "You can't let him out again. If you do, he'll come straight for you. For Jamal and Mama Jean."

"I know," she whispered, reluctant acceptance shining in her eyes. Both our hearts were breaking with the weight of the impossible choice. It was either the entire world or me. And she had to fulfill her duty. It's what she did. It's who she was. And I wouldn't have her any other way.

Maybe I'd have her on that arcade joystick one more time though. I made strange, cracking sounds as I amused and aroused myself in my last moments.

"I wish we had more time," she confessed with a trembling voice.

I struggled to maintain any semblance of levity as my body threatened to implode from the intense pressure raging inside me. "Time is overrated."

I'd had a near eon of it and it was wasted without Miranda in it. Timothy's warning had sunk into my bones. My future was borrowed time with Miranda and it would have never been enough. The prospect of walking this earth for all eternity without her was too unbearable to comprehend. It was better this way.

"You're going to be okay," I said with a lopsided smile. "Afterall, you are a badass."

"Truth or dare," she said, tears streaming down her face as her body shook almost violently.

That threw me. "Truth?"

"I love you."

If I weren't already burning from the inside out, I would be now. "I love you, too," I managed to whisper. "But the game is over, sweetheart."

The steam only thickened and molten fingers reached out from my inside. Aten was making his way out of me.

I wanted her to shut her eyes. I didn't want her to watch

what she was about to do, but in true Miranda form, she stared straight into my eyes as she plunged the blade through my body and into Aten's.

A different, sharper pain sliced through me as death blackened the edges of my vision, and the bright burning sensation went out like the flick of a light switch.

CHAPTER 36

THE BEAST

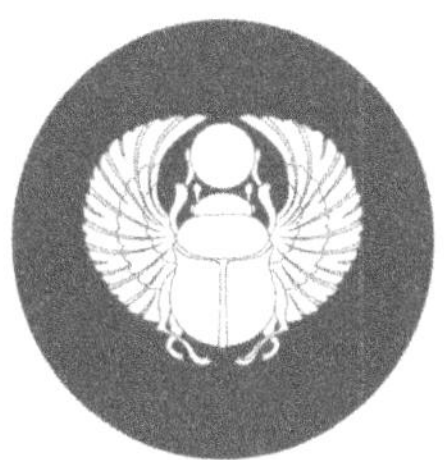

Death felt a lot like living, or so I thought as my eyes fluttered open in Grim's penthouse. Someone had a death grip on my hand and I felt strange, different. Like my senses had been muted and I no longer held that internal thrum of power I'd always known.

"Welcome back," I heard Grim's voice from over my shoulder.

I didn't turn to look at him. Not when a certain cat-eyed goddess sat at my side, staring at me like I was some kind of miracle.

"Miss me, sweetheart?" I grinned.

Then Miranda threw herself on me. I wrapped my arms around her even as I sat both of us up on the couch.

"I thought I killed you." Her words were muffled into my shoulder.

Vivien gave me the thumbs up and dragged Grim out of the room, leaving us alone.

I held Miranda, rocking her back and forth, giving her soothing hushes even as I inhaled her scent like it was oxygen.

She pulled away to meet my gaze, tears shining in her eyes. I brushed away a tear that trailed down her cheek with my thumb. I was awed to see her vulnerable enough to cry not only in front of me, but over me.

"Is Aten..." I was still dazed and confused by waking up.

"He's dead," she assured me. "Or rather, he's trapped in Bob again."

I let out a sigh of relief. "Good. I wouldn't have wanted to die for nothing. That being said," I patted my chest. "How am I alive?"

Miranda gave me a lopsided smile. "It was a gift from Bob."

"Oh really?" Now this I had to hear.

"Instead of taking you whole, he took your godhood." Her face twisted in distress and worry, her eyes searching mine as her voice dropped to a whisper. "You're mortal Xander."

I stiffened.

"What?"

"I'm so sorry," she rushed to say. "He didn't ask, he just did it, and I know it's probably not what you wanted but—"

I jumped to my feet and took Miranda with me, twirling

her around in my arms. Her laughter filled the room, infectious and pure. I felt lighter than air.

Mortal.

The realization washed over me like a wave crashing onto shore. It was both terrifying and exhilarating.

As I stood there with Miranda in my arms, I became acutely aware of the dullness in my senses. Colors were less vibrant, smells less potent. And when I reached for my powers within, they were noticeably absent.

But that also meant the harsh lights no longer pierced my eyes like vengeful lasers and the noises no longer drowned out my inner thoughts.

In this mortal form, I could finally experience life without constant distractions and overwhelming sensations. "Okay, okay, I get it. You're not mad about it. Now put me down, you psycho."

Dropping to the couch, I nuzzled her neck. "Oh, but I'm *your* psycho, sweetheart."

"Is it safe to come out now, or are you guys humping like rabbits?" Vivien called out from the hall.

"It's safe." Miranda extracted herself from my grip though I refused to let go of her hand.

"*Is* it safe?" I waggled my eyes suggestively. I got a smack on the chest for that, but I caught her fingers and dropped kisses on them.

Grim and Vivien entered the living room again, he with a serious gait while the auburn-haired vampire practically bounced on her feet.

She threw her arms around us. "Come here you guys." She squeezed until I actually couldn't breathe.

"Viv, too much," Miranda squeaked out.

"Oops! Sorry."

I rubbed at my throat. "Is this what all mortals feel like?"

"Annoyed by overly affectionate vampires?" Miranda said dryly. "Not all of them, but I imagine some."

"You love it," Vivien tossed back before wrapping her slim arm around her big, tall, and dark husband.

"How are the others?" I asked Grim. All of the gods had been taken hostage by Aten, and I didn't know if they'd survived.

He nodded. "Everyone is fine. I can't say I'm thrilled that all of the dark ones from the Blade of Bane are in the cradle now, instead of Miranda's weapon. Eventually they will rise again and may have to be dealt with."

"Try not to be so dark and cynical, honeybuns." Vivien patted Grim on the chest. "There's a lot to celebrate! Being released from prison, Xander's new mortality, and a brand spanking new magic show on the Strip."

I shook my head, not understanding the significance of that last bit.

Miranda answered. "Apparently Sheshem is happy to star in a show with Max and Alfonso as long as they feed him all the shrimp and syrupy pancakes he wants and promise not to interrupt him when he feeds."

My mouth opened, then closed. "Okay, then."

Miranda's lips pursed as she shook her head like she didn't get it either.

"So..." Vivien turned to me. "What now?"

"Give him time," Grim said with restrained impatience. "He just learned that he's mortal."

Vivien pouted.

"No need to put her off, Grim. I do, in fact, have plans."

"You do?" Miranda said, looking up at me.

I swung an arm over her shoulders with a grin. "I have a dinner date."

THIS WAS the worst bet I had ever won.

I did get Miranda to invite me over for that dinner, and she did in fact cook. But I also did not realize she lacked any culinary talent. The chicken was dry and the spinach was overcooked, and it took a lot of soda to wash it all down.

And yet, I was the most fantastically happy man on the fucking planet.

Not god. Man.

I was Miranda's man, and she was my woman.

"What's for dessert?" I asked.

Miranda raised an eyebrow as she set her napkin on the table and got up. "What makes you think I made dessert for you?"

I encircled her waist as she walked by, drawing her onto my lap. "Because you always treat me to a little something sweet."

"You," she poked me in the chest, "are ridiculous."

"And you," I said, punctuating kisses on her full luscious mouth, "love it."

I kissed her deeply, angling her head back to get deeper. She moaned and came away breathless. "You couldn't have worn a nice shirt?" She flicked one of the buttons on my Hawaiian shirt.

"This is the nicest shirt I own," I said. "My girlfriend got it for me."

Girlfriend.

If you had told me a couple months ago I would end up

mortal with the most badass woman with a built-in family, I would have laughed myself to death that night.

"You sure Jamal isn't going to ask to come home?" I moved to kiss down her neck, enjoying the silky delicate skin there. When I found the right spot, her fingers dug into my arm.

"He's good to stay at his friend's for the night." Jamal and Heinz both went to one of his friends' houses for a sleepover, and Mama Jean was back at her own.

Thankfully, Mama Jean only thought they'd been attacked by house looters and had no idea there was a supernatural element to it. As it started to really shake her and affect her sleep, I went and asked Fallon if he could do something to ease her mind. He was gruff and appeared reluctant, but he did so.

Which meant everyone was safe and sound, and we were alone for the night.

"I lied and I cheated," Miranda said from where she writhed on my lap. "Dessert is in the fridge. I got Mama Jean to make a chocolate cake."

"Later. I need something sweeter first." With that, I hauled her up and carried her to the bedroom, laying her down on her lavender quilt.

Our clothes were soon discarded, forgotten in the growing heat between us. Miranda's skin was soft and warm under my touch, her breath coming quick as she pulled me closer. There was a hunger in her eyes that mirrored my own, a need that had been building between us for far too long. We hadn't been alone together since she defeated Aten.

"I love you, Miranda. And if you let me, I'm going to grow old and die with you."

Half her mouth quirked up. "Kind of romantic, kind of dark."

"Dark," I pushed hair back from her face, "would be having to face an eternity without you."

At that she pulled me to her and kissed me, reassuring me we were together in this moment.

"What's irritating is you'll still probably look hot with wrinkles."

"Oh, you bet your sweet ass I will. And wait until you see how good I look with a mustache."

All humor fled from her face. "No mustache."

"Oh, come on," I tickled her sides, but she slapped at my hands. "It will really complete that Magnum PI look I've got going."

"You're crazy."

"You love it."

Before she could fight me anymore, I gently stroked her breast, brushing my thumb across her nipple until it hardened under my teasing. Miranda moaned into my mouth, her hands threading through my hair, holding me closer. I slid my hand over her body, slipping my fingers down until I found her hot, ready, and wet for me. My finger parted her lower lips and sunk into her, making her gasp, sending blood to my fast-stiffening cock.

"You can't imagine how good this feels, being with you in your bed like this. Like we are just two people." I added a second finger and stroked faster.

"We are just two people," she said even as her breathing turned ragged and she fought to keep her eyes open.

"Oh god, that's so hot," I said, pulling back.

She giggled even as I removed my fingers, but she stopped as I dropped between her legs and licked up her slit slowly. Her breath hitched as I continued to lap at her, my tongue swirling and twirling around her sensitive areas. I could feel her pulse quicken, her desire for me becoming more desperate. It was in this moment that I felt truly alive, that I knew I belonged to this woman, that I was home.

Fingers wrapped around my hair as she held on for dear life, nearing her breaking point. I didn't realize how much I needed this connection, this moment of pure intimacy with Miranda, until I felt my tongue dancing over her most intimate places. She tasted sweet and salty, her skin warm and soft against my touch. I licked and suckled, savoring every taste and every moan she let out, drinking in her passion like nectar.

Her moans grew louder, and I knew she was close. I slipped a finger inside her, matching the rhythm of my tongue, and she let out a scream, her body convulsing as she arched against my face. I drank in her climax, savoring every drop, every sensation.

I continued to gently lap at her until she recovered, and then she rolled us over, so she was on top.

Gazing up at her beauty, I found my rock, my North Star —and I would do anything to keep her safe, happy, and content.

Straddling my hips, her gaze met mine. Slowly, she lowered onto me, surrounding me like a hot velvet glove. I threw my head back and dug my fingers into her hips.

Being mortal didn't make sex any less mind melting, as it turned out. She rode me like she owned me, which she absolutely fucking did. We came shaking and crying out together until all the pleasure had been wrung from our bodies.

In the end we lay naked, sweaty and satisfied, limbs curled around each other.

"I still want that cake," I said into her neck.

"Perfect. You go get it and bring it back here with a couple forks," she said, with a contented sigh. "And a big glass of water while you're at it."

"What do I have to do to get you to do it?" I said, feeling too boneless to get up.

She held out a fist. "Rock, paper, scissors. Loser gets the cake."

"Game on."

EPILOGUE

MIRANDA

"You can play video games when you guys are done with the dishes," I said, stopping both Xander and Jamal from creeping away.

"I made dinner," Xander pointed out with more than just a little too much smug pride. He had, and it was ridiculously delicious. Rustic lamb ragu and pasta. Xander was more than a fast learner and had become something of a chef in short order.

"Fair enough. You're off the hook."

Xander dropped a kiss on my cheek, then took my hand

and dropped a kiss right on the knuckle next to the diamond ring he'd put on it a couple weeks ago.

He would have done it sooner, but I insisted we take things slow. Xander disappeared to the living room where Mama Jean was already waving a controller at him, ready to race some cars.

Heinz barked excitedly beside her. He loved when everyone got riled up in front of the television.

Xander hadn't been wrong. That dog made life more fun with loving licks, simple requests for treats, or for me to throw a ball. Playfulness and lightheartedness had been growing and expanding inside me in more ways than one.

Xander moved out of Grim's basement and in with Jamal and me. And while I didn't need as much help with childcare, Mama Jean came over even more now.

Neither Xandar nor I figured out how this would work, but it turned out the answer was one day at a time. And our family grew even more close knit.

While his powers and immortality were gone, Xander still had a lot of mental health issues to deal with. Living in isolation for so long had really caused a disruption in his mind, but we found resources to help him learn how to deal with any attacks of anxiety or confusion. When he worried he didn't deserve me or he was more trouble than he was worth, I reminded him he had to deal with my fiercely independent nature and my tendency to stonewall. We were perfectly imperfect together.

I was still working on being vulnerable and taking life a little slower. Which of course still included morning coffees at the Perkatory with Vivien and Aaron.

"Looks like it's you and me on dish detail, kid," I said, ruffling a hand on Jamal's head. He flapped his hands to get me to stop. At thirteen, his limbs had shot out and elongated from his body until he was almost as tall as me.

"Rock, paper, scissors for it?" he suggested hopefully.

"Not on your life."

"Why can't we just hire someone to do the dishes?" He dragged his feet all the way over to the stack of dirty pans.

"Xander is rich, not us," I said. Xander may be mortal, and lived with us, but he still owned the Atlantis hotel and had exorbitant funds from living for so long. I only asked that he split rent and utilities, though he splurged and spoiled us every chance he got.

"But after you get married—" Jamal tried to reason.

"Hey, you better cool it on the Christmas list this year, you hear me? Do not ask him for jet skis again."

"Aw, come on, you know he would love them," Jamal said, his eyes sparkling.

My phone buzzed so I just shot him a warning finger as I picked it up and walked into my bedroom to take it. "Hey."

"Hey my bestest, best, best friend in the whole wide world," Vivien's voice poured over the phone like butter and sugar. Looks like someone needed my help mediating a dicey situation between some gods and vampires. It sometimes helped to have someone there as back up, especially when that person had a weapon that could inflict some real damage to immortals.

"I'll be right there."

"Thank you, thank you, thank y—" I hung up, cutting her off.

Going to my closet, I retrieved my sword. Drawing Bob from his sheath, I asked, "You're always going to be here with me, right?"

"It's very likely that one day you'll turn around and I just won't be there. I come and go according to the magic that dictates where and when I'm needed. But that could be tomorrow, or it could be in ten years."

I didn't like the idea of Bob not being there. He'd changed my life in both good and bad ways, but I had a lifetime to spend with Xander now and I could never thank him enough. Though he certainly enjoyed it when I tried.

When I stepped into the living room, Xander saw I was dressed to go out and handed the controller over to Jamal—who had already abandoned dish duty.

"Vivien needs some help."

"I'm coming with you. You okay to stay with Jamal for a few hours?" Xander asked.

Mama Jean waved a hand in consent before trying to ram Jamal off the racetrack. Heinz trotted up and gave us a sincere look as his tail wagged wildly, as if to tell us he also understood the assignment before heading to Jamal's side.

It was hard to let Xander come along knowing that he was mortal now and our time could be cut short in other ways. But Xander did have eons of fight training and knew about the politics of gods. I nodded, and he was right there with me, locking up the house.

Maybe there will be a time when we will switch to a totally normal life, when my job didn't entail threatening with a god killing blade with my badass fiancé who didn't let anyone fuck with me.

But today was not that day.

Want to experience an unexpected turn? Get a bonus with favorites Timothy and Aaron.

Head to www.hollyroberds.com and check out the bonuses to read!

WANT A FREE BOOK?

Join Holly's Newsletter Holly's Hot Spot at www.hollyroberds.com and get the Five Orders Prequel Novella, The Knight Watcher, for FREE!

Plus you'll get exclusive sneak peaks, giveaways, fun lil' nuggets, and notifications when new books come out. Woot!

A Letter from the Author

Dear Reader,

Thank you for reading!

I love my Vegas Immortals world, and while I had planned to write a book 3 for Miranda and Xander, I found the story naturally concluding in two books and decided not to fight it.

And while I may step away from this world for a moment to go play with my fairytale retellings, I assure you I haven't forgotten about Timothy and Aaron's unrequited love. I shall return to Vegas to take care of them in some shape or form in the future.

Loved this book? Consider leaving a review as it helps other readers discover my books.

Want to make sure you never miss a release or any bonus content I have coming down the pipeline?

Make sure to join Holly's Hotspot, my newsletter, and I'll send you a FREE ebook right away!

You can also find me on my website www.hollyroberds.com and I hang out on social media.

Instagram: http://instagram.com/authorhollyroberds

Facebook: www.facebook.com/hollyroberdsauthorpage/.

And closest to my black heart is my reader fan group, Holly's Hellions. Become a Hellion. Raise Hell. www.facebook.com/groups/hollyshellions/

Cheers!

Holly Roberds

About the Author

Holly started out writing Buffy the Vampire Slayer and Terminator romantic fanfiction before spinning off into her own fantastic worlds with bitey MCs and heart wrenching climaxes as well as other errr climaxes...

Holly is a Colorado girl to her core but is only outdoorsy in that she likes drinking on patios in Denver.

She lives with her ever-supportive husband who helps by feeding her culinary miracles, lets her cry and rant about the injustices of the editing process, engages in inappropriate brainstorming over happy hours, and makes sure she takes breaks to play Dungeons & Dragons.

For more sample chapters, news, and more, visit www. hollyroberds.com